W0246417

the TRESPASSERS

ALSO BY JENNIFER LYNN ALVAREZ

Lies Like Wildfire

Friends Like These

FOR MIDDLE-GRADE READERS

The Guardian Herd Series

Riders of the Realm Trilogy

the

TRESPASSERS

JENNIFER LYNN ALVAREZ

DELACORTE PRESS

Delacorte Press
An imprint of Random House Children's Books
A division of Penguin Random House LLC
1745 Broadway, New York, NY 10019
penguinrandomhouse.com
GetUnderlined.com

Text copyright © 2025 by Jennifer Lynn Alvarez
Cover photograph copyright © 2025 by Willie Dalton/Stocksy

Penguin Random House values and supports copyright. Copyright fuels creativity,
encourages diverse voices, promotes free speech, and creates a vibrant culture. Thank you
for buying an authorized edition of this book and for complying with copyright laws by not
reproducing, scanning, or distributing any part of it in any form without permission. You are
supporting writers and allowing Penguin Random House to continue to publish books for
every reader. Please note that no part of this book may be used or reproduced in any manner
for the purpose of training artificial intelligence technologies or systems.

Delacorte Press is a registered trademark and the colophon is a trademark of
Penguin Random House LLC.

Editor: Wendy Loggia
Cover Designer: Casey Moses
Interior Designer: Ken Crossland
Production Editor: Colleen Fellingham
Managing Editor: Tamar Schwartz
Production Manager: Shameiza Ally

Library of Congress Cataloging-in-Publication Data is available upon request.
ISBN 978-0-593-90061-1 (trade) — ISBN 978-0-593-90063-5 (ebook)

The text of this book is set in 11-point PT Serif.

Manufactured in the United States of America
10 9 8 7 6 5 4 3 2 1

The authorized representative in the EU for product safety and compliance is
Penguin Random House Ireland, Morrison Chambers, 32 Nassau Street,
Dublin D02 YH68, Ireland, https://eu-contact.penguin.ie.

Random House Children's Books supports the First Amendment and
celebrates the right to read.

For the homes I've left behind

The blood of the covenant is thicker
than the water of the womb.

—**HEINRICH DER GLÏCHEZÄRE**

ONE

FINLEY, NOW

I squeeze the throttle on my snow machine and speed across the flat, scrubby Alaskan taiga. When I find them, they will tell me the whole truth about Valentine's Day—about what happened to Jason Walker—and then I will turn them over to the police.

Best friends aren't always the *best* friends.

My blood races as I imagine Mya, Eli, and River having another secret meeting without me. I don't trust them; maybe I never could. The trouble the four of us got into as children rushes back to me—sneaking out, cutting school, poaching salmon, and lying. The mischief ended after my dad died and Mom and I fled Alaska. Mom believes Dad's last act scared me straight, but that's not it. In LA, I met better people. It's that simple. I followed *the* rules instead of *Mya's* rules. Then I moved back.

"You ruined my life, Mya!" I scream into the wind.

And Jason Walker's life.

As I skim the flatlands, the spindly trees blur past and the pale northern sun reflects off the snow. There's the charred spruce Eli set fire to years ago. It's become a landmark on River's wilderness property. It means I'm close to the frozen pond and the fishing hut.

A wind gust tries to blow me off my seat. I slow the machine and scan the terrain. No matter what I find out about Jason, I'm in massive legal trouble. Nothing can change that now.

I gun the engine and the snow machine launches off a snowdrift and lands with a thump that tosses my body into the air. I miss the seat on my way down. Panicking, I squeeze the throttle tighter and the machine drags my legs through the snow. My shin strikes a rock and pain sizzles up my leg. Then the sled's double runners slide onto the smooth frozen pond, propelling it faster. Ahead is a brown shape: the fishing hut.

My hands break loose and I tumble free. The snow machine veers off as I slide face down across the ice like a hockey puck.

When my body eases to a halt, I flip over, gasping for air.

Three figures stand outside the hut, their heads covered in hooded jackets—Mya, River, and Eli. Coldness engulfs me. One of the boys is carrying a hardwood bat used to bludgeon fish to death. He twirls it, and his spiked boots grip the ice as he walks toward me. The girl—Mya—has wide, rounded eyes.

"Finley!" she shouts.

I curl into a ball and cover my head. Blood drips from my leg. "Stay back," I rasp.

"You're the one chasing us." Then they surround me.

My best friends.

TWO

Whoever said you can never go home again was wrong because here I am, back in Alaska. Mom and I spent the past four years in sun-soaked Los Angeles, and when we arrived in Anchorage last week, I expected the Last Frontier to chew me up and spit me out. But no. Alaska welcomed me into her frozen arms with a fond, if vampiric, hug.

Our two-story townhome borders a nature park with walking trails and an icy lagoon. Behind it the snow-veiled Chugach Mountains scrawl across a purple sky. It's morning, but sunrise is hours away. We moved back in the middle of winter and my last semester of high school. I left behind two favorite teachers, two great friends, and that lovely orb we call the *sun*. Here, daylight will rise and fall while I'm at school. I'll see the sun on weekends, if it's not snowing.

"You got this, Finley Dunn," I say as I apply my lip gloss in the mirror. Soon, I'll be face to face with my old friends Mya Green, River Madden, and Eli Kalluk, and things with

3

them were not good when Mom and I left. We've kept in touch, but it's not the same as hanging out every day. I can't gauge their true feelings about my return. They claim they're happy, but . . . I don't believe it. I blow out a breath and hunt for my boots. Unable to find them, I burst into Mom's bedroom. "I can't find my mukluks."

She eyeballs me while curling her hair. Mom starts her new job today, and her bathroom counter looks like a bomb went off. "We just bought them, Fin. Ouch! Let me get ready." She sucks her finger where she burned herself on her iron.

"But have you seen them?"

Mom waves one arm. "Look at my mess. Am I the one you should be asking? I can't believe you unpacked and organized your entire bedroom but lost your brand-new boots."

My dad's mother died a few months ago and left me this townhome in her will. Now Mom's bedroom is piled with stuff Gran collected over the past eighty years. She's right, it's a mess.

"Never mind." Pulling out my phone, I message my group chat with Mya, Eli, and River: How cold is it gonna be?

Bro, it's winter, Eli writes back.

Cold, says Mya.

Message received. Don't ask dumb questions. I slide my phone back into my pocket. River didn't respond at all, which is not unusual. He's never been glued to screens, but his silence worries me. My return will spark memories—not all of them good. I need to make things right with him, but I don't think there's anything I can say that will return us to the way we were.

The four of us met in preschool, the only kids in class

who weren't cheechakos, the Alaskan term for newcomers, or military brats from Elmendorf Air Force Base. Our parents got along too, and our families did everything together—parties, vacations, adventures, and sleepovers. We were insular, communal, and a little bit criminal. Eli's family grew black-market weed, River's dad avoided paying federal taxes, Mya's mom bribed the town council, and my family poached salmon out of the river behind our house. We were wild, but I felt safe. Protected.

It was fantastic, until my dad did what he did and Mom and I got the hell out of Alaska.

We never planned to return to *Los Anchorage,* but after Gran died she left me her townhome, five thousand dollars, and a 2012 Volvo. Her will states I can't sell the house until I'm twenty-five, so here we are. If the LA struggle taught Mom and me anything, it's that you don't pass up free housing.

I tread downstairs, pack my lunch, and message the group: Who wants a homemade skinny hazelnut latte? *Kill them with kindness,* I think.

Your California is showing, Mya writes back.

"Wait until you see me," I mutter. I spent every dime I earned in LA erasing the old Finley Dunn—new clothes, trendy makeup, teeth-whitening strips, latest phone model, orthodontics, and hair treatments. I was full feral when I left Alaska, and while no one in LA bullied me to my face, I heard the whispers: *Are those Wranglers? Do they sell hairbrushes in Alaska? Did she live outside?* By the time I entered high school, feral Fin was dead and I had two new best friends, Olivia and Imani.

My phone pings. I want a latte, writes Eli. As a kid he would eat literally anything. It's comforting to know he hasn't changed even though I have.

Still no response from River. Is he upset about my return or just being a dude? Stomach gurgling, I craft two lattes and pour them into travel mugs.

Outside the kitchen window, lighted lamp poles pierce the darkness, revealing piles of months-old brown snow. Gran used to babysit us in this house, and my friends and I pretended to be Iditarod huskies, played tag between the cars, or raced across the street to explore the lagoon. Dad smoked salmon filets in the driveway with Mom hugging his waist. My chest tightens because I miss my dad. I have good memories before everything went to shit.

Mom appears downstairs. "Check the car."

The memories dissolve. "What?"

"The mukluks. Check the car, and please don't miss the bus, Fin. I don't want to be late for my first day." It irks me that I have to ride a school bus, but Gran's old Volvo is in the shop getting "road-ready" for me.

I search Mom's car and find my new mukluks. They're a bit *extra* for a school day, but it's January, and I'm about to stand at a bus stop in Alaska in the dark, so who cares about fashion? I rip off the tag and pull on a neck gaiter, a beanie, and a long down jacket, completely covering my cute outfit. I leave the house dressed for *skiing,* not high school. "Bye, Mom, love you."

"Love you too!"

Outside I slam into a wall of freezing wind that rips the breath from my lungs and blasts stinging ice particles at my

6

face. The lamp pole light struggles to pierce the darkness, and the snow blows sideways. My nostrils freeze shut. Balancing the two lattes, I trudge toward a group of younger students, none of whom are wearing mukluks. I wish I'd asked my friends to pick me up, but I was too chicken.

The students watch me approach. "Are you new?" a boy asks.

His friend bops him. "Have you seen her before, shithead?"

New is a slur in Alaska, and my chin juts. "I'm not *new*. I grew up here." The group absorbs the fact that I'm dressed to summit Everest, and their eyebrows shoot up. *Cheechako,* one mouths. Whatever. When I get Gran's Volvo, I'll honk at these fools each time I drive past.

Headlights veer into the complex. I prepare to board, but it's not the bus. It's a lifted Ford Bronco with snow tires. The driver revs the engine and a deep, obnoxious rumbling assaults my ears. "Get a muffler," I grumble. Then the window rolls down, revealing dimples, white teeth, and sandy brown hair.

My stomach somersaults. "River?"

He grins at me. "Hey, Finley."

Even though I follow his account and have seen his recent photos, I expected him to look like he used to: wire-rimmed glasses, a skinny boy's body, and tangled hair flopping over one eye.

He taps the Bronco. "Get in."

"Uh, okay." I race to the passenger side and climb into the warm car. "You didn't tell me—"

"I wanted to surprise you." His lips quirk as he helps

me wrangle my heavy backpack onto the seat between us. "What's in there, rocks?"

"Books."

He shrugs and shifts into first gear. The Bronco jerks forward and I fly deeper into my seat, spilling droplets of latte onto my jacket. The younger students watch us drive away, shivering in the cold, and I decide not to honk at them when I drive by in the future. River nods toward my hot drinks. "Is one of those for me?"

He seems so . . . comfortable. Also not what I expected. "No, but if you ever checked your phone, I would have made you one."

Emotions swirl behind his gold-flecked eyes. "Damn, Fin, it's good to see you."

My throat knots. "Really?"

He nods. "Yeah, really."

When Mom and I left Alaska, River was in bad emotional shape. He'd ceased speaking to anyone and yanked out his eyebrow hairs one by one. He snapped out of it about a year later and the four of us started our group thread while I was living in LA. I'm not convinced his recovery is complete, or that he forgives me for what happened, but he looks good— *really good.*

Recalling our first kiss four years ago, I sip my latte and try to act cool. "You've changed."

River smiles. "I'd say you've changed too, but I can't tell beneath that sleeping bag you're wearing."

"It's cold!"

"Maybe to you."

I lean back and enjoy the fact I'm sitting next to River

Madden, in Anchorage, after four long years apart. His artful hands grip a steering wheel instead of handlebars, and his muscular legs press a clutch instead of bike pedals. Childhood memories overcome me, changing him from man to boy, boy to man. Mom always liked River best. "That kid plays as well indoors as he does outdoors. The others are wilder than a pack of raccoons."

It's as if my time in LA were a dream, except that my California pals, Olivia and Imani, sent me a message this morning: good luck on your first day 🌝. They seem a million miles away.

"You remind me of a girl I used to know," River says. His mood is reflective as the dark road unfurls ahead of us. "She was tiny and cute. She glowed when she was happy."

"Was she a firefly?"

"Yeah. She was always bugging me, a total pest."

"I was not a pest."

"You were, but who says I was talking about you?" He winks, and I laugh. Jesus, when did River learn to flirt?

We arrive at school, and Bartlett High looms like a cruise ship at port—a two-story structure of gleaming glass windows, welcoming throngs of student passengers into its hull. Even though it's January, Valentine's dance posters and decorations cover the glass and unexpected pleasure courses through me. I learned to enjoy school while I lived in Los Angeles, and Bartlett has been remodeled since I left. It looks more like a well-resourced college than a high school.

We're early, and River idles the Bronco to keep us warm. I unzip my jacket and pull off my beanie, releasing my long blond hair. His gaze rakes across my loose jeans, tan skin, and fitted white top. His voice deepens. "LA looks good on you, Fin. Remember when we—"

"Kissed?"

His cheeks darken, and the car cabin shrinks. Our breathing is like the wind, gusting between us. His fingers trace down my forearm, then pull away. "When I think about the past, that kiss is what I remember. The rest is behind us, Fin. I can tell you're worried, but don't be. I'm okay. I'm not gonna break down or anything. Promise. I'm good and I don't blame you for what happened."

My heart judders. He's told me this over text and I didn't believe him, but hearing it out loud is different. He's not mad. Maybe there's a chance we can pick up where we left off. Four years and thirty-four hundred miles haven't driven our kiss out of my head. It's as if we're fourteen again and back in his bedroom. My gaze falls to his lips.

A banging sound startles me as a massive human wearing an FTP beanie pounds on the windshield. My hand jerks, spilling my latte. "Is that . . . ?"

River cuts his engine and sighs. "Yup, that's Eli, and there's Mya."

A disoriented feeling descends as Eli draws back from the window. He's so much larger in person than in his photos. A girl stands beside him, staring at me. She's pale and wire-thin, but taller than she was when I left. She wears thick makeup, and her black-dyed hair frames fierce eyebrows. I catch the glimmer of a diamond nose stud. It's Mya.

Eli pounds the glass again. "Unlock the door. We're freezing out here."

River unlocks his doors, and they climb into the back seat. Eli shakes my shoulders. "You're home, Finny. I can't believe it. How the fuck are you? You haven't grown an inch."

"You calling me short?" I hand him his latte.

Mya chews her lip, and her dark gaze invokes our past. It's too much. The bad memories crash into River's truck like floodwaters. The summer party at River's house. Gunshots. Blood splattered across dusty floorboards, and sirens piercing the Alaskan night. News crews at our door. The headlines blaring:

MURDER IN THE BACKWOODS

**ANCHORAGE MAN KILLS
BEST FRIEND IN SHOOT-OUT**

**BUSINESS DISPUTE LEADS TO
GUNFIRE**

My daddy shot River's daddy.
That's why Mom and I fled Alaska.

THREE

MYA

Finley Dunn is back. Mya knew she was coming but still can't believe it. Her childhood friend sits in River's truck with shiny blond hair, flawless makeup, and a little shell-pink mouth, cuddling her homemade latte. The scent of brand-new composition books and college-ruled paper wafts from Finley's spotless backpack. Mya struggles to merge this girl with the one she grew up with. That girl was scrawny and musty, with colorless white hair and eyes too big for her face. She ate roe straight out of salmon bellies, pined for a sled dog, and wore the same iron-on horse T-shirt every day.

Finley 2.0 is a living doll.

It's been a minute, four years to be exact. Mya should be happy Finley is back, she's one of her best friends, but Mya is not happy. "You glowed up," she says, the words spilling out like an accusation. Their collective breath creates steam that drips down the inside of the Bronco's car windows.

Finley blushes. "Thanks."

Mya sneaks a glance at River in the front seat. *He's* the reason she's concerned. It took him over a year to rebound from his father's murder, and she worries Fin's return will send him spiraling again. Finley's dad received a defensive wound that night that sent him into a coma. He died in the hospital without ever waking up or getting arrested for the murder. The police believed a business dispute caused the shooting, but they were wrong. It was about River's dad beating the crap out of him.

The truth about their horrid past is as fragile as ice, and Finley is like the sun. Her appearance in Alaska could melt the shield Mya has constructed to protect them. There is more to the shooting that night than Finley knows—things Mya hopes to keep secret.

She gnaws on her lip as her fears flicker like candlelight. River catches her concerned look. *I'm fine,* he mouths. She shakes her head. She doesn't believe him. None of them are *fine.*

"Do you like the latte?" Finley asks Eli.

He licks the foam off his lips. "Yeah, it's sweet. Thanks, Finny."

Mya's gaze slides to Finley's mouth. Her once crooked and overcrowded teeth are straight and chemically whitened. Her clothes and backpack are in pristine condition. Finley, who almost failed seventh grade, is enrolled in AP and leadership classes at Bartlett High. Mya's feelings bounce inside her. This is not the same girl who left.

"No one comes back from Outside," says Eli.

"That's the truth," says Mya. "Let's celebrate. School blows anyway."

Finley chokes on her drink. "I can't skip school."

Eli snorts. "Since when?"

"It's not skipping if you haven't officially started yet." Mya glances at River through the rearview mirror. "Can we ride your snow machines? I mean, Finley's got the outfit for it."

They laugh, and River backs out of his spot. Finley doesn't protest as Bartlett High vanishes behind them. Mya is pleased that time has not inoculated Finley to them. Beneath her flawless makeup, matching outerwear, and the sprinkle of freckles across her nose, she is still the little girl who does what the group wants. She is still their blood sister.

When they were eleven years old, the four of them took a friendship vow at Salmon Lake, near Nome. It was during a summer camping trip with all the families. The tundra was flat scrubland, and the wind whipped the wildflower-studded plains from the sandy shore of Salmon Lake to the distant Kigluaik Mountains. That camping trip is one of Mya's favorite memories:

Her friends collapsed on the shore, laughing after having a mud fight. Sunshine flickered on the lake's surface, and fish leaped and splashed where it was deeper. They finished Eli's deer jerky, and River hummed a song while muddy water dripped from his bangs. Back at the campsite, their parents fished and the older kids chatted by the fire. "I wish you guys were my family," Finley said.

"We could be," Mya said. "Blood is thicker than water. I read about it in a book."

Eli opened one eye. "What does that mean?"

"It means a blood oath is stronger than family ties. I saw a movie where kids cut their palms and became blood brothers. We can do that. It's better than being related." Mya slid her Swiss Army knife out of her pocket.

"Will it hurt?" Finley asked.

"I mean, a little, but it lasts forever."

For lack of anything better to do, they agreed.

Mya made them wash their hands in the lake and then gather in a circle. Wincing, they took turns slicing small gashes into their palms. Then they pressed their hands together and squeezed, mingling their blood. The cobalt sky spanned overhead, and the wind swept their words away as they repeated Mya's verse: "The blood of the covenant is thicker than the water of the womb."

Afterward, Mya nudged Finley. "We're sisters now. We're family, just like you wanted." Finley grinned and warmth flooded Mya.

"The last one in is a rotten egg!" said Eli. He raced toward Salmon Lake.

They chased him, and River was the last one in. They dunked him and he came up sputtering. They splashed and chased each other as the dark mud ran off their bodies, leaving them clean, cold, and exhilarated beneath the midnight sun.

Mya sighs. Her friends are back together, the shooting is behind them, and River seems fine. Maybe having Finley back will be good for him and good for the group.

River steers his Bronco toward home while Finley chatters about LA. In the back seat, Mya feels Eli's eyes on her.

She nudges him away, but he shimmies right back to where he was. His leg is warm against hers, and he smells like body wash. He's been extra-sweet to her since their . . . encounter, which is annoying. If he doesn't stop flirting, Mya's going to sleep with him again and it will be *his* fault. She opens her mouth to blast him, but Eli smiles—his real smile—and her insults die on her tongue.

"Stop staring at me," she hisses.

He stares harder.

Mya turns away, a grin blossoming on her face.

FOUR

FINLEY

"You cut school on the first day?" My mom plods up the garage steps to confront me.

I meet her in the kitchen, holding out a glass of red wine. She balks. "You're *drinking,* too?"

"Calm down, it's for you." I hand her the glass. I've been home for over an hour, and I'm still processing my first day with my old friends. Mya seems conflicted, and I get it. Mom and I left a trail of destruction behind us, but the boys are happy I'm back.

We drove to River's house and rode the snow machines and everything was . . . *good.* When I left, River gave me an extra-long hug. His body was warm and solid, and he smelled like snow. My insides are still glowing. Maybe I am a firefly. Mom, however, is glowing with anger. The school must have called her when I didn't show up.

"What did you do today?" she asks.

"Um . . . I hung out with my old friends."

She accepts the wine and tosses her purse onto a chair. "You've never cut school before."

"God, that's not true. I cut all the time in junior high."

She sighs. "I meant in LA. You didn't play hooky with Imani and Olivia. Don't resurrect bad habits, please."

"I'm a straight-A student. I can miss one day."

She follows me into our tiny family room. "Being a good student doesn't mean you can do whatever you want."

I return to the hot chocolate I left steaming on a side table and cradle it in my cold hands. Outside, the snow drips off the trees, warmed by the Chinook winds. "It kind of does. You said I can make my own choices if I get good grades. I'm an adult."

"Turning eighteen doesn't make you an adult."

"You might want to write your congressperson about that."

"Don't get smart. You're not—"

I cut her off. "An adult as long as I live under your roof, I know, but my friends haven't seen me in four years. They wanted to hang out, and the teachers posted the homework online. I already finished it and DoorDashed dinner. It'll be here in fifteen minutes."

Mom collapses onto the recliner and enjoys a hearty sip of her wine. "China Haven?"

"Yep. Your old favorite."

She shifts in her chair as feelings glide like clouds across her eyes. She's thirty-five, and I'm eighteen, and we get "Who's the mother and who's the daughter?" comments— mostly from men. With our matching blond hair, freckled faces, and blue eyes, we're intimidating to absolutely no one. "Where did you guys go?" Mom asks.

I blow on my hot chocolate. "To River's house."

"How was it being *there* again?"

"Not bad. They tore down Bart's old shop." A visible tremor rolls through Mom's shoulders because the shop is where her husband shot River's dad in the back.

"Being near the old shop must have brought up terrible memories," she says.

"It's fine. Everyone's cool about it."

Her pretty face twitches. "Ah, Finley. I don't believe that and neither should you. Other than Mya's mom, no one has called to welcome us back. Not a single one of them. Your friends' parents were my best friends too, you know."

"Not even Connie Kalluk?" Connie is Eli's mom. She's nosy and social and likes to be liked. She'll talk to anyone.

"Not even Connie," says Mom. "They didn't stay in touch while we were in LA, so it's not a surprise, but I assumed they'd at least say hello now that we're back."

"I'm sorry. Are you sad?"

She draws another sip of wine. "Not sad. No."

"Then what? You look sad."

Her eyelashes flutter. "Being here makes me miss your dad even more. That's all. But I need to make new friends. It's time I moved on."

Mom's lonely, and that's worse than being sad. "You have me," I say.

She smiles. "Yes, and Cookie Green. I'm grateful Mya's

19

mom gave me a job. She's very understanding about . . . what happened in the past."

"Did you guys talk about it?"

"Nope. She poured me a glass of champagne, welcomed me home, and got straight to business. No talk about before, no funny looks. Just started teaching me about real estate. She knows I don't want to talk about it."

Mya's mom hired mine to work at her housing development. Cookie is unpredictable, unconventional, and filthy rich, but she's also the woman you want on your side if you're in trouble. "How did your first day go?"

Mom considers her wine. "I'm going to need another glass. It was . . ."

"Busy?"

"The opposite. Cookie must have hired me out of pity, because not much is happening there. Northwood Estates is her crown jewel, but she hasn't presold a home in three months. The economy is not good and interest rates are sky-high. No one wants a McMansion in Alaska right now, and if they do, they can't afford it."

I glance out the frosty window to the lagoon, where people are ice-skating in the moonlight. "We're lucky we have this house. It was worth moving here to know that no one can kick us out. Not ever again."

Mom and I experienced homelessness last year after our apartment pipes burst and she lost her job in the same week. We got evicted and ended up in a shelter after first living in her car. We ate at a soup kitchen and accepted handouts. I attended school with a hollow stomach and a racing mind and pretended everything was fine. It was embarrassing and scary, but I'm glad there is help for people who lose every-thing. Now I own a home. It's small, but it's paid off and it's mine. No one can take it.

Mom's eyes moisten. "I'm sorry I couldn't afford LA. I know you liked it there."

"Don't feel bad, Mom. No one can afford LA." We laugh, but it's not funny. The terror of our ordeal still clings to me. It was like falling, but I didn't hit bottom or die—I just fell. That's when I threw myself into school. If I could control my grades, I could control my future. Getting evicted would never happen to me again.

Mom reaches for my hand. "We've been through so much, honey, but don't lose sight of the ball. You have to graduate and go to college. I like Mya, Eli, and River, but I don't like that you skipped school with them. Don't end up like me."

Mom blames her lack of education for our financial struggles. She dropped out of high school after she got pregnant with me, and Dad's death made things worse. He died from injuries he got while committing a felony, so Mom didn't get his life insurance money. Guilt washes over me. "I won't skip again."

"Thank you." Mom sips her wine and untucks her feet. "Cookie's opening the first model home in two weeks and that should kick things into high gear. She's been trying to sell the houses based on three-dimensional models, but I think people prefer to walk through a real house before they spend that much money. Speaking of jobs, did you hear back from Mama Moose's?"

"Yep. I have an interview after school tomorrow." Mama

Moose's is my favorite restaurant in Anchorage. I applied online the day we arrived and the owner, Clodagh, texted me today to set up an interview. Right then, my phone alerts with a DM from River and my heart soars: I'll pick you up again tomorrow, he writes.

Only if you put a muffler on that Ford.

Done

Wow, that was easy. I grin at my screen as the warm glow reignites inside me.

"Making plans?" Mom asks, trying to sneak a look at my phone.

I blacken my screen just as the doorbell rings. "Dinner's here."

FIVE

MYA

"Mom! Did you sign my math test?" Mya's voice echoes through the halls of her cavernous lodgepole pine home. Two weeks have passed since Finley's return, and it's going better than expected. River has kept his shit together, and the group has been eating lunch at school, riding the snow machines, ice-skating, and watching movies. Today, they're going to the 5th Avenue Mall to make Valentine's Day plans. It's senior year, and Mya wants to make the evening *extra-special*. But first, algebra.

She pads through her six-thousand-square-foot house, hunting for a parent. Her older sister, Brittany, is in the shower, their dad might be at his morning spin class, and their mom could be anywhere. No one answers Mya's calls.

She shuffles back to her bedroom. If she doesn't pass Algebra II, she might not graduate from high school. Mya tries hard not to care about this as she pulls on black tights, a flouncy black skirt, and a red Ramones T-shirt she bought at a thrift store. She yanks old combat boots and a black cardigan out of her closet and then sits at her vanity and confronts her small, pointed chin and big ears. How can she adore these features on her father and hate them on herself?

She slathers foundation over chalky skin, lines her eyes in kohl, and applies red eyeshadow, flaring it out like wings, a mask she hides behind at school. Mya's popular at Bartlett High the way cats are popular. People like to be around her but she does her own thing. She might enjoy the attention if she weren't so focused on keeping her fucked-up friend group together—first, because she loves them, and second, because she's afraid of what might happen if she steps away. Nothing binds people tighter than their secrets.

She chooses red for her lips and clunks down the stairs. "Mom?" Her sister is the only one home. Mya drives herself to school without a signature on her math test.

. . .

At the mall, Eli leads them straight to the food court, where they order meals from Chopsticks. When the checker asks for fifty-two dollars, Eli and River step aside for Mya to pay the bill, but she spreads her empty hands. "No bread. My mom cut me and Brittany off."

Eli lifts his eyebrows. "Come again?"

"You heard me, idiot."

Finley slides a debit card from her purse. "I got it. There are things called jobs, you know. I've been here two weeks and already got hired at Mama Moose's. You three don't have to be broke."

24

"I got a side hustle," says Eli.

"Plowing driveways isn't a side hustle if you don't have a main hustle," says River. Eli feints with a right hook that River dodges.

They find a table and spread out their food containers. "Why'd your mom cut you off?" River asks.

Mya slumps lower in her chair, remembering last night's argument between her parents. It happened in the kitchen:

"We're underwater three million dollars," her mom said to her dad. "If one more thing goes wrong with Northwood Estates, we're looking at bankruptcy. You can mail your nephew a present, but you're not flying to Singapore for the wedding. Wake up, Vaughn. The damn economy has changed."

Her dad's face turned scarlet. "Staking that development with our money was the stupidest thing you've ever done."

Cookie dragged her eyes over her husband's fluorescent spin outfit. "It wasn't the stupidest."

Mya's sister slammed the refrigerator door. "Stop fighting."

Mya's parents have been arguing about Northwood Estates for years. The housing development at the edge of Anchorage was supposed to make them richer, but instead it's sucking them dry. Mya stirs her mixed veggie bowl with a chopstick and answers River's question. "She cut me off because her business is in the shitter. My parents are fighting all the time. They don't do poor well."

"Does anyone?" asks Finley.

"No, but if things get any worse with Northwood Estates, we'll end up in a homeless encampment. You're right, I should get a job."

"Hold up," says Finley. "There are homeless encampments in *Anchorage*? I don't remember seeing any before I moved. I mean, it's a huge crisis in LA, but it's warm there."

"I think it's a thing everywhere," says Eli.

Finley toys with her straw. "My mom and I stayed in a shelter once." Her words silence the friends and her cheeks turn a scalding pink. "It was just a few weeks. Anyway, I think affordable housing is important." She picks up her soda and peers at Mya.

Mya's face grows hot. "I didn't say it wasn't important."

A second resounding silence follows her statement. Eli fills it by grabbing the fortune cookies off the table. "I'm gonna read your fortunes."

"Don't touch mine," says River, snatching his back.

"Sheesh, I was just gonna open it for you." Eli breaks his cookie and reads the tiny paper inside. "Beware of all enterprises that require new clothes." He tosses the paper down. "That is some wise shit."

Mya rolls her eyes, but with Eli's distraction, the tension dissipates.

As they dig into their meals and slurp their drinks, Mya forces a smile. "Let's talk about Valentine's Day. No one wants to go to the dance, right?"

"Verdad," says Eli.

"I could skip," says River, but his gaze slides toward Finley. "Unless you want to go?"

"Whatever you guys want."

"Good," says Mya. "My mom's interior designer finished decorating the Chateau last week. Let's hang out there one last time before Mom opens it for showings."

Finley balls up her napkin. "What's the Chateau?"

"It's the model home at Northwood Estates," says Mya. "We'll go there instead of the dance."

Eli nods. "I'll do whatever as long as I don't have to see my ex."

Mya witnessed his ex yelling at him at school a few days ago and enjoyed it, which bugged her. She never used to care about Eli's love life. Their unexpected encounter a few weeks ago continues to gall and confuse her.

"Your mom lets you hang out in her model home?" Finley asks.

Mya waves her hand. "Not exactly. I found the code to the front door lock a few months ago, and as long as her lame-ass security guard doesn't spot us, she won't know. It's the perfect place to party. Everything in the house works—the refrigerator, the bathrooms, the fireplace—and it will be furnished. We just have to pack out our trash. Leave no trace."

With the plan made, they finish their meals, and Mya drives Finley home from the mall.

"I was wondering," Finley says when they arrive at her townhome. "Is River really okay with me being back? I mean, he says he is, but . . . seeing me must make him think about his dad."

Mya's nerve endings tingle. She's got to shut this down fast. "Fin, I think Bart is on River's mind whether you're here or not. Don't worry about it."

"But what happened is my fault." Tears wash her eyes. "River begged me not to tell."

Mya nods as understanding dawns. Finley feels guilty for siccing her father on River's father. On that horrible night, she informed her dad that Bart beat River so hard River was peeing blood. And it's true that River begged her not to tell her parents, but Finley didn't listen. She told her father and he confronted Bart while they were each drunk and armed. The detectives called what followed an "execution-style" killing.

It was a messy, gruesome murder. It's got to be why Finley tries so hard to look and act perfect—to disassociate herself from her father's legacy. She wants absolution. Mya meets Finley's sky blue eyes. "It wasn't your fault and River doesn't blame you. Leave it in the past."

Finley releases a huge breath. "If you say so."

"I do. See you tomorrow, okay?

Finley nods and steps out of the car. Mya sends a quick DM to River: Finley's worried about you. Are you sure you're ok?

Yep, he writes. I'm perfect. I'm glad she's back.

Ok. Call me if you want to talk.

River doesn't respond and Mya drives away, thinking about the fatal shooting and the lie she told the police about it. Finley's not the only one who carries blame. Mya's guilt about that night was difficult to bear when Finley was in LA. It's almost impossible now that she's back.

SIX

MYA

It's Valentine's Day, and Finley insists on picking everyone up in her gran's old Volvo with the *AK907* sticker in the window. She beeps her horn in Mya's driveway.

Mya pops out of her bedroom and bumps into her sister in the hallway. Brittany eyeballs her black lace hoop dress, black boots, and dark makeup. "It's Valentine's Day, not Halloween."

Mya ignores her, and Brittany crosses her arms. "You *are* going to the dance, right? Or did you lie to Mom?"

"Shut up."

"You lied. What a shocker. It's going to storm later, Mya. Don't get caught in it." Brittany wiggles her fingers at her. "Tell Eli to use a condom."

Mya's cheeks warm. "I'm not..."

Her sister laughs. "No one cares. Have fun with your boy toy, I have a date with a *real* man." Brittany slams her bedroom door.

29

Mya shuffles down her curved staircase and onto the front porch with her black dress swishing around her ankles. She feels pretty in the flowing lace and dramatic makeup. Brittany relies on her body for attention. Mya prefers the *unusual*.

She lifts her wide skirt and patters down the steps to Finley's turquoise-green Volvo. She glimpses sequins through the window. "Oh my God," she mutters.

Mya yanks open the passenger door and slides onto the leather seat. Yep, she was right. Finley is wearing a skin-tight, pink-sequined minidress. Her red fingernails are embellished with tiny pink hearts, her long yellow hair is curled into loose waves, and her cleavage is squeezed into two half-moons. She looks like a piece of candy.

Finley is equally speechless about Mya's solid black attire and sparkling red headband. "You look great," they say at the same time, and then bust out laughing.

"Actually, you look like a prostitute," says Mya.

"You look like Wednesday Addams."

"Thank you!" Mya preens in her seat. "Did you tell your mom you're going to the dance?"

"Sure. Did you?"

Mya's mother didn't ask where she was going or remember that it was Valentine's Day. Cookie returned Mya's goodbye without even looking up from her computer, so Mya ignores the question. "This car is so ugly. I love it. Drive, woman!"

Finley picks up Eli first. The sheen on his green shirt matches Fin's car *exactly*. "Oh, hell no," Eli says. He marches back into his house and returns wearing a white button-down. "I'm not twinning with a fucking Volvo." His eyes stutter across Finley's sequin-wrapped curves and miniature waist. "Holy shit, Finny. You look..." He doesn't finish.

Finley laughs. "Um... thanks?"

Mya feels a stab of envy but can't blame Eli for noticing Finley's beauty. Anyway, Mya isn't supposed to care who Eli likes. She glowers at him for existing, and Eli winks at her. "Stop," she hisses.

Finley turns onto Seward Highway and drives east to River's house. The waterway called Turnagain Arm spans to their right. It's low tide, and silver moonlight reflects off the tidal flats. To their left, the Chugach mountain peaks are white and rugged. The first sign of tonight's storm appears when fat snowflakes drift to the earth, weightless yet falling. It's how Mya feels, weightless yet falling. Riding with Finley in her gran's Volvo is like sliding into the past.

No outsiders. No cheechakos. Just her best friends.

Like old times, but not.

River pops into Finley's car last, carrying his guitar case. His gaze sticks to Finley's cleavage, and a huge smile lights his face.

"Jesus, they're boobs," Mya grumbles.

River settles into the back seat with Eli, and they return to the main road. As they're driving, Eli texts Mya: I wish it was just us tonight. I brought protection.

Her cheeks burn as she sends him a stop sign emoji. She hasn't known what to think since she and Eli had unexpected, drunken sex during winter break. It happened on a Saturday night when River was busy and before Finley moved back.

Eli stole a bottle of rum from his house and brought it to Mya's. They hung out in her bedroom, where he mixed the rum with Coke. Mya drank it like water.

Soon they were wrestling on her floor, and Eli showed her different clinches and holds. When her face ended up in his armpit, she yelled at him to let go. He flipped her over and rested on top of her. Their gazes clashed. His jaw muscles fluttered, and his thick brows drew together. He watched her with an intensity that reached the base of Mya's spine.

"Am I pinned?" she asked.

Eli pressed her shoulder to the floor with one finger. "Now you are." His other hand slid to her waist.

Mya wiggled to get more comfortable. Feeling relaxed and uninhibited, she traced the muscles on his back. Eli's large and powerful body had fascinated her longer than she cared to admit. She squeezed his softball-sized biceps. "You're so ... big."

His smirk vanished. He spanned one hand across her flat stomach and gripped her hip with the other. "You're so small."

In the dark, under the soft haze of alcohol, Mya's reservations spun loose. She brushed her lips against his, and Eli made a noise she'd never heard him make before. Their bodies melded, and she closed her eyes, her mind in flames.

What happened next was as easy as rolling down a hill.

They tugged off their jeans, Eli slipped on a condom, and he pressed into her. She felt a sting and then euphoria. Mya clutched his back as if she might fall off the planet. "God," she cried, tears springing to her eyes. He filled the universe.

Eli's weight held her down, but they seemed to float off the floor anyway. When it was over, reality cascaded in on Mya. *Oh no*, she thought.

Eli handed her a towel from her bathroom. "You're bleeding. Are you okay?"

"What?" She stared at the blood that trickled down her leg. She knew this could happen the first time, but it caught her off guard. Her bedroom spun like Dorothy's house in the tornado, and saliva filled her mouth.

"Oh shit, hold on." Eli picked her up, carried her to her en suite bathroom, and set her down next to the toilet. At the sight of it, she vomited rum and Coke into the porcelain. "Sorry," she gasped.

"No worries." He stroked her dark, damp hair. "You're not the first girl to throw up after sex with me."

"It's not funny." She vomited again, feeling confused and a little frightened. "Don't tell River. Don't tell anyone."

His face fell. "Why not?"

"Promise me, Eli. This is our secret."

He smoothed his expression. "We might forget it anyway. We're pretty hammered."

But they didn't forget it. They did it again a week later, and there was no excuse that time. They weren't drunk or stoned or the last two people on Earth or besieged by aliens—they were just really fucking horny, and it felt really fucking good—and now Eli wants to do it again. It's turning into a situationship, and Mya doesn't know what to do about it.

From the back seat of the Volvo, his eyes burn holes into the back of her head. Her traitorous body angles toward him, but she's determined not to give in a third time.

"Turn right," Mya says to Finley. They've arrived at Northwood Estates on the outskirts of Anchorage. Mya drove here earlier and decorated for the evening—a surprise for her friends. She's not a fan of manufactured retail celebrations like Valentine's Day, but she decorated because she believes it will make the night more fun and keep the group cemented in the present. They need to look forward, River most of all. If they don't look back, the truth can stay buried.

A gravel road appears in Finley's headlights. "That's the service road," says Mya. "It runs along the back of the houses. Take it so the guard doesn't see your car. They drive by at two in the afternoon and two in the morning."

Finley steers her Volvo onto the indicated gravel road and parks. The four friends jump out. A chain-link fence and dozens of no-trespassing signs surround the property. The snowfall is light because the worst of the storm is still hours away. Finley and Mya carry their party shoes in one hand and tromp through the crunchy snow in their boots. Eli peels back the chain link as they slide through it.

The bougie model home backs up to hundreds of acres of wild taiga and evergreens that reach for the stars. The Chateau looms like a movie set. It's painted and landscaped

34

but surrounded by unfinished houses and construction dirt. The scent of sawdust lingers in the frosty air.

Finley slips out of her boots and into pink heels.

Mya punches in the code and opens the front door. "Our palace for the evening."

The four friends—dressed to kill—enter the Chateau.

SEVEN

FINLEY

My breath catches as I walk through the front door. "Is this for real?"

The house is professionally decorated with designer furniture, artwork, and a table set for an imaginary dinner—crystal plates and goblets, dark blue chargers, candles, and baubles. It's also decorated for Valentine's Day, but not by a professional. A chain of pink hearts dangles from the fireplace mantel, tea light candles glow from various vantages, and rose petals are scattered on the kitchen island, which is laden with snacks—trays of heart-shaped cookies, bowls of chips and colored popcorn, platters of cold cuts and bread for sandwiches, a punch bowl, and paper dishware.

River gapes at Mya. "Did you do all this?"

"I didn't know you were so romantic," says Eli, grinning.

Mya winces. "I came by earlier to turn up the heat and get everything ready. It's not a big deal."

"I think it's nice," I say. It's obvious Mya did something

out of character, and the boys shouldn't make a fuss over it. She went all out, and I suppress the envy I feel at her wealth. Her family owns a private gated estate in Anchorage, a new hunting cabin in Sitka, *and* a housing development. Mom and I couldn't afford one stupid apartment in LA.

What's harder to swallow is that Mya can go to any college she wants and doesn't care. I'm stuck with whichever one gives me the best financial aid package. It's another reason why I try so hard in school, that and because my mom would die of disappointment if I didn't attend college. She dropped out of high school to have me, so she expects me to do better. I watch Mya light her candles—privileged and oblivious—and release a breath. It's not her fault she's rich. I hook my arm in hers. "Let's take a photo by the fireplace."

We pose in front of the charming stone fireplace—me in pink, her in black—and Eli takes pictures. Then the boys join us for selfies. River unpacks his guitar and tunes it.

I stroll around the first floor. The model home has vaulted, wood-beamed ceilings, chandeliers, and a grand staircase. There are towels in the bathrooms and a library stocked with books. It's sumptuous and designed to impress. Everything is real except for the fake books. I return to the kitchen. "It's like a life-sized dollhouse. What's upstairs?"

"Bedrooms," says Eli, adding a wink.

"I didn't decorate up there," says Mya.

Eli helps himself to a cup of punch and grins. "It's spiked."

"I thought of everything," says Mya. She connects her phone to a wireless speaker and music pipes from it. The blinds are drawn and the music is soft even though there's no one for miles to spot us and the guard doesn't drive by until two. Mya is taking no chances. River picks up his guitar and plays along with the music.

"I thought of something too," says Eli. He pulls a plastic bag out of his pocket and jiggles it. It contains tiny, colorful tablets of ecstasy.

A wave of unease washes over me. "I don't trust that stuff."

"What about gummies?" Eli pulls a second plastic bag from his pocket, withdraws a gummy, and moves to feed it to me.

My muscles clench. "What's in it?"

"THC, nothing else. Didn't you party in LA?"

Mya drops a tablet of ecstasy onto her tongue. "Finley doesn't want it."

My cheeks warm. I'm making this a thing, and it's not a thing. I've eaten pot gummies before. I glance at River. We've been texting every day but we haven't been alone since our first car ride to school because Eli joined our carpool, then Mya. It's almost as if they don't want me to be alone with River.

So my plan is to get him to myself tonight. Beneath River's muscle growth, facial hair, and new confidence lurks my shy best friend and our first kiss. I want that boy back. Maybe a little weed will ease my nerves. "All right, give it to me." Eli feeds me the pot gummy.

As I chew the laced candy, Mom's words drift back to me: *Don't resurrect bad habits*. River's dad used to pour alcohol into our hot chocolates when we went ice fishing, and

Eli's family grew weed and fed us pot brownies a few times. These are bad habits, old habits. I gave them up in Los Angeles after meeting Olivia and Imani. I took on their *good* habits. We hosted study parties, not drug parties; arrived early to school instead of late; peer-reviewed one another's papers instead of copying off the internet; attended local trivia nights instead of pulling pranks; and entered online chess tournaments instead of watching porn on Eli's dad's computer. In LA, I was an angel.

A sudden, mournful longing for Olivia and Imani rips through me. My behavior is backsliding fast without them. I catch sight of myself in a decorative living room mirror and wonder if I'm the person who would jump off a bridge if their friends did. But it's too late. I've swallowed the gummy. The ride has begun.

EIGHT

MYA

Mya leans on the kitchen island and watches Eli scarf down her artfully displayed appetizers. His big hands disorder neat rows of crackers and cold cuts, and he drops whole deviled eggs into his mouth as if they're grapes. Using the back of his sleeve, he wipes his mouth and grins at her, his dark hair gleaming in the candlelight. "I didn't know you could cook," he says.

Unexpected affection wallops Mya's heart. "The food is store-bought, idiot." Doesn't he notice that the party platters are still in their grocery store trays?

"You'd never know," he says, dragging a carrot through ranch dressing.

He looks cute and Mya shakes her head. "I must be high," she mutters.

Mya pours glasses of spiked punch and offers them to the others. River passed on the ecstasy and the pot gummies, but he accepts the punch. "Why aren't you partaking?" she asks, nodding toward the ecstasy tabs on the counter.

River scowls. "My mom volunteered me to fish the Gulf with my cousin. They're down a deckhand, and I start at four in the morning. Crab season opened early. This will be my weekends for the next few months."

"Why didn't you tell us?" Mya cries. "You should be in bed if you have to get up that early."

"It's Valentine's Day. I didn't want to ruin it." River gives a pointed glance toward Finley. "Besides, if I don't go to bed, I technically don't have to wake up."

Mya groans. "Does your cousin know you get seasick? And what about the storm?"

"My mom gave me seasick pills, and it's an inland storm. The water should be fine." River sets down his guitar and runs a hand through his hair. "I fucking hate the ocean."

Mya knows why he hates it. When they were seven, their families drove to the Cook Inlet for a picnic. Eli spotted a plateau of large flat rocks far out on the wet sand, a perfect formation for playing king of the hill. They ran out to play, including Eli's brothers and Brittany.

It was a fierce game, lots of shoving and falling and laughing. The fun ended when Finley's head smacked a rock and blood dribbled down the back of her skull. She fell into several inches of seawater that hadn't been there when they started playing. Seconds later it reached their knees. "Run!" Mya yelled. She grabbed Finley's arm and yanked her upright.

The Alaskan bore tide rose like a bathtub filling as the

friends tried to outpace it. Soon the freezing sea swamped them and floated them off their feet. Their hands broke apart as they dog-paddled toward shore.

Finley went under and stayed under.

"Help!" Mya screamed.

River's dad, Bart, and Finley's dad, Dusty, ripped off their shoes and jackets and rushed into the basin. They dove under multiple times until Bart broke the surface with Finley clutched in his arms. Bart dragged her onto shore and Dusty started CPR on his daughter, but Finley was okay, just stunned. It was a happy ending, but it left River and Finley with a fear of the water. It was also the first time their fathers, who were best friends and co-owners of an HVAC business, made the papers.

The second time was when they got into the argument that ended Bart's life. To this day, police believe their gunfight was over the HVAC business. The men were trying to sell it and arguing a lot, but the truth was far worse. Bart beat his son, and his wife couldn't stop him, and that evening was no exception. After Finley told her dad what happened, Dusty confronted Bart and both men fired their hunting rifles during the exchange.

Mya witnessed the whole thing, but she didn't tell police the truth about the killing. She will take that to her grave. She can't let anyone find out, especially Finley.

Mya shakes off the horrible memory. "Play a song," she says to River. She flips on the gas fireplace and they each sit cross-legged on the family room rug. Between bites of food, River plucks at his strings.

As the ecstasy tablets work their magic, Mya plays with Finley's hair. "Do you miss your friends in LA?"

"Yeah, of course. I don't miss the traffic, though."

Mya's mind and body begin to dissolve. The edges of her vision blur, and the music sweeps through her like wind. River starts a new song, but the mood is depressing. "Let's play truth or dare," she says.

"Hard pass," says Eli. Mya glares at him until he caves. "Fine, one game. Truth or dare?" he asks her.

"Truth."

"Did you plagiarize that essay you swore to me you didn't plagiarize?"

Mya's eyes narrow as she grabs her lower lip in her teeth. This is the Eli she wants to smack. "AI does your homework. Why do you care?"

River jabs her. "Answer or take the dare."

"God." Mya rips off her red headband and then slips it back into place. "Yeah, I fucking plagiarized it. I think you already knew that, Eli."

"Just wanted to hear you say it. Play goes to the right. You're next, Finny. Truth or dare?"

"Truth."

"Are you a virgin?"

Mya's teeth scrape harder on her lip. "Why do you want to know if she's a virgin?"

"I wonder that about everyone," he says.

"You are so fucking weird," says River, but Mya can tell he wants to know too.

Eli prods Finley. "Come on. Answer."

"Pass," she says.

Mya smiles. "Finley Dunn can keep a secret."

"Yeah, her own. Big whoop. You have to take the dare, Finny." Eli hands her a cold beer and pops the top. "Drink this entire can in one gulp."

She fails, of course, and everyone laughs when she burps.

They play six rounds of truth or dare, and after the first round they mostly choose dares—things like Eli singing a child's lullaby, Mya naming all fifty states (she got forty-five), River pulling up his shirt and belly dancing, and Finley cussing like a sailor for thirty seconds straight. When she can't think up enough swear words, she finishes her sprint with "Fuck, fuck, fuck, fuck." Eli and River collapse with laughter.

River wins the game because he only passed once, and it wasn't when Eli asked him if *he* was a virgin. He answered yes without a trace of embarrassment. There was a moment of silence for that, then more laughter.

After the game, they zone out, and River plucks at his guitar, creating melodies that float around the living room. Finley becomes transfixed by Mya's sparkling ruby-red headband. "There's no place like home," she murmurs.

"Finley's out of it," says Mya. She switches the music to Pink Floyd, keeping the volume low in case the security guard drives by early. The blinds are closed and the light is dim. River puts his guitar away, and they each lie back and stare at the ceiling.

The lyrics of "Another Brick in the Wall" speak messages into Mya's ears. "I want pudding," she says.

Eli laughs so hard that he curls into a ball. "I'm dead, bro, dead."

"I have to pee." Finley stands up too fast and sways on her feet. River jumps up to help her. Other than the fireplace and the light from a few candles, the house is dark.

"There's a flashlight on the kitchen counter," says Mya.

River grabs it and sticks it beneath his chin, casting his face in shadows. "Be right back." Then he helps Finley to the first-floor bathroom.

Before Mya can register their departure, Eli is on top of her, squishing her flat. "Hi," he says, flashing his delighted smirk.

"No," she sputters. "Go away."

To her shock, he does. He rolls off her and sits with his back to the sofa. His brown eyes shine in the firelight. "I want you to come to me."

Mya's quick retort dies on her lips. Eli is serious. No smirk, no cocky banter. He holds out his arms. "Please, Mya." Her name sounds delicious on his lips.

Mya creeps forward.

NINE

FINLEY

River follows me to the first-floor bathroom, supporting me along the way. My tight dress feels like the only thing holding me together. "Can you do it on your own?" he asks at the door.

I snort. "Sure. I think so."

After I finish and exit the bathroom, River hands me a water bottle with a gentle smile on his face. "Drink this, you'll feel better." I lean against the wall and guzzle the water. "I take it your LA friends don't do drugs," he says.

"We drank a lot of Red Bull."

"Yeah, not the same thing."

River morphs in my head from a teen to a child, like the age progressions you see on TV but in reverse. This is my chance to get him alone before he leaves for the fishing boat. I peer toward the grand staircase that leads to the bedrooms. "Want to show me what's up there?"

He startles. "Sure." He tugs me by the hand and I follow,

46

fixated on the golden hairs gleaming on his arm. We pass through the white marble foyer and confront the ornate staircase. River releases me. "Ladies first."

I duck past him and start climbing, and when I miss a riser, his hands reach up to support me and land on my hips. They remain there a beat longer than necessary, and anticipation races up my spine.

At the top of the stairs, we pause at the double doors leading to the primary bedroom. The space is very dark, and the shutters are closed, but I make out the shape of a giant, king-sized bed centered between two windows. "Is this the first stop on the tour?"

A smile plays on his lips. "If you want it to be?"

"I do."

He sweeps me up so fast that I flounder in his arms. "What are you doing?"

"Quiet." He carries me across the threshold like a bride and pries opens the shutters with his fingers, allowing moonlight to splay across the unmade bed. He lays me on it and flops beside me. A small cloud of dust wafts off the haphazard coverlet. He coughs.

"I think the cleaners missed this room," I say.

The wind picks up outside. My phone jabs my hip, so I toss it to the carpet.

"You feel okay?" he asks.

"I feel . . . really good." I press my forehead to his. His body goes still. His eyes search mine. His breath is scented with punch and alcohol. His pupils are huge and dark, surrounded by topaz. "I can see outer space in your eyeballs."

His grin turns sultry. "You're high as shit, Fin."

"No, I see outer space. I do. There's a universe inside you, River."

His gaze lopes across my face, then drifts to my lips. "All I see is you."

The moonlight filtering between the shutters casts our bodies in cool shades of silver. My skin tingles. I lace my fingers through his, and I remember this so well—hanging with River, no need to speak, and feeling safe with a best friend. I remember his candy-scented breath the night we kissed and how our lives imploded afterward. My weightless body grows heavy beneath these thoughts.

River rests his head on my half-bare chest, tracing a finger across my collarbone. "I missed you every single day you were gone."

"I missed you too. Can we talk about what happened before I moved?" I ask. His muscles tense, but I plow ahead. "I don't understand how you forgave me."

His eyes drop. "Jesus, Fin, it's not that difficult and I . . . don't want to talk about this. I'm serious."

"But . . ."

His voice grows husky. "Please, Fin." He pulls me tight and presses his lips to mine. Our horrid past dissolves as I return his punch-sweet kisses. When his stubble grazes my chin, sparkles dance down my back. His hands find the curve of my waist. "I've always loved you, Fin."

I can't speak, can't breathe. My heart swells to the point of bursting.

River breaks off the kiss to study me and his eyes grow darker. "I don't deserve this. I . . . I should tell you—"

Thump.

I lift my head. "Did you hear that?"

"Hear what?"

I push him away and sit up. The air feels cool after the heat we created. Holding up a finger, I listen.

A creak.

A wheezy breath.

The sound of running water in the attached bathroom. The door is closed, but the movements are coming from inside the room.

I grip River's hand. "We're not alone."

TEN

FINLEY

River and I slide off the bed and crouch beside it. "Maybe it's a raccoon?" he whispers.

"In the bathroom?" I shake my head just as a person clears his throat.

"Oh shit." River adjusts his grip on the flashlight, and we creep toward the closed door. Mya's music drifts up the stairs, along with a sound I can't place. Something rhythmic.

The water in the bathroom turns off, and we freeze. The person's breathing grows louder, a wet, rasping sound. My heart hammers and tingles rush down my legs. The THC I ingested muddies my thoughts.

When we reach the bathroom door, River tries to whisk me behind his back, but I won't have it. Our eyes collide in the moonlight. "What if he has a weapon?" I whisper. River tightens his grip on the flashlight just as the door swings open. A surprised male grunt emits from the darkness. The stranger rushes us.

I scream, and River swings his fist, but the man is quicker. He tackles River, knocking him onto his back, and the flashlight rolls across the carpet. The stranger's voice rustles like crushed leaves. *"Get out."*

My heart stutters. I snatch up the flashlight and shine it on the trespasser. He leaps up. He has a bearded, grizzled face and a deep cleft in his chin. His glazed eyes peer into mine and his lips draw back as he lunges.

I swing the metal flashlight and strike his temple. *Thwack!*

The man shoves me and I smash face-first into the wall. My head rings. Shock waves rock my body, and stars dot my vision. My cheekbone throbs.

River lurches to his feet and throws a punch that lands on the man's jaw. The stranger kicks him in the chest and River flies backward into the bed frame. He collapses with the wind knocked out of him. "River!" I scream.

"Run," he gasps.

The man, who is strong for his small size, swings toward me.

"Go away!" I stagger off the wall, arc the flashlight down, and just miss his face.

Downstairs, the music stops.

A throttled roar rushes from the stranger's mouth. He charges but stumbles. I rush past him and into the upstairs hallway. He chases me. *"Get out!"* His hand snakes into my hair and grabs a clump. I scream as he jerks me backward.

A handful of hair rips from my head and pain sparkles across my scalp. Gasping, I break free and race for the stairs with the intruder on my heels. *"Get out,"* he rasps again. I whirl to face him and the moon's glow reveals his scrunched face and gritted teeth.

River wheezes in the bedroom behind us, still winded and unable to stand.

The man opens his mouth as if to say something. We're at the peak of the staircase with nothing between us but air and the torn blond hairs that dangle from his fist. River gasps my name because he can't catch his breath. Worry for him flips a switch in my brain. This stranger hurt River the way his dad used to hurt him. I flash back to four years ago when River's father threw him backward into his dresser and almost killed him. Fury flames down my arms to my hands. I shove the man with both hands. His feet fly out from under him, and horror wings across his face.

Arms pinwheeling, he flies backward into the dark open space of the stairwell.

ELEVEN

MYA

Mya's hand freezes on Eli's buttock. "What's that noise?"
Their bodies are entwined on the sofa with his pants pooled
around his ankles and her dress pushed up to her chin. Mya
tried very hard not to have sex with Eli a third time. Now
her passion fades. Her neck hairs stand on end. "Someone's
upstairs."

Finley screams.

Mya and Eli rocket to their feet. He tugs up his pants and
she smooths down her dress. They rush to the foyer. "Oh my
God," says Mya.

They arrive in time to see a strange man's body cart-
wheel down the staircase. He issues sharp, horrifying yelps
along the way. He slams onto the marble floor and slides
headfirst into the solid-wood front door with a resounding
crack.

Finley stands at the top of the stairs, her mouth an open
circle. River appears beside her, holding his stomach.

"What the fuck?" Eli turns on the foyer light, pointing at the downed man. "Who is that?"

Mya slams the light switch back off. "No lights. It's almost two. The security guard!"

Finley and River descend the staircase and the four of them surround the unconscious man. Mya's gaze skitters across the horrific scene. Fresh blood halos his head. He lies chest down, his cheek smashed to the floor. Finley clutches the hem of her tiny pink dress. Black mascara streaks her face. Her left cheek is red and swollen. River is breathing hard, and his knuckles are raw. He cups Finley's face. "Are you okay?"

"I—I'm fine," she says, but Mya sees that Finley is not fine. She's trembling with shock.

"What happened?" Mya asks.

River aims his flashlight at the man. "He was in the bathroom. He attacked us."

"He was in the *bathroom*?" Mya repeats.

River glances at Finley again, wincing as he turns his body. "Yeah. Oh fuck. That's why the bed wasn't made. He's been sleeping here."

"You're shitting me," says Mya. She studies the ten-foot-tall front door. It was locked when they arrived, she's sure of it, and she locked it behind them. The interior designer decorated about a week ago, and the cleaners haven't come yet. This man must have broken in after the furniture delivery last week. He's a squatter, and her mother will lose her mind. No, no. She can't tell her mom. Mya is high on X, and they aren't allowed to be here.

She prods the stranger's limp body with her toe. His jaw

54

is red and bruised, and he has an angry mark on his forehead. He holds a clump of Finley's long blond hair in his fist. "Jesus," she says, holding her stomach.

"Is he dead?" Fin asks. Her eyes are bloodshot and hazy from the pot gummies. Two spots of color brighten her cheeks. A bruise blooms across her cheekbone.

"He looks dead." Panic slithers through Mya's stomach. The foyer's a mess, her mother's first open house is in a few days, and Mya promised not to party here. She wrings her hands. She can't leave this blood, or this injured man, for the housecleaners to find.

Eli kneels closer. "He's breathing but smells bad, like he's sick or something."

Fear and anger cycle inside Mya, mixing unpleasantly with the ecstasy she took. She doesn't know what to do.

"I think we should get out of here," says River.

Finley sways on her high heels. "Should we call nine-one-one?"

Mya shakes her head. "My mom can't know we're here. Fuck, look at this mess. Can you guys get him out of here?"

"And do what with him?" Eli nudges the man. "Creeper."

River rubs his forehead. "We could drop him at a hospital or something."

"I'll drive." Finley spins to grab her purse from the entryway table and almost falls over.

River takes the purse and steadies her. "You're in no shape to drive, Fin."

She sniffles and squats beside the man and Mya's heart rate kicks higher. "Hey, don't get too close. He could be dangerous or, like, contagious."

"What if he dies? This is my fault." Finley prods the man's shoulder. "Sir, are you okay?"

His eyelids fly open. He snatches Finley's arm and yanks her so hard that her neck snaps back. *"You . . . ,"* he growls, then convulses into a coughing fit that spews blood across Finley's dress.

"Get off her!" River rushes to help, but Finley wrenches herself free. The stranger's fingernails leave long red welts on her forearms. She scoots away, trembling harder. The man's head falls back with a thump, and his eyes dart side to side.

Eli yanks Finley to her feet. "Jesus, Finny, stay away from him."

A wail pours from the man's mouth, filling the foyer. "Ahhhhhhh!" He twists from side to side. "Ahhhhh!"

He reaches into his pocket and pulls out a silver knife. *"Go away!"*

Mya screams: "RUN!"

TWELVE

FINLEY

The stranger pushes to his feet, waving the knife. Blood trickles down his face and my legs turn to rubber. I hurt him, and now he wants to hurt me. I can't move.

Mya and Eli race out the front door. River picks me up like a doll and carries me down the porch steps, joining the others on the driveway. Freezing air brushes my skin. My breath is trapped in my chest.

The man stands inside the dark maw of the Chateau, his knife glinting in his hand. The weapon is smaller than it first appeared. A pocketknife? My brain catches up to my body and I start to breathe again, start to think.

"Get to Finley's car!" Mya cries. She flees and her heel catches on her long dress. She crashes onto the snowy street. Eli helps her up, and the frost glitters on her black lace like diamonds.

A vehicle drives into the neighborhood and the intruder slams the front door, closing himself in the house.

"It's the security guard," says Eli about the approaching vehicle.

Relief floods me. I lift my hand to wave him down and Mya grabs it. "Don't," she snaps. "We have to hide."

"But that guy has a knife!" I cry.

Mya glances at the front door, which remains closed, and whispers, "He's a squatter. He wants the house, not us. See, he's not coming out."

The guard's headlights draw closer. "Are we hiding or what?" Eli asks Mya.

"We're hiding."

As the black security Jeep coasts through the neighborhood, we vanish into the landscaping like sea creatures into a reef. Northwood Estates sits on a hill, so we're looking down at the guard's vehicle several streets away. Storm clouds have rolled in fast, and they diminish the moonlight. A fresh inch of powder covers the streets, and I clench my jaw against the cold because we ran outside without jackets. I can't believe we're not flagging him down. Cookie hired a security guard for this exact purpose—to catch trespassers. "Mya," I hiss. "Please stop him."

Her eyebrows draw closer and her gaze is like a slap. "No. The police can deal with him tomorrow, when we're *not here*."

The security guard completes a turn and cruises past the model home. He taps his steering wheel and sings, paying no attention to his surroundings like he should be. I let out my breath and a long plume of steam rises from the bushes toward the sky.

The driver's head swivels. He slows and squints at the landscaping. Crap. Mya glares at me from behind her bush, and I hold my breath as the guard peers in my direction. When nothing more happens, he continues on his way. Once he's out of sight, we explode from the bushes.

"Fuck, that was close," says Eli. He rubs his arms and gazes at the model home. "Now what?"

"Do you have your car keys?" Mya asks me.

"I have them," says River. He's still holding my purse after grabbing it from me.

"Let's talk in her car, where it's warm."

We scramble through the chain-link fence and hustle to the gravel road where I parked my Volvo. River starts the engine and turns on the heat as we jump inside and shut the doors. My stomach sloshes. Mya rests her face in her hands and groans. "What just happened?"

Eli notices my injured cheek. "Are you okay, Finny? Did he hit you?"

"He pushed me into a wall." My voice cracks. "Did you see his blood?" Now that River and I are safe, a sob climbs up my throat. I pushed a man down a flight of wooden stairs onto a hard marble floor. He went unconscious, then coughed up blood. I did that *on purpose*. I was so . . . angry. "He needs an ambulance," I say.

"No, fuck that asshole, he pulled a knife on us," says Eli.

"Agreed," says Mya. "We need to get him out of the house without calling anyone."

"We ruined his hiding spot. He'll leave on his own," says River.

Mya snorts. "Did you hear him? *Go away,* what an ass."

Eli wipes his face. "He was a freaky-looking fucker, wasn't he? A crackhead or something."

I remember green eyes and brown hair, a straight nose, ruddy cheeks, and a deep cleft in his chin. His teeth were even, his beard thin and unkempt—a young man. Was he about to speak to me when I pushed him? I don't know. I was terrified and then so upset I couldn't think straight. A glance in the rearview mirror shows me I have his blood spatter on my face and dress.

"Are you okay?" I ask River.

He rubs his sternum. "Don't worry about me. I'm fine."

My brain fog begins to clear as I process what happened. The intruder is *not* Bart Madden. He's not a father who attacked his son because he was drunk. Maybe he is terrified too. He didn't expect us to show up at the model home any more than we expected him. We caught him off guard. A dawning fear that I overreacted rises in my chest. "We need to call someone. He could die. I think his head is broken."

Mya spins toward me and her voice cracks like a whip. "He's not going to die, and I said *no*."

"But—"

Her nostrils flare. "Stop feeling guilty. You're lucky *you're* alive, and I don't want a police report about this. That guy could sue my mom, the development, or you. You pushed him, and you're high. You won't pass a drug test. This is a bad, bad situation for us. Even though he trespassed, he was there first. He could say he defended himself. It won't matter that he broke in, that's not how the law works. No police."

The boys nod.

I lace my hands together and take deep breaths. I forgot about the pot gummy, the beer, and the spiked punch.

If I fail a drug test my mom will freak, and I could get arrested. The colleges I applied to could find out. A shiver rolls through me. "You really think he's okay?"

"He was okay enough to pull a knife," says Eli.

Tears brim and spill down my cheeks. I don't believe the stranger is okay, but I don't want to upset my mom or get myself or my friends in trouble. I was scared, then angry, and now I'm scared again. It's confusing. I have to trust them. "I don't feel good," I say.

Mya's eyes turn to glittering slits. "Yeah, you're a mess, and River needs to catch his boat soon. Let's get you guys home. Eli and I will come back and figure this out."

"What do you mean *figure this out*?" I ask.

"Clean up and get the stuff we left inside," says Mya. "River's right. We probably scared the guy enough that he'll move on. I'm gonna go home, get supplies, and sober up. Then I'm coming back. If he's gone, great. This night never happened. If he's still here, I'll tell my mom. Okay? But I'm not doing anything until this X wears off."

"I'll come back with you," says Eli.

My friends make a plan to pick up River's car, drive me home in my car, and then drop off Eli and Mya at her house. River will go to work with his cousin, and the other two will come back to the model home in Mya's car.

I'm exhausted, and my injured cheek throbs. "Fine, let's go."

The Volvo's all-wheel drive engages as River grinds his way back onto the main road. "I'll check on you after my shift," he says to me.

"Thanks." I rest against the back seat, watching the

Chateau get smaller behind us, and realize that things could have turned out worse—the stranger could have pushed *me* down the stairs. But when I close my eyes, I remember that he was about to speak and his hands were down. My breath hiccups. I sent him flying because he hurt River. Mom believes Dad killed Bart for the same reason, to protect River, but that wasn't the first time my dad had lost control. People talk about mothers becoming mama bears to protect their children. My dad was a papa bear.

When I was ten, he punched a stranger in the face for talking to me at the Fur Rondy festival in Anchorage. The festival marks the beginning of the Iditarod race, and we attended with the other families. I got lost when I followed a musher through the city, begging to pet his sled dog. Panicked, Dad searched until he found us at the mouth of a dark alley. The man had crouched to my level and held out my hand to his Samoyed:

"Get the fuck away from her!" Dad brushed past me and punched the dog musher in the face. The man flew against the brick building.

Hands grabbed my shoulders and spun me around. It was Mom, her blond hair powdered with snow. "Finley, what are you doing? Who's that man?"

Eli had trailed along and stood behind her, holding cotton candy he'd bought for me, his eyes bulging.

"I was just asking about his dog," I said. I broke free of her arms and cried as my dad punched the man over and over. A blow to the man's jaw sent a tooth and blood flying out of his mouth.

"Get outta here before I call the cops. Fucking perv!" Dad yelled.

"I could call the police on you, asshole," said the musher, holding his face. "I didn't do nothing wrong. She followed me. Keep a better eye on her."

"You had your hands on my daughter!" Dad railed. He puffed to twice his size and his blue eyes looked black.

The musher glared at me, then yanked on his husky to follow him, muttering that my dad was crazy.

I bawled harder. "He was going to let me feed her."

"You know better than to wander off," Dad growled. He marched us back to the nalukataq, the traditional whale-sighting blanket toss.

Eli tried to hand me the pink cotton candy. "I don't want it," I said, still crying.

Mom held my hand tight and looked at Dad. "You didn't have to attack him, Dusty. She just wanted to feed the sled dog. I don't think that guy was going to hurt her."

"Would you bet her life on that?"

Mom gasped and shook her head.

For the first time since Bart's murder, I understand how easy it is to act without thinking. What if the stranger doesn't survive his injuries? Will I be a killer too? He charged us first, but we snuck up and surprised him. It's not clear who is to blame. None of us had permission to be in that house. Each of us was a trespasser.

Groaning, I rub the spot where the man yanked out my hair.

I wish Mom and I hadn't returned to Alaska.

THIRTEEN

FINLEY

My friends stop by River's house for his car and then drop me and the Volvo at my house. I teeter through my front door, dazed, stoned, and still wearing heels. The snow has soaked my feet and it's like walking on ice blocks. A few hours ago, my biggest problem was a piece of glitter stuck in my eye. Now I'm jacketless, shivering, and afraid I killed a man.

Mom is asleep, and the kitchen clock reads 2:41 a.m. Our heater whirs, and the warmth drags my eyelids lower. I have a shift at Mama Moose's later this morning and I'm too new to call in sick. I swallow two tablets of ibuprofen and stumble straight to my bedroom. After stripping off my dress, I take the hottest shower of my life and break into deep sobs.

I've never injured another person. It was so . . . violent. A bruise has risen below my left eye, and my cheekbone is swollen. The man's dirty fingernails left raised welts on my forearms.

Stepping out of the shower, I towel-dry my hair, spray it with keratin oil, and slip on a clean T-shirt and soft sweats. My Valentine's dress is ruined. I gather it and my heels, wrap them in an old shopping bag, and toss them into the back of my closet to throw away in the dumpster later. I can't let Mom find my bloody dress and start asking questions, not after lying to her about going to the dance. She warned me about resurrecting bad habits and this is why. Bad habits lead to bad outcomes.

I have no energy to ice my bruised face, so I crawl beneath the covers. The mattress creaks and my bedroom shrinks around me.

When I close my eyes, the stranger's face appears in my mind. His wails fill my ears and the sound of his skull striking the front door resounds in my head.

I flip to one side, then the other. Just as I decide I'm never falling asleep, I do. The world blackens, the man disappears, and the silence brings utter relief.

. . .

Something startles me awake. I jolt upright and turn on my nightstand lamp. Dim yellow light brightens my room, but there is nothing here. It's dark outside my window and clouds veil the moon. I swallow hard. The pot gummy has turned my mouth into a dry, chalky pit.

I reach for my phone, but it's not here. I remember tossing it onto the floor of the model home's primary bedroom.

Crap.

Mya and Eli said they would return to the Chateau for

our stuff, but they don't know I left my phone upstairs. If they don't find it, the cleaners or Mya's mom will and we'll all be in trouble. I pick up my laptop and message Mya through Instagram. After ten minutes without a response, I'm too anxious to wait any longer. She must be at the house.

I have to go back.

. . .

When I reach Northwood Estates, I turn off my headlights and glide onto the gravel road. The fresh snowfall erased our earlier tracks as if we were never here. I park and crawl through the chain-link fence with the wind battering my face and numbing my cheeks. The storm is not as bad as predicted, but the snow falls fast and heavy. I pull my mom's jacket tighter around me.

Parked in front of the Chateau is Mya's SUV and my muscles unwind. My friends are here, which means the intruder is gone. Since the security guard already made his rounds, the lights are on in the house. I trot up the porch steps, open the front door, and reel backward. "Oh God."

The foyer is awash with blood.

Mya is crawling across the marble with a bucket and a sponge. Adding water to dilute it, she scrubs the stranger's fluids off the slab floor. Mopping and squeezing, the blood drips into the bucket like water.

Eli vacuums the living room. "Do you want me to save the decorations or throw them away?" he calls to Mya.

She notices me in the doorway and cusses up a storm.

"Holy fuck, shit, crap—you scared me, Fin. What are you doing here?"

"I—I left my phone upstairs."

Eli appears in the hallway, carrying a trash bag, and we stare at each other.

Mya wipes her nose with her forearm. "I found your phone. It's right there with your jacket." She nods toward the entry table, then looks at Eli. "Yes, you can throw away the decorations. Fin, shut the door. It's freezing." Blood from the sponge trickles down her arm.

I close the front door and grab my phone and jacket off the table. My eyes bounce from the family room to the stairwell to the foyer. "Where is the *guy*?" I whisper.

"Gone," says Eli.

"Gone where?"

Mya squeezes red liquid into the bucket and crinkles her nose. "He was gone when we got here, but we found his . . . nest." She points toward the second floor. "He's been sleeping in the main bedroom and keeping his stuff in the closet. We found a broken window in the basement. That's how he got in." She grimaces. "He was probably here when I decorated. I could have been killed."

I glance at the small pile of belongings in the foyer, which includes a camp stove, a dingy green backpack, and a transparent plastic bag full of canned food. Something about this collection of things is familiar. I struggle to catch up. "He left his stuff behind?"

"Yeah. I'm going to throw it away," says Mya.

I plop onto the wooden staircase, notice dried blood

droplets on the wood risers, and leap back up. "Where did you get cleaning supplies?"

"Grabbed them from my house before we came back," says Mya as she resumes scrubbing.

My mind clicks back to the man's belongings—canned food, backpack, and a camp stove—and I crinkle my brow. It hits me where I've seen items like this—at the homeless shelter where Mom and I stayed in LA. Many unhoused people lived in tents on the streets, but they came inside during heat waves. They had little stoves and nonperishable canned food. I witnessed firsthand the fierce bond unsheltered people have with their possessions. "Do you think he could be homeless?"

Mya grunts. "More like a fugitive or a thief."

I shake my head. "Thieves don't carry camp stoves. He might be homeless. We shouldn't throw his things away."

Mya narrows her eyes. "He can't live here, Fin, and he didn't exactly leave a forwarding address. What am I supposed to do with his stuff?"

"I don't know." Now that the terror and the THC have worn off, everything looks different to me. "Do you think he broke in to escape the storm?"

Mya shakes her head. "He could have stayed at a shelter like you and your mom did. We have places like that here, too, you know, but he chose to trespass. That's a crime."

"What if the shelters were full?"

Mya wipes her brow, smearing blood onto her forehead. "You could have thought of all this *before* you pushed him down the stairs, Fin. It's too late to feel bad, so just stop. I don't want any trace of him here."

But I do feel bad and walk toward his pile of abandoned things. We hurt this man and scared him into the cold snow. He's alone and injured. My heart squeezes. No. I hurt him. It was me. "I'll take his stuff and drop it at the homeless shelter downtown. Maybe he'll get it back."

Eli sets down his bag of garbage and begins vacuuming. Mya grips her lip in her teeth. "Fine, turn his things in if you want, but don't tell the shelter where you found them."

"Why?"

"Hey, Finny." Eli drops the vacuum and crosses the foyer. He puts his hands on my shoulders, forcing me to look into his deep-set eyes. "This is the thing—the dude is gone, and it's best he stays gone. He's not our problem, okay? If he shows up at a hospital or you tell someone where you found his stuff . . . it could appear that we beat the shit out of him and then abandoned him on purpose. Do you see how bad that looks? It's too late to come clean, yeah? No one will believe it was an accident, and you're the one who, you know, did the damage."

My stomach plummets.

"We're not blaming you." He pats my shoulder. "But it doesn't look good."

My mind reels. They aren't blaming me. What does that mean? "It *was* an accident," I say, but my voice warbles. The stranger wasn't touching me when I pushed him. He might have been trying to talk to me. Shame heats my core.

Eli shrugs. "There were four of us and one of him, and we ditched him with a head wound. If the guy says we hurt him, it won't be a lie, and Mya doesn't want her mom to know we were here. So drop it, okay?"

I gaze at the red-smeared marble floor.

Eli's eyes soften. "Head wounds bleed a lot, Finny, even when they aren't serious. Maybe he called someone to pick him up. Maybe he has a tent in the woods. If we're lucky, we'll never find out."

If *we're* lucky? A chill sweeps my body. "Did you look for him in the woods?"

"No, we didn't." Eli picks up the vacuum. "Go home, Finny. We gotta clean up so Cookie can sell these homes to rich bastards. You good?"

I swallow thickly as it becomes clear—the bloody sponge, the cleansers, the garbage bags—my friends are cleaning up a *crime scene*. By not calling for help right away, we incriminated ourselves. I step backward. "This feels wrong."

Mya rears up. "Jesus, we're doing this for you." She waves at the diluted blood at her feet. "This is *your* mess. I didn't touch the guy. All you have to do is *nothing*."

Tears obscure my vision. She's right, she didn't touch him, yet here she is with blood on her hands. Confusion clouds my thoughts. I start to shake.

Mya's iron will looms over me, so familiar—just like it did when we were kids. She doesn't let me tell the truth. She lies to protect me. She protects all of us so we never get in trouble. It's familiar, but not in a good way. Mya grips my arm and tugs me closer. "You're eighteen. Do you want to go to jail?"

My jaw goes slack.

"It's a yes or no question, Fin."

"No," I say, lips trembling.

"Good." She peers into my eyes. "Time for a new pact. We're going to promise not to tell anyone what happened here. Put your hands out." She and Eli stack their hands. "Promise," she says to me. I hesitate and she narrows her eyes. "Do you think River's mom, or yours, can handle another tragedy?"

My head snaps up. Anger slithers beneath my fear, but it works. Guilt has always worked on me. I squeeze my eyes shut and stack my hand on theirs. "Okay. I pr-promise."

Mya drips the man's blood onto our piled hands and my stomach heaves. "The blood of the covenant is thicker than the water of the womb. You know what that means." She peers at each of us. "It means we tell no one, not even family. It means we are bound by this secret."

"What about River?" I ask.

"I'll talk to him," she says. "He was here too and he's one of us."

My muscles turn to rubber. She's trying to help me, I know that. I offer a weak smile and nod.

Mya grimaces. "Now go home."

I collect the man's backpack and the rest of his stuff and exit the Chateau while my friends resume cleaning.

As I place the stranger's belongings into my trunk, I replay the attack in my head. Violence against unhoused people is a problem in LA, and it could be a problem here, too. If the guy is homeless, it's not surprising he was armed and fearful of us. To top it off, Eli thought he might be sick. The stranger lost a lot of blood in the foyer, and we're on the outskirts of Anchorage, miles from help. I glance at the woods behind the model home. If he's alone and on foot, he's in trouble.

With a loud flurry, the wind blows a hunk of snow off a birch tree. I peer deeper into the wilderness. Perhaps he's hiding in the trees, waiting for us to leave. My pulse pounds in my head. Using my phone flashlight to illuminate the darkness, I call out to him. "Hello? I have your stuff. I can leave it here."

No answer except the resonating hoot of an owl. The snow flocks my hair, and my loose tendrils turn to icicles. "Are you out there?" If I leave his stuff on the ground, the snow will cover it within the hour. He may never find it.

I hike to the edge of the storm-blown woods, sweeping my beam of light. There—footprints! Two sets lead into the wilderness, and the snowfall is already starting to erase them. Blood droplets sprinkle the prints, but why are there two sets? Eli said he and Mya didn't search the woods. Did he lie, or is the stranger with a friend? If he's with a friend, then there could be two people in the woods, watching me watch them.

There is movement in the trees. Something big and loud. I sweep my phone light side to side as I back toward my car.

The bushes thrash and shift. A creature bursts from the forest.

I whirl and run.

FOURTEEN

FINLEY

My feet slide on ice and I fall hard. Stumbling forward, I reach my car and yank on the door handle. It's locked. "No, no, no." I fumble for my key fob.

The creature runs toward me. I flip around, arms up to defend myself.

Two huge eyes meet mine and my body sags against the car. It's a black-tailed deer with antlers. A buck. After a steamy snort, he bounds away, leaving me alone. A relieved laugh bubbles up my throat until I consider that *something* scared the buck out of the woods. Whatever it was—the stranger or another beast—it could come for me next.

I unlock my door, slide into the Volvo, and start the engine. The headlights beam into the woods, lighting the trees and pristine white snow. If there's anyone out there, they're hiding from the lights. My car is still warm, so I hold my numb, wet hands to the heater vents. Moments later, my fingertips tingle as hot blood flows through them.

I consider returning to the Chateau to ask Mya and Eli about the two sets of footprints, but I'm cold and tired. If they lied to me about looking for the stranger, they'll just lie again. It's pointless.

I drive away with the man's things in my trunk. There's a homeless shelter near Mama Moose's called Safe Spaces, and I work a shift later today. I'll drop his things there.

Fighting against the wind that threatens to blow my car off the road, I drive home and then bring the stranger's backpack into my bedroom. After changing into dry clothing, I pull on a pair of glove liners, open the top flap of his backpack, and snake my gloved hand through its contents, praying I don't stab myself on a needle.

My search produces unwashed clothing, a pen, and slips of paper picked up from town—brochures, menus, and flyers. I search the smaller pockets and find a few bus tickets, gum wrappers, and loose change. Nothing here identifies the stranger or his associates.

Digging into the final pocket, I discover a cellular phone. It's dead, but I have an old charger that fits it. After a few minutes, it powers on, showing me a locked screen. "Damn it." I try five generic but common passwords, and none of them work. I power it back off, tuck it into the bag, and find a journal.

There's a handwritten poem on page one with the author's name: *Jason Walker*. I read the poem out loud:

A Heart Too Broke

Clouds glide
drift through my mind
a soul too sad
flying.
Sunlight falls
burns through my skin
a heart too broke
crying.
Dreams fade
sift through my soul
drifting, burning, dying.

I set the poem on my lap, and my chest grows tight. The stranger has a name: Jason Walker. I photograph the poem and read it again. These lines seem like the sentiments of a sad person, not a violent person. My head slides into my hands.

God, what have I done to this man?

FIFTEEN

MYA

Mya arrives home at five in the morning. Her back aches and her knees throb from crawling on the hard white marble floor. Her stomach churns from scrubbing the stranger's blood. It's still dark, and the sun won't rise for many hours. She stands beneath the lodgepole pines that surround her house. Their straight trunks grow toward the sky, perfect and blameless, silent observers of good and evil. These trees will remain standing long after Mya and her family have turned to dust. She sighs. She still has much to do.

Before leaving the model home, she changed into the fresh clothes she'd grabbed when she collected her father's cleaning supplies. She washed her face and hands in the Chateau's bathroom and sealed the rags, the sponges, and her bloodstained party clothes in a black garbage bag so that the man's DNA would not transfer to her Range Rover. Now she slips around to her backyard firepit, carrying the bag.

Heavy snowfall has eased into soft, fat, drowsy flakes,

and the flagging wind blows in intermittent, gutless bursts. Mya shovels fresh snow out of the firepit and grabs dry wood from the covered woodpile. Her breath puffs like a steam engine in the cold. She stacks the wood in the pit, then empties the bag of clothing, rags, and used sponges on top. She squirts them with lighter fluid and sits on a cedar Adirondack chair. What has she forgotten?

She flies through the model home in her mind. She and Eli vacuumed, dusted, mopped, and sprayed, using cleansers she borrowed from her neat-freak father. She tossed their party trash in a random apartment dumpster on the way home. She deleted all the photos and texts about the evening and messaged Eli, River, and Finley to do the same.

"Finley," she mutters. The way her friend stood in the Chateau's entryway, watching Mya sponge the floor with her big eyes bulging, had made Mya want to smack her. It's not the first time Mya's cleaned up for Finley—there was the time she broke her mom's favorite glass-blown vase and Mya was quick-thinking enough to blame the breeze from an open window, the time she lost control of a grocery cart and dented a Lexus and Mya had to force Finley to flee the shopping center, and the time Finley gave Eli a bottle of her dad's whiskey and he got alcohol poisoning. Mya had called Eli's older brother to deal with it.

Finley is careless and uncoordinated and . . . weak. When she screws up, she becomes immobilized by guilt, leaving the rest of them to deal with the fallout, and then she wants to confess. It all comes crashing back to Mya, why she can't trust Finley. The girl is a coward.

This thing with the trespassing man is so much worse

than a dented Lexus, though. Mya and Eli can never tell Finley what they did to fix her mess. If she finds out, she'll break, and if she breaks, she'll confess for sure. Like a drowning person, she'll drag them down with her. She's that weak-minded, that shortsighted, and that airheaded.

Finley's lucky she has Mya.

Mya will rescue her. She'll wash away the blood and burn the evidence. She'll do whatever it takes to protect Finley and the boys. It sucks being the responsible one, but their past has bound them. Not just their childhood covenant but Mya's desperate lie four years ago. It is the Jenga piece that holds the group together. If the truth ever comes out, their worlds will collapse. She owes it to her friends to make sure that never happens.

Mya clicks the lighter and sets her bloody clothes and cleaning supplies on fire.

The flames roar up, then lower to a gentle flicker. Fire cleanses. It erases. Mya slides an ID card from her pocket. It's an expired driver's license she stole from the stranger's backpack. The man in the photo is handsome with soulful eyes, olive skin, long brown hair, and a straight nose. Mya reads the information about him. Jason Daniel Walker, born July 7. Sex: male. Height: five feet eight inches. Eyes: green. Address: Fairbanks.

She Googled the Fairbanks address and found pictures of an average one-story home but no information about its owner. The driver's license is expired, so the address could be an old one. She searches his name and city and finds an old article about a Jason Walker who was in a snow machine accident. The photo shows the crumpled sled but not the rider, who was hospitalized but survived.

Whoever Jason Walker is, he broke the law when he trespassed on private property, and Mya doesn't feel bad for him the way Finley does. He's a grown man who made a bad choice. Mya tosses his expired driver's license into the flames. "Goodbye, Jason." As the plastic melts, so does his face, curling at the edges and folding into itself like a roly-poly bug. Then gone. *Poof.* No more Jason Walker.

She messages Eli: It's done.

Come over, he writes back.

He wants to finish what they started on the sofa, and a delicious warmth fills Mya's stomach that she ignores. I'm beat, she writes back.

His answer takes a minute. Do you trust Finny not to tell

No, but I'll handle her

I want to handle you

Mya grins and leaves Eli on "read."

SIXTEEN

FINLEY

I wake up later that morning hungover and starving. The man's rasping voice scrapes across my brain like a nightmare, but then reality crashes through. "No, no. It wasn't a dream." His name is Jason Walker and I watched his blood run out of Mya's sponge. His backpack sits at the foot of my bed.

I rush to my toilet and vomit. My hunger vanishes.

Messages from Olivia and Imani in California populate my notifications. They went to their Valentine's dance last night. They send a photo of themselves dressed up and making kissy faces. We miss you, they write. Affection for them awakens my longing to return to LA, to sunshine, and to friends who bring out the best in me. Miss you too, I write back.

I wonder why I'm so easily influenced. I could have said no to skipping school, lying about the dance, and getting high. I could have ignored Mya and flagged down that security guard last night. Instead, I let her pressure me. I've always let Mya pressure me. But not just her. Olivia and Imani pressured me too—they encouraged me to go to school, tell the truth, and study hard. Am I a mere reflection of whoever I hang out with? Who is the real Finley Dunn? I have no idea.

God, the time!

My shift at Mama Moose's starts in less than an hour. I pull on black jeans and a long-sleeve sweater to cover the scratches on my forearm and then fix my hair. A quick online tutorial shows me how to cover my bruised cheekbone with makeup. I load Jason Walker's things into my trunk and sneak out before my mom wakes.

The main roads have been cleared and salted, and the drive to Mama Moose's is quick. When I enter the rustic, wood-paneled restaurant, I bump into the owner. Her name is Clodagh, and she's an Irish woman with dark hair, freckles, and deep wrinkles around her eyes.

"Careful, lass." She sticks her hands on her wide hips and frowns. "What happened to your cheek?"

A flush creeps up my neck. I guess I didn't do a good job following the makeup tutorial. "I fell on the ice."

Clodagh looks skeptical. "On your face?" I nod. She doesn't seem to believe me but lets it go. "Aw, child. You're not in LA anymore, are you?"

"No, ma'am."

I tie on my apron and grab my order pad and a pen. I wave at Josie, who works the dining room. She's a junior at Bartlett High and in my leadership class. She waves back.

My job is to serve the counter, which seats seven individuals, plus I'm responsible for operating the register and packing the to-go orders. The restaurant is cheerful and the customers are friendly—a mix of tourists and locals—and what happened last night feels like another life. My first customer, a bearded man with raw pink cheeks, has just sat down. I hand him a plastic menu. "Good morning. Would you like some coffee to get you started?" He accepts the offer and studies his menu.

Josie sashays up to me, her turquoise hair in two rope-like braids. "I wish you'd come to the Valentine's dance last night. It was fun." Her gaze skims across my injured cheek. "What did you and your friends do?"

My stomach rumbles, hollow from skipping breakfast, and anxiety claws at me. "We had a game night," I say. A vision of the stranger tumbling down the stairs and his head slamming into the solid wood door makes me flinch.

"That's cool." Josie moves on, delivering her OJs, and I imagine how my night would have been different if I'd hung out with her instead of Mya. The regret stinks like betrayal. Mya is my oldest friend, but it's all coming back to me: the bad things we did—skipping school, shoplifting, drinking, and lying to cover it up.

I am very worried about Jason Walker. My concern is that Mya or Eli followed his footprints into the woods, found him dead, and are afraid to tell me. *The dude is gone, and it's best he stays gone,* Eli said. The snow that night would have quickly buried Jason's body, and he might never be found. It's not difficult to disappear in Alaska.

If he's dead, my friends will never tell me the truth.

Mya thinks I can't keep a secret, but that's not true. She doesn't know I kissed River the night his father died, and she doesn't know I pushed the stranger in a fit of anger. She believes it was an accident.

A tide of customers rushes in—the breakfast crowd—and my heart kicks up a notch. Grateful for the distraction, I take orders and deliver food for two hours straight. Sweat collects in my armpits. Invisible bacon grease coats my face.

Despite my exhaustion and a few mixed-up orders, my shift passes quickly and keeps my mind off last night. Clodagh snatches frequent glances at my bruised face, so I plaster on my biggest, fakest smile to reassure her. After the second rush ends, a few customers linger, but the counter is empty. I sterilize the surface, refill the condiment packages, and wipe down the plastic menus. When that's done, Josie and I order our complimentary meals as the last customer departs with a friendly wave.

Clodagh approaches me, her warm eyes crinkling with worry. "Here, put some ice on that cheek."

"What happened?" Josie asks, looking closer at my face.

"Nothing," I mutter. "Sorry, Clodagh, but I have to run." I take my ice and my meal to go and scoot to my car. The homeless shelter is down the street, and I pray that Jason Walker isn't there. *No, no.* I want him to be there. I just don't want to run into him.

I drive two short city blocks and park on the curb. The storm ended this morning, but the Arctic wind has picked up again. The breeze is numbing. I huddle inside my jacket and enter the shelter called Safe Spaces, carrying Jason Walker's belongings. The shelter smells like the one where

Mom and I stayed in Los Angeles, a mixture of commercial cleansers, mildewed clothes, and human odors. The humiliation, gratitude, and fear I felt in LA come rushing back.

Mom and I spent our first two nights sleeping in her car because the shelters were full. On the second night, a man tried to open our passenger door. My eyes flew open and I screamed. Mom woke and shined her phone light in his face. She snapped a picture. He ducked and bolted. Mom's hands shook as she started the car and sped to the police station, using the last of our precious gasoline. She filed a report about the attempted break-in and then burst into sobs. The cops got us into a shelter that night. "They don't turn away mothers with children, even when they're full," he explained.

Once we were settled on a full-sized cot with a privacy screen to shield us from the dozens of men in the shelter, Mom cried harder and hugged me. "I'm sorry. I'm so sorry."

"Mom, we're safe. Don't cry."

Now, standing in this shelter in Alaska, I wonder if River and I struck the same terror into Jason Walker's heart when we crept up on him in the bathroom. I wrap my arms around my chest, feeling small and wretched.

"Can I help you?" A Native Alaskan man pops out of a small wood-paneled office, startling me.

"Um, yeah. Do you work here?"

A grin creases his cheeks. "I do. My name is Panuk."

A curtain hangs in the hallway, shielding my view of the living space for unsheltered people, and I'm grateful. If Jason made it here, he won't spot me.

"What brings you to Safe Spaces?" Panuk eyeballs the frayed green backpack, food bag, and camp stove.

"I—I found these items and don't know what to do with them. They must belong to someone, right?" My cheeks warm because I *know* they belong to someone.

Panuk's smile vanishes. "Bring them in here." I follow him into a small office and set the items on a cluttered metal desk. He touches the worn pack, examines the camp stove, and peers into the canned food bag. His dark eyes turn grave. "Whoever these belong to could die without them."

My voice falters. "Oh, I didn't know."

"Did you find them near a tent or a snow shelter? Or were they in the city?"

My mouth pops open. Why didn't I foresee these questions?

Panuk frowns and shakes the backpack. "These belongings are crucial to their owner's survival. You should have left them where they were and called the police."

"They—they looked abandoned, and I didn't see a tent. The snow last night would have buried them." I shut my eyes against my deceit. He's right; we should have left his stuff where we found it, but Mya was going to throw it away. Tears collect and threaten to fall.

Panuk pinches the skin between his eyes. "Do you know what happens when the snow melts in Alaska? That's when we find the bodies. Unsheltered people do not survive winter without help. They freeze to death."

My hand flutters to my chest.

"Did you look through the backpack? Is there an ID?"

"No, but there's a poem inside with a name on it—Jason Walker."

Panuk purses his lips. "I know Jason. He's sheltered here before, a younger guy. Haven't seen him in a while."

Panuk confirms my suspicions. Jason is not a fugitive, a thief, or a lost hiker. I attacked a verified unhoused man. My stomach lifts and floats. "So he's not here now?"

"Sit down." I sit while Panuk makes several phone calls, asking the other shelters about their inhabitants. Then he hangs up and says to me: "Jason didn't check into any shelters last night. I'm concerned about how he became separated from his possessions." He shifts my attention toward a map of Anchorage on his wall. "Tell me where you found his things and I'll send a team to look for him. This might be a matter for the police. Go ahead, point out the location."

I edge toward the map with dread pressing hard against me. Cookie Green's housing development borders the wilderness. It would be so easy to point there. But what if they find Jason dead in the woods? Dead because of me.

Fear scatters my thoughts and I stab the trailhead to Flattop Mountain with my finger. It's a rural area where I used to hike as a kid. "Here," I say.

"When?"

"Y—yesterday."

"Okay, but what time?"

"I don't remember."

He lets out a long breath. "I don't mean to interrogate you, miss. Thank you for bringing the items here. We'll search the area, and perhaps Jason will show up." He retrieves a pad of paper and a pen. "Write down your name and address, please."

"Why do you want my name?"

"In case I or the police need to follow up."

I walk backward through his doorway. "I don't want to get involved." Turning on my heels, I speed-walk out of Safe Spaces. Glancing up, I spot a blinking security camera and duck my head. Freaking perfect. I looked right at it.

I race to my car, slip on the ice for real, and smack my tailbone. Being more careful, I rise and climb into my car, my heart galloping. My phone pings with an alert. It's River: I'm back from crabbing. How are you?

I gasp with relief. He's the only person I can talk to. Terrible. Can I come over?

A pause and then: it's not a good time. My mom is having a spell

His mother has bipolar disorder, and she's also addicted to pills. Her spells range from manic outbursts to lethargic depression to being doped out of her mind. Her condition got worse after my dad killed her husband, and now River takes care of her. My shame expands at this reminder of how I destroyed River's life when I sicced my dad on his. I can't put more burdens on him. I write back: Sorry to hear that. I'm fine. Just had a crazy day at work. TTYL

Tears sting my eyes. God, this isn't fair. That man broke the law when he snuck into the model home. I should not feel guilty about what happened next. I rub my eyes with the back of my hand. I might be overreactive and easy to influence, but I'm a good person. I know I am.

The worst drama I suffered in LA was when I kissed

Olivia's ex-boyfriend at a party. She blew up at me, even though they'd been broken up for eight months. Olivia and I reconciled after a few weeks, and it was over.

This is so much worse than that. My guilt grows heavier and tears well in my eyes. I don't want to keep this secret. I need Mya. She has to fix this.

SEVENTEEN

MYA

"Where were you last night?" Cookie asks.

Mya rolls over in her bed. "Huh?"

Her mom flips on the bedroom light and thrusts open the curtains, letting in rare winter sunshine. The Valentine's storm is over. "I know you didn't go to the dance," she says.

"How do you—"

Her mom smirks. "I have my ways. Where were you, and who were you with?"

Mya's teeth hurt from clenching them—a side effect of the ecstasy—and she wonders if she looks as rough as she feels. "I drove around with my friends and went to Denny's. The dance was stupid."

"You told Dad you were going."

Mya meets her mother's hot gaze. Cookie is clutching her leather briefcase, but she's nothing like the business-women Mya sees on TV. She wears boots, jeans, and utility belts. She has a rifle rack on her truck, and she cusses. She dresses fancy for client meetings and dates with Dad, but Mya can't remember the last time her mom did either.

Cookie lets out a breath. "I don't care about the dance, I care that you lied to your father."

Mya shrugs. "You know how he is, Mom. Dad wants me to do 'all the things' senior year because he thinks I'm going to miss out, but I don't care about football games and dances, and it bugs him. He thinks I'm strange."

Cookie nods, thoughtful. "He thinks the same about me. Your father doesn't understand my aversion to twisting myself into a yoga pretzel or riding imaginary bikes with him."

"Stationary, not imaginary," says Mya.

Cookie grins. "He's the strange one, right?"

"Yeah. You and I are totally normal." A few hours ago, Mya mopped up a strange man's blood, then burned his ID. What she did was not . . . *normal*.

"Get up, okay? Time in bed is time wasted." Cookie departs and Mya falls back on her pillow. Her mom suspects nothing, and as long as the security guard didn't spot them or report them, and Jason Walker stays missing—which he will—all is well.

. . .

Later that day, Finley stops by Mya's house without calling first. She bangs on the door and rings the bell so many times that Brittany pulls out her earbuds and shouts, "Whoever that is better be on fire!"

"I'll get it." Mya opens the door.

Finley stands trembling on the porch. Her nose is red,

and her eyes are swollen. She's covered the bruise on her cheek with makeup, but not well. Loose hairs spring from her messy ponytail as she gulps for air.

Mya drags her into the house. "Why are you here?"

"His name is Jason Walker. He's homeless," Finley blurts out.

Mya blanches. "Shhh, my dad . . ."

Her father pokes his head into the great room and smiles. "Finley! We were wondering when you'd stop by. How are you adjusting to life back in Alaska?"

"F-fine," Finley stammers.

Vaughn's forehead crinkles and he walks toward them. "Are you all right?"

"She's good, Dad. She's here to see me, not you." Mya drags Finley across the room and downstairs to the basement recreation area and shuts the door. "My dad thinks we went to the dance. You can't come in here yelling about a homeless guy, and how do you know he's homeless? How do you know his name?" Mya burned Jason's driver's license. She's sure Fin never saw it.

"I found this poem." Finley holds out her phone, displaying a photo of a handwritten page.

Mya reads it and notices it's signed with the name *Jason Walker.* She peers at Finley and observes the guilt scrawled on her pretty face. Damn it. This is what Mya hoped to avoid—Finley's guilt. *Deflect,* she thinks while crossing her arms. "So, he has a name. Most people do."

Tears wet Finley's cheeks and drip from her nose. "The manager of the homeless shelter knows Jason. He said he didn't check into a shelter last night. He said he needs his supplies to survive." Finley swallows her tears. "He walked into a storm with *nothing*, Mya." Finley collapses onto an oversized chair by the pool table. Her body trembles as if she's freezing.

Mya drops to her side and gnaws her lip. "You're hysterical, Fin. Calm down."

Finley's blue eyes are dark violet, like the sky before a thunderstorm. "We should have called an ambulance." Accusation threads between her words.

Mya rears to her feet. "Not this again! Stop looking backward, Fin. He scared you. He scared all of us, and then he left on his own two feet. He isn't hurt as bad as you think he is. Just stop this, this . . . sadness." She waves her hands at Finley's blotched face and wet nose. "It's not like you planned to hurt him. Why do you feel so damn guilty about it?"

Finley's mouth falls open.

Mya shakes her head. Finley's biggest fear is getting into trouble. She believes she's a good person and she wants everyone else to believe it too, especially after her father murdered River's dad. The way to control her is to terrify her, and Mya is not afraid of tough love. She sinks next to Finley's chair and locks eyes with her childhood friend. "If the trespasser is dead, like you think he is, it's your fault. You will be in the most trouble, and then River. He landed a solid punch on that guy. He's an accomplice."

"Don't say that," rasps Finley.

Mya holds her gaze. "Your bad choices led to me cleaning up fucking *blood*. If you want to go around thinking you killed a homeless guy, go ahead, but don't *say* it. Don't tell anyone. I'm serious." She draws air through her teeth. "We were doing fine until you moved back."

Finley recoils. "*I* was doing fine until I moved back. Now I'm skipping school and breaking into homes and, and . . ."

"We didn't break in. My mom owns that place. *He* was the trespasser."

Finley's head drops into her hands and she slumps, weeping. "My mom can't deal with another killer in the family."

"God, you are so dramatic!" Mya cries. "We don't even know he's dead." But her scalp tightens, and her stomach plummets. Scaring Finley was the wrong move. Mya needs to course-correct before Fin weakens further. She hugs Finley as tight as she can. "Shhh," she whispers. "You defended yourself. You didn't mean to hurt anyone. I'm sorry I yelled at you and scared you. I know you're upset."

Finley sobs onto her shoulder for a long time, then pulls back. Mya wipes her friend's damp hair out of her face. "You feel bad because you're a good person, Fin. Please don't worry about Jason. He walked away. He's fine."

Lies. Lies. Lies. Mya can taste them on her tongue—not just the ones about last night, but the ones about the murder in their past. It's all swirling together and making a mess. Jason Walker is not fine, but she can't tell Finley that. Mya can't remember the last time she told this girl the truth. She wishes Finley had stayed in Los Angeles.

"I'm sorry too," says Finley. "I just wish we'd called an ambulance. We could have helped him. Safe Spaces is sending a search team to look for him now. I—I didn't tell them where I found his stuff, I promise, but I could call back and let them know."

"It's too late, Fin. You already lied and he's long gone. Let it go." Mya's chest squeezes. A search party—that's not good, but she understands where Finley's desire to help Jason comes from. She wants to redeem her family name, not reinforce her status as the daughter of a killer. She's also identifying with Jason because she was homeless too.

And Finley's not wrong. They should have called an ambulance, but it's too late. Mya blames the drugs for her not thinking things through. The problem now is that Finley 2.0 cares more about what other people think than what Mya thinks, which means Mya can't trust her. "You should go home and rest," she says.

Finley nods. "I wanted to go to River's, but his mom is having one of her episodes."

"That sucks," says Mya, but she's glad. Finley needs to leave River out of this. He may not show it, but he hasn't recovered from the past either. His stability is precarious. This crime isn't the same as what happened to his dad, but it's close enough to rub his wounds raw.

After Finley leaves, Mya calls Eli. "Is it possible the trespasser survived after . . . you know, the stuff Fin doesn't know about?"

Eli has her on speaker and breathes hard through his mouth. "I mean, it's possible, but not likely. Why?"

"Fin says people are looking for him."

Eli snorts. "Don't worry about it. I'm not."

Mya hears the clanging of weights. "Are you exercising?"

"Yeah. I'm lifting in the garage." There's another clang as he sets his weights down. "You want to come over?"

"The model home was the last time, Eli."

He huffs into the phone. "I'm inviting you to dinner. Jeez, all you want is my body."

"Really? Just dinner?"

"I mean, if you're offering more . . ."

"I'm not."

He chuckles. "Yes, just dinner, but the model home doesn't count as a *time*. We didn't finish."

She imagines his smirk and the heat in his eyes and her insides melt. "Asshole," she whispers.

Eli laughs. She hangs up on him, but her heart is lighter. He isn't worried. She shouldn't worry either.

River and Fin are the wild cards. They're fragile, and if they crack, everything Mya's done to protect them could come crashing down.

EIGHTEEN

FINLEY

It's Sunday and I need to talk to River. His mom's spell should be over by now and he should be home from his second day of crabbing.

My heart flutters, erratic, as I cruise down Seward Highway, the sky unraveling overhead. Mya is hiding something from me. I know it. It's how she chewed on her lip yesterday when we talked. She does that when she's lying or omitting something important, except I'm not used to her lying to *me*. River is the only one I trust.

His gravel driveway is a quarter mile long. Tall snowdrifts border each side of the road. The forest is thin at the front end of his property. Sitka spruces, hemlock, and birches stand against the backdrop of the Chugach Mountains. The storm left a rare sunny day in its wake, and the fresh powder is bluish and sparkling.

River's time capsule of a home rears into view when I

round the final bend. Orange sunlight reflects off beaten gutters and dirty windows, and a man in a hat sits on the front porch, whittling in a rocking chair. My chest tightens. It's Bart Madden, River's father.

The last time I saw Bart, he was face down and dead, shot "execution style." One bullet to his spine and one to the back of his skull. Compliments of my father.

The ghost on the porch lifts his head and my heart resumes beating. No, it's River, wearing his dad's hat. I park near the porch and exit my car.

His eyes widen. "I didn't know you were coming over."

"Sorry. I had to talk to you. Why are you sitting outside?"

"My mom's taking a nap. Have a seat."

"Oh." His mom is either still in a depressive episode or knocked out by pills. She's famous for her "naps." As kids, we got into a lot of mischief when she fell asleep while watching us. I take the empty rocker beside River. His big hands fiddle with the piece of wood he's carving. It looks like the beginning of a dog or a bear. "How was the boat?" I ask.

His topaz eyes find mine, then look away. "Scary." He resumes whittling.

Shit, I should have called first. River is sullen and tired, and when he gets stuck in his head, he has difficulty getting out. If I can get his feet moving, I can get him talking. He has the same idea. "You want to see something cool?"

"Who doesn't?"

"Here, wear my mom's boots. The snow is deep."

I exchange my Converse for his mother's rubber bunny

boots and put on the mittens I store in my jacket pocket. It's warm by Alaskan standards, almost forty degrees, but feels cold to my unacclimated Southern California blood.

"Come on, cutie." River's bare hand takes mine. Feelings jumble inside me as I remember our kiss on Valentine's Day. That beautiful moment was marred by the stranger. I don't know if River and I can get it back or if he wants to get it back. We aren't . . . lucky together.

He diverges off the snow-trampled path and veers toward the hills. The forest becomes denser, the trees taller. The white powder slows our progress, but my feet remain dry in his mom's boots. The sun drops fast, casting the blue snow in shades of gold, and the forest is silent, gagged by winter.

We climb higher, and when I look back, I spy River's pond and, beyond that, the concrete scab that is Anchorage. River's property lies at the base of the mountains near the shore of Turnagain Arm, and the inlet is visible from the slope. The unfrozen sea glitters pink in the sunset. This climb is kicking my butt, and I pause to breathe. "Your land must be worth a fortune now."

River nods. "Mom'll never sell it, though. She says dad is still here." He looks green as he says this. Then he shakes it off, tugs me to his side, and wraps his arm around me. "We can't get any closer or we'll scare them off."

"Scare who off?"

"Clark and Lois." He slides a small set of binoculars out of his jacket pocket and points to the top of a massive black cottonwood tree. "They live in the penthouse."

I press the binoculars to my eyes in time to observe a

large brown bird land on a huge nest. I recognize the white head—a bald eagle. A second eagle stretches its long wings and switches places with the new arrival. I peer at River. "Clark Kent and Lois Lane?"

His dimples flash. "Yeah. I think they have eggs, because they take turns sitting on the nest." As he speaks, the second bald eagle walks along a lone branch, screeches, and leaps into the air. Its wings spread wide as it glides toward Turnagain Arm. "That was Clark," he says. "Lois takes the longer shifts. She doesn't trust him."

"Boys," I say.

River chuckles. "We're not good egg-sitters."

"Have you tried, though?"

"Fair." He wipes the snow off a boulder and we sit facing the tree, watching the sunset. A few clouds float in the sky, and they're backlit by the solar glow of orange and salmon pink. He holds my hand. "You seem stressed."

Is he joking? My heart knocks harder in my chest. "Of course I am. Aren't you?"

"Yeah, but there's nothing we can do. It's over."

"I don't think it's over." I describe my trip to Safe Spaces and what I learned there. "His name is Jason Walker and he's homeless. A team is looking for him."

River grimaces.

"I know you're dealing with your mom right now, but this isn't going away. If I ask you something, do you promise not to tell Mya?"

There's a reluctant pause from River, so I push forward. "Please, River. I need to talk to someone."

"All right, shoot."

I bluster on. "Okay . . . I think it's weird Jason left without his stuff. The guy who works at the homeless shelter says he can't survive winter without it. I think Mya and Eli lied to me."

River watches me, waiting for more.

"I found two sets of footprints leading into the woods and a trail of blood. Mya and Eli said Jason was gone when they got there, and they didn't go looking for him, but *some-one* was with him or followed him. Did they lie? Was it one of them?"

"No. I mean, how would I know?"

"Mya tells you everything. Did she mention following him?"

He snorts. "First, no . . . she doesn't tell me *everything*. Second, she didn't mention following him. Maybe the guy met up with a friend."

"During a storm?" I stamp my feet in the snow, frustrated. "Mya was going to throw away his stuff. She made me delete my photos and swear on his blood not to tell. What if . . . what if she or Eli followed his footprints into the woods, found him dead, and they're afraid to tell me? What if I killed a man, River? I deserve to know the truth."

"Jesus, Fin, no wonder you're stressed." He squeezes my hand. "You don't need to feel guilty about this, okay? He shouldn't have been there in the first place."

"God, none of you understand what it's like to lose your house. You can't blame Jason for trying to survive. Mom and I . . ." Sudden tears wash my face. "It was awful, River. Our building was red-tagged after the pipes burst and our stuff was ruined. We had nowhere to live. It was so unsafe.

You have no . . . worth when you don't have an address. People won't even look at you, and when they do it's with pity."

"Hey, don't cry." He wraps his arm around me. "Why didn't you call me or Mya's mom for help? Cookie would have given your mom money."

I stiffen against his embrace. "We found a shelter and made it through, and you're missing the point."

"Sorry."

I sigh and change tactics. "Look at this." I show him Jason's poem on my phone. "The point is that Jason is not a bad person. He probably has people who love him."

As River reads the poem, his eyes glisten. I hoped he'd respond to it, artist to artist. I continue. "It was scary finding a stranger in the house, but it's not like he was spying on us. He was using the bathroom. I think we should have tried to talk to him, you know, instead of attacking him. Am I crazy?"

"Okay, stop. Hold on." Blood rushes to River's dark cheeks. His topaz eyes melt into golden pools. "He didn't ask for help, not even after you pushed him down the stairs. He pulled a knife and told us to go away. We were legit scared, Fin. Not all homeless people are safe. He could have robbed us, hurt us, we don't know. It might be clear now, but it wasn't then."

My confusion thickens. "But it was a pocketknife."

"Hindsight, Fin. I wouldn't do a thing different. No way was I gonna have a conversation with that guy. My only fucking regret is that it was you and not me who pushed him down the stairs." River's body vibrates with emotion.

"I wish I'd punched him unconscious. You probably don't want to hear that."

River never fought back against his father, but his knuckles are still raw from punching Jason. "Did the fight trigger you?" I ask. "Because it did for me. After he hurt you I wanted to . . . I wanted to kill him."

God, I admitted it out loud. I wanted to hurt that man like my father hurt Bart. "I'm sorry," I whisper. "You probably didn't want to hear that either." I stand up and startle the nesting eagle. River peers at me, looking pained. Our pasts are tangled with love and death. "I'm bad for you, River. I can't believe you still talk to me."

He launches to his feet and hugs me so tight I struggle to breathe. "It's not your fault. Nothing is your fault." He kisses the top of my head. "You and your dad tried to protect me. I wish I were worthy. I don't deserve you, Fin. That's the truth."

River's pupils expand. His pulse flutters in his neck. He's sincere and I relax. I offer a half smile and return to the subject at hand. "I get your point about hindsight, but Jason is out there somewhere. What if he's alive and angry. Do you think he can find us?"

"See, Fin, you're still afraid of him."

A gust of wind blows snow off the pines, and the darkening sky hangs like a ceiling. I feel as if I'm trapped in a snow globe. Jitters rock my stomach. Is it cabin fever? Am I going mad?

River traces my bruised cheekbone with his thumbs. "I'll keep you safe from now on. I won't let this ruin things for you, Fin."

When we're together like this, we time-travel. We're fourteen again and not ready to grow up. He's the boy with glasses, floppy bangs, and candy-scented breath. I'm the girl with tangled hair, muddy knees, and crooked teeth.

We're children who have fathers.

Our first kiss was the last precious moment of my life. Then my father murdered his. Our second kiss on Valentine's Day was a return to "normal," but then the stranger appeared, and I pushed him down the stairs. I toss out one last truth before this moment passes. "Do you realize that every time we kiss, someone dies?"

He blows out a breath. "Stop assuming he's dead. You're driving yourself crazy. He moved on and broke into some other house or hunting cabin. I'm sure he's fine, but look, trespassing is dangerous. He's not completely innocent."

"You're right."

With the mood killed, we walk back to River's house. The eagle named Clark returns with a fish wiggling in his talons and envy scorches me. That bird will never grapple with a moral dilemma. He will never do a wrong thing. He will never regret his choices. I grip River's hand tighter. "I can accept it wasn't our fault he broke into the house and got hurt," I say, "but everything that happened afterward was our fault."

River's eyes glitter as the sun dips below the horizon. His lips draw tighter. "What happened afterward?"

"We covered it up."

NINETEEN

FINLEY

Two strained weeks pass after the horror of Valentine's Day. My friends and I eat lunch together at school, but tension lurks in the things we don't say. River treats me as if I'm made of glass—walking me to the lunchroom, buying me coffees after school, sending me song recordings, and sharing photos of his nesting eagles. Mya and Eli treat me as if I'm made of dynamite—acting too nice, making small talk, and avoiding eye contact.

I can't concentrate and my grades slip. I start half-assing my homework, and my AP English teacher calls my mom. Mom attempts to diagnose me one night after dinner:

"Are you getting cabin fever, Finley? An Alaskan winter is a huge adjustment after LA."

"How the hell would I know?" I snapped.

"Irritability is a sign," she said.

Unlike River, I don't believe Jason is chilling in an empty hunting cabin or in someone's warm attic. He walked into an Alaskan storm with a massive head injury; the only way he survived is if someone helped him, and that isn't likely. Northwood Estates is located on the outskirts of Anchorage at the edge of a forest. More and more, I believe Mya and Eli lied to protect me from the truth—they followed Jason's footprints into the wilderness and found him dead. The man at the shelter, Panuk, said, *Do you know what happens when the snow melts in Alaska? That's when we find the bodies.*

Paranoia blooms like mold. My heart thuds at the sight of cop cars on the road. I wait in dread for a knock at my townhome door. The only thing worse than Jason dying is Jason living. I'm scared that he'll tell on me or, worse, seek revenge. I have nightmares about freezing to death in a storm. I scream and scream, but my mouth is full of snow.

Other than my nerve-racking guilt and faltering relationships, my life overflows with normal shit: leadership meetings, shifts at Mama Moose's, chores, and quiet dinners with Mom.

As the days blur into one another, locked in the darkness of winter, my longing for the LA sunshine and my friends in California expands. I obsessively watch their stories. We FaceTime and talk for hours. I miss debating lip gloss choices and hiking Runyon Canyon. I miss afternoons in the library and movie matinees. I don't miss the money stress that clung to Mom and me like a bad smell. We are financially better off in Alaska, but the benefits end there.

· · ·

On Saturday I'm at Mama Moose's and the strain of the past two weeks has eased. I haven't been arrested, and Jason's body hasn't been discovered. Perhaps Mya told the truth—Jason was gone when she got back to the Chateau, and he's fine. New guilt for not trusting her takes the place of the old.

I slide my pen out of my work apron and face my thick-bearded customer. "The usual?" I ask, already writing it down: *ham scram with xtr cheese, w/w toast.*

The fisherman, aka Ham Scram, eats breakfast here each weekend. Today he changes his order. "I feel like an English muffin today."

"You look like an English muffin today."

He chuckles, and I amend his order from whole wheat toast to an English muffin and attach it to the order wheel. He returns to his conversation with the woman sitting next to him, another local. It's the usual talk—politics, gas prices, and the real-life moose that's been walking around Anchorage as if she owns the place. Clodagh calls her a "moosance," to everyone's delight. The fearless cow moose, famous for gazing at her reflection in store windows, is discussed on every local Facebook page and earned a feature in the *Alaska Daily*. Someone nicknamed her Princess Fiona, and it stuck.

Josie breezes past me. "Poached Eggs just asked me out."

We refer to our regulars by what they order, and I glance at the customer in question, a man in his forties. "Gross," I say.

"Right?" She grabs two hot plates off the dock, delivers them, and returns.

Last night, Josie and I went to the movies together. We had a good time, and before I think better of it I blurt out, "Do you want to eat lunch with me and my friends on Monday?"

A smile flutters across her lips. "I don't think they'd like that, Fin. Your friend group is tight, like 'the Cullens from *Twilight*' tight."

"What does that mean?"

"Oh." She blows out a breath. "You'll think I'm a gossip."

"Speak freely, please."

She pushes back her turquoise bangs. "It's just, I hear your friends have eaten lunch together since, like, kindergarten. Sure, they hang out with other people—like Eli . . . I can't name a girl he hasn't dated. Except me," she adds with a quick laugh. "But no one gets invited to lunch. I don't know how you managed it."

"You're joking, right?" I had no idea people felt this way about us.

Josie's pursed lips tell me she's not joking. "They're like siblings, you know, but . . . closer. You can't mess with one without setting them all off."

"Isn't that true of most friend groups?" I refill my apron with straws.

Josie pulls a face. "I guess so, but most friend groups that old would have blown up by now." She makes an exploding noise while spreading her fingers.

Josie's family is military and moved to Alaska last year.

As accurate as her intel is, she doesn't understand that I'm a "Cullen" too, one who moved away and then came back. I finish counting my cash tips and mess with her. "If they're the Cullens, does that make me Bella Swan?"

She curls her lip. "I hope not. They wanted to kill Bella."

"Eat her," I correct, and we laugh.

The cook rings a bell, and Josie picks up a fresh order. "It's going to be sunny on Monday. Let's see if your friends show up." She winks and sashays back to her tables. I watch her go, smiling but disturbed by the comparison. When Edward Cullen kills Bella near the end of the book, she's totally okay with it.

"Hi, can I get a menu?"

A deep voice draws me back to my job. "Uh, sure." I grab a clean menu and slide it onto the counter. "Can I start you off with a drink?"

"Coke, please."

I glance up, and my order pad falls from my fingers. My scalp prickles. Green eyes. Straight nose. Cleft chin. It's *him*. It's Jason Walker. My hands begin to shake. "Oops." I bend down to pick up the pad, and my heart slams my chest. *He's alive, he's alive.* I can't believe it. What if he recognizes me? What if he's here *because* of me? My hands shake harder and the restaurant spins. "One Coke coming up," I say without looking at him.

"Behind you, lass," Clodagh tuts when I bump into her wide body. The order she's carrying teeters but doesn't fall.

"Sorry." I fill a glass with ice and Coke and set the glass in front of Jason. I dare another peek at his face, which is partially obscured by a baseball cap.

He doesn't look at me, because he's reading the menu. He's wearing jeans and a faded pullover. His longish brown hair is clean. His bruises, like mine, have healed and vanished, except for the scratches on my forearms, which are faint red welts.

His clothing appears fresh. The shelter isn't far from here; I remember it has a shower and laundry facilities. I glance around for his backpack and catch a glimpse of the frayed green bag hanging off his chair. He's alive, that's good, but does he recognize me?

Jason smiles as his green eyes lift. "I need a few minutes."

"Oh, okay." My face grows hot as I retreat. I refill drinks, remove plates, and deliver orders to my customers, all regulars and locals, except for the man I shoved down a staircase two weeks ago.

I wonder what Jason will do if he recognizes me? He could accuse me—tell everyone in the restaurant I pushed him down the stairs and abandoned him, but I could accuse him of breaking and entering. The people here would side with me. But what if he's more subtle? What if he waits for me to get off work and confronts me outside the restaurant when I'm alone? My legs feel rubbery with fear, but also relief that Mya didn't lie to me when she said he left the model home on his own two feet. God, I've been terrified and paranoid for nothing.

Jason sets down his menu and withdraws a small, folded stack of papers from his jacket pocket. He starts reading them. He looks ready to order, so I approach. "What can I get you, sir?"

Deep creases appear when he smiles, but he's not old, maybe in his late twenties. "Cheeseburger with fries," he says.

"It comes with lettuce, tomato, onions, and pickles."

"No pickles, please." I nod and take the menu from him. One of his loose papers catches my eye. It's a pamphlet from Safe Spaces, the housing shelter down the street. Good. He's accepting help, and I have to admit the transformation is impressive. On Valentine's Day he was yelling at us to *get out* and wheezing for breath. He was either high or sick or both. Now he's calm and centered.

Fifteen minutes later, I serve Jason his cheeseburger and refill his Coke. When he finishes, I remove his plate and meet him at the register to ring him up. He pays with cash and leaves me a five-dollar tip. "Thanks, Finley."

My head jerks back. "How do you know my name?"

He tilts his chin, offering a confused smile. "Because I can read."

I follow his eyes to my name tag. "Oh yeah. Have a nice day, I'm glad you're all right." My mouth clamps shut. I can't believe I just said that. He's going to recognize me if I keep acting weird and drawing attention.

His eyes rake across my features. "Have we . . . met before?"

"I don't think so," I say, breathless.

He exits the restaurant and I let out a massive sigh. Jason Walker is alive.

Holy fuck, I am *not* a murderer.

TWENTY

MYA

Mya and the boys receive a message from Finley on Saturday afternoon: Can we hang out? I have news!

Mya reads the message with mixed feelings. Finley's been sullen and unhappy since Valentine's Day, and it's really fucking rude considering what Mya did to protect her. Unlike the boys, Mya enjoys a good grudge, but their group is too small to be petty, and she misses how easy things were the first few weeks with Finley. Besides that, she's curious about Fin's news.

River messages back first: let's meet at the hut

The hut is where River ice-fishes on his pond. Mya would rather go hot-tubbing at her house, but she relents because the group always does what she wants: I'm in, but I'm low on gas. I need a ride

Eli's response is immediate: I'll pick you up

That evening, Mya's doorbell rings. She lets Eli and a blast of chilled air into her house. He's carrying a case of beer. "Can we put this in a cooler? It's warm." He glances around Mya's great room, realizes they're alone, and drops the box.

"What . . ."

His breath tickles her ear. "Do we have time to go to your room?"

She pushes against him. "Eli, we're not . . ."

"We're not dating, I know. You say that every time." He scoops her off the floor and wraps her legs around his waist, making her laugh. His gaze burns into hers. "Whatever it is we're *not* doing, let's keep not doing it." An infectious grin lights his face. "You like me. Admit it."

She shakes her head.

"Well, I like you." Eli teases her mouth with kisses, and her body goes limp in his arms. A contented noise escapes her.

"What's this?" comes a voice.

Eli releases Mya, and she falls butt-first onto the box of beer. "Hi, Mrs. Green," he says, wiping his mouth.

Cookie shakes her head at him. "You break my daughter, you buy her."

Eli laughs, and Mya scowls at them. These two adore each other, and it drives her mad. She stands up, hoping her mother overlooks the beer.

Brittany pops out of the kitchen and crosses her arms. "I heard you two kissing. Gross."

"Not as gross as you and the pedophile," says Mya, referring to the middle-aged man her sister is dating.

Brittany narrows her eyes. "Mom, they have beer."

"I see it," says Cookie. "Party tonight?"

"Yes, ma'am," says Eli, because Cookie is the one person he won't lie to.

Cookie nods. "Good, be safe. Mya, call your dad if anyone needs a ride home. I'm celebrating with Finley's mom. We presold a house today with all the upgrades, and two couples are touring the Chateau next week. One is from California. Things are looking up."

"I said they have beer," says Brittany. "You didn't let me drink at that age."

Cookie shushes her with a glance.

"That's great news about the sale," says Mya. She's been concerned about her parents' fighting, but positive cash flow is the grease that keeps their marriage from squeaking. "Where's Dad?" she asks, wondering why her parents aren't celebrating together.

"He's on a cleanse and can't drink. He's in the yoga studio if you need him."

Cookie says this without an ounce of her usual venom, and Mya smiles. "Have fun, Mom."

"You too," she says, winking at Eli. "But not too much."

"You're supposed to keep boys *away* from her," Brittany points out, but their mother is already out the garage door. Brittany lifts her shoulder. "At least Mom cares what I do."

"Don't you have a date with your groomer?"

"Fuck you."

"I love your family," says Eli.

"Let's go," says Mya. Cute as he is, she is *not* sleeping with Eli again. For real this time.

• • •

An hour later, Mya, River, and Eli blast into the wilderness atop three snow machines, with Finley riding behind Mya. They head toward the ice-fishing hut at the east end of River's property. Mya's lithe body bends like a wire as she hunches over the handlebars, ducking to avoid low branches.

Finley grips her waist as they fly across the sparse taiga snow forest. The sun is setting, and the sky is hung with stars. Warmer Chinook winds roar down the Alaska Range, kicking up fresh powder like fairy dust. The friends blast through it, and Mya hollers louder than the boys. She hopes Fin is having fun too, but the girl is quiet behind her. When Mya fishtails around a turn, the ski bounces over a series of mounds that send shock waves up her spine. The ride turns smooth when they hit the ice and skim onto River's frozen pond.

"Hold on!" Mya jerks the handlebars and the ski twirls into a spinning slide. The breeze lifts and tangles her hair. Her stomach falls and floats away as the world revolves around her, cold and crystalline. The snow machine eases to a halt beside River's ice-fishing hut. She cuts the engine and faces Finley. "Did you like that?" Finley's face is green, and Mya slouches against her handlebars. "Are you okay?"

Her friend staggers off the machine. "Give me a minute."

"Sorry, Fin. You used to like going fast."

"I guess I've changed."

River frowns at Mya and puts his arm around Finley. "Let's get inside and start a fire."

Mya doesn't like how he babies Finley 2.0, treating her

like the doll she's become instead of the girl she used to be. Scowling, she follows them toward the homemade fishing hut. The words *Madden About Fishing* are spray-painted on the side. They spent many winter days as kids in this hut, dragging salmon and trout out of the icy water. Beyond the hut, the sun sizzles toward Russia, and total darkness descends fast.

"Is the ice safe?" Finley asks as they tread across the frozen pond.

"It should be," says River.

Mya hopes so. This time of year, the lake's surface is thick enough to drive a car on, but accidents happen. Ice is unpredictable. Falling through it and becoming trapped has got to be one of the worst ways to die. Eli reaches for Mya's hand, but she shrugs him off. Fin called this meeting for a reason, and until Mya knows why, she won't relax.

River opens the old wooden door, and Finley gasps as they enter. "It's exactly the same."

"Still a shithole," says Eli.

The fishing hut is about the size of a large bedroom. There's a cutout for the chimney, and wooden benches are built into the walls. A garbage can firepit rests in the center. The hut is strapped to sled runners so it can be pushed to different locations on the lake. The floor is the frozen pond itself. Huge, fat fish swim below the ice layer, out of sight.

Old photos are nailed onto the wooden walls, showing them as kids. They're proudly holding up dead fish or playing hockey on the ice. A bludgeon, several nets, fishing poles, a long gaff hook, a hunting rifle, and three augers hang on one wall. The augers vary in size between a twelve-inch, an eighteen-inch, and a twenty-four-inch. The larger ones drill holes big enough for people to fall through, so they're not used often. Mya scans the ice floor for active puncture sites but there are only circular echoes of past holes that have frozen over. It's safe.

"I'll start the fire," says River. The garbage can is pre-filled with scrap paper and chunks of wood, and he lights it fast. He spreads a colorful blanket across a bench for them to sit on.

Eli sets his cooler down and grabs the smallest auger off the hut's tool wall. "Let's get a line in the water. I'm itching to catch something."

"Besides an STD?" says River.

"Ha ha." Eli flips him off, and River laughs and then passes out beers from the cooler.

"Are you still the fastest ice hole driller in Anchorage?" Finley asks.

Eli shrugs off his jacket. "Nah, Finny, the whole state." He jabs the auger into the pond's surface and twists the handle. The metal spins and his big hands blur. His rounded muscles flex and shift beneath his T-shirt. When the drill punches through the bluish ice seconds later, he raises his fist like a rodeo calf roper. "That's how it's done, baby."

The pond water bubbles up and sloshes onto the floor. Eli scoops out floating ice chunks. "Grab a rod, it's on."

Finley sips her beer. "Seriously, guys, I remember this warmer."

"Remember how Bart used to spike our hot chocolates?" says Eli. Silence falls on the group. Mya glances at River. His expression is controlled and blank. They try not to bring up his dead father in front of him, and it's extra awkward with Finley here.

Eli baits a hook and drops it into the cold pond, and the spring bobber floats on the water. He winks at Mya. "Want to hold my pole?"

"There is nothing I want less."

Eli settles back to watch his line and lights a joint. As he finishes his toke, he hands it to River. "Here you go, man."

Finley wrinkles her brow. "I thought you were crab fishing with your cousin every weekend."

"Not every weekend," says River, inhaling the joint.

Mya's muscles unclench. Fin looks much better than she has in the past two weeks. She's pulled her shiny yellow hair into a high ponytail, and she's not wearing makeup. Mya thinks she's prettier this way—natural and glowing. "So what's the big news?" she asks.

"You will not believe it," says Finley, breaking into a smile. "Jason Walker is *alive*. He ate at the restaurant today. He's fine."

"Who's Jason Walker?" asks Eli.

Mya smacks him as Finley explains. "You know, the guy who fell down the stairs."

So now Jason fell, thinks Mya. She leans forward, seeking clarification. "Jason came into Mama Moose's to *eat*? Like as a customer?"

Finley beams. "Yes. Can you believe it?"

Mya leans back, chewing her lip. "Are you sure it was him?"

"I'm positive. He has the same eyes, the same crease in his chin, the same old backpack."

River looks as shocked as Mya feels. "Did you, like, talk to him?" he asks.

"Yeah, I took his order. He had a brochure from Safe Spaces. He's getting help."

"Jesus," says Eli. "Did he have money to pay?"

"Of course."

"You're positive it was Jason Walker?" River asks. "It was dark at the Chateau, and we didn't see him well."

Finley's relief wafts off her like smoke, but Mya doesn't feel it. Not yet. "Yes. It's the same guy," says Finley. "I shined the flashlight on his face, remember? How come none of you are happy?"

River lifts his beer and exhales a huge breath. "I'm happy. I'm very fucking happy. The past two weeks have been hell. He made it. He fucking made it through that storm. He must have nine lives."

"It's over," says Finley. She and River clink their cans together.

Mya pokes Eli with her foot and he nods at her. They will talk later.

The bobber jerks on the fishing line. "Hey, I got something." Eli leans back and tugs. "It's a king."

River snatches the fish bat off the wall. "I'm ready." It's always been his job to bludgeon their catches to death.

Moments later, a king salmon's head appears through the ice hole with gray eyes, silver scales, and spots across his topline. Eli yanks him out of the pond, and the fish flops on the ice with his mouth open. River lifts the wooden bat over his head.

A sound like a locomotive emits from Finley's mouth. She grabs the fishing pole from Eli and throws it down. "Don't kill him!"

The fish slides into the water and almost takes the pole with it. Eli catches the rod before it slips into the pond. The fish frees itself and the line goes slack. Everyone gapes at Finley and River lowers his bludgeon.

"Why'd you do that?" Mya asks.

Eli pokes her. "I was going to eat that fish, Finny."

She gazes at the ice hole. "I don't want him to die."

"It's a fish, not a *person*," says Mya.

"Well, this was a bust," Eli mutters.

Mya shakes her head. The whole night was a bust. Finley's news is *not* good. If Jason Walker is alive and he talks to the police, they are royally fucked.

TWENTY-ONE

FINLEY

The good news about Jason didn't land like I expected. And when River brings me home drunk from ice fishing, my mom's elated mood after celebrating home sales with Cookie shifts like a spring storm. "I'll speak to you in the morning," Mom says to me. She thanks River and sends me to bed.

Sunday, I wake early and rush out the door. Mom's lecture can wait, and I don't care if my friends believe me or not. Jason Walker is alive, and that's all that matters. I feel a hundred pounds lighter.

Mama Moose's is busier than usual. I take over the phones, the register, and the new customers who arrive at my counter, serving them with gusto. "There's a big sale at the mall next weekend," Josie says as she brews a fresh pot of coffee behind me. "Want to check it out with me?"

I beam at her. "Yes. Love to."

A customer plops onto an open stool at my counter.

"Morning," he says. I reach for a menu, and then the smile slides off my face. It's him. Again. Shit. As glad as I am that Jason's alive, I hoped I'd never see him again. "Would you like some coffee?"

"Coke, please. Easy on the ice." His green eyes slide across my face—his brow wrinkles.

Does he remember me from the Chateau? Unease flickers down my spine. I fill a glass with ice and soda and set it before him, my order pad in hand. "Would you like a cheeseburger again today?" I watch his mouth to avoid his eyes.

"I'll try the tuna melt and moose fries."

The thought of greasy moose fries smothered in cheese sours my stomach. "Got it. Thank you."

After scurrying away, I spend the next forty minutes attending to him and my other customers while avoiding eye contact with Jason Walker. Almost everyone in the restaurant is talking about the wild moose, Princess Fiona.

"*She shut down West Ninth this morning.*"

"*Can't believe no one's shot her yet.*"

"*No rack; why would they?*"

"*Anyone who shoots Princess Fiona will have to answer to me,*" says Clodagh, her round chin lifted high.

I smile along with the excited banter while anxiety crawls like maggots under my skin. Jason watches me work. When I ring him up, he pays in cash. It's rare for anyone to use cash these days, even here in the Last Frontier. Mya might be right that Jason is a criminal.

"Finley?"

"Hmm?" His rasping words from Valentine's Day fill my head: *Get out.* I swallow and brace for Jason to accuse me in front of the whole restaurant: *You shoved me and left me for dead!*

"I got a question for you," he says.

"Okay." My eyes fall to his shoes. They're clean and new, and my nerves hum. I'm suddenly not so sure that Jason is homeless. He could be a thief, a drug dealer, or an escaped convict. Perhaps he left his stuff behind because he steals whatever he needs, and now he's here to get rid of me so I can't identify him to the police.

I take a giant step backward. "I have an order up, sir." I sink my hands into my apron to hide their trembling.

"Finley, this might sound strange, but do you . . . recognize me?"

My breath hitches. Shit, here it comes. I battle to keep my expression flat. "Um, no, I don't think so."

His cheeks darken, a hint of embarrassment or anger, I'm not sure which. I let out a breath and my nerves unravel. If he tells on me, I'll tell on him. We both trespassed. Neither of us is innocent here.

"You look at me as if you know me," he says.

I push out my best smile, the one I reserve for difficult teachers. "I'm just friendly, but I have to go. I have customers."

"Hold on." Jason retrieves a loose paper from his notebook and hands it to me.

Is he giving me his phone number? He wouldn't be the first customer to ask me out. "No thank you," I say without looking at it.

His expression hardens. "Yesterday, you said you were glad I was all right; what did you mean?"

"I don't remember saying that."

He shakes the paper at me. "It's just—I'm looking for my brother, see? We were supposed to meet two weeks ago and he never showed up."

Brother? I snatch the paper and gape at it. It's a missing person flyer. It features a photo of the man standing right in front of me. "But that's you."

He chuckles. "No, that's my twin. Jason."

Twin? I reel backward as his words take root. I'm speaking with Jason Walker's *twin,* which means Jason is still missing. Dear God in Heaven, I am going straight to hell. "I—he looks just like you." Tears burn the backs of my eyes.

"Yeah, we're identical," he says. "I'm Brady, this is Jason. You recognize him, don't you? I can tell you do."

I glance around for Josie or Clodagh or anyone to save me. "No. I'm sorry."

Brady's hands clench, creasing the paper. "Please think harder. My brother's been a drifter for years, but he called me for help. The shelter down the street had his stuff, said someone found it and turned it in." Brady gestures toward Jason's backpack. "When I showed them my brother's picture, they remembered Jason sleeping there a few times. Maybe he came into this restaurant? It's possible, right? The shelter's just down the street. He would have been alone and sat at the counter. Please try to remember if you saw him. I'm worried, Finley."

My heart tumbles, but I can't deal with this right now. I have drinks to refill and dishes to bus. "I'm really sorry," I say, and turn toward the kitchen.

"Wait." He rubs his jaw. "Look, when my brother called

me on Valentine's Day, he said he was sick and wanted to quit getting high. We agreed to meet at the library the next day, but he didn't show up and he stopped answering his phone. I—I pay for it, so I know it's active. He left it in this backpack." Brady rattles the bag at me. "I send him money through that phone. It's his lifeline. He'd never leave it behind."

He drops his head and inhales a steadying breath. When he looks up again, his eyes are wet. "I've searched all over Anchorage. None of the shelters or hospitals have him. He's not at any of the encampments, parks, libraries, hospitals, rehabs, or churches either. I've spoken to people living on the streets and at the camps. They haven't seen him in weeks. My brother is out there without his phone, stove, or food. He needs help, Finley, and I can tell you've seen him before. Where was it?"

"I have no idea where he is and I don't know him," I say, telling the truth. Clodagh whisks behind the counter and refills my customers' coffee cups. She frowns at us. My orders are backing up.

Brady sighs. "I don't want to keep you from your work. Take this. Please." He pushes the flyer into my hand and points to a phone number at the bottom. "That's my number. Call me if you remember anything. Can I post a copy on your bulletin board?"

I agree without bothering to check with Clodagh, because she lets people post flyers whenever they want on the corkboard she calls the Antler Rack.

"Thanks, Finley. This isn't a normal bender for Jason. He'd never abandon his phone or his food. I filed a missing person report with the police, but all they can do is keep an eye out for him. They don't have the resources to search for a nomad." Brady's jaw tightens. "If you remember seeing my brother, call me."

While he posts the flyer on the Antler Rack, I stuff the one he gave me into my apron. "I will. Have a good day."

He nods and exits the restaurant. The bells jingle. I pull the flyer out of my pocket. It says Jason Walker is twenty-eight years old. There is a one-thousand-dollar reward for information, and the details read: *Jason is homeless and not dangerous. He may be very ill. He contacted his identical twin brother on February 14 and requested to meet at the public library on Denali Street on February 15. Jason did not appear.*

I cover my mouth. *Not dangerous, very ill, homeless.* I envision a scenario where my friends and I help Jason instead of assault and abandon him. Guilt chews at my stomach. I should have known better.

Clodagh taps my shoulder. "Did that man bother you, lass?"

"N-no. His brother is missing." I nod toward the flyer.

Clodagh leans over the counter to examine it. "Poor lad. He's missin' and in this weather." She gives a sad cluck of her tongue.

Poor dead *lad,* I think. Maybe I did kill Jason Walker.

TWENTY-TWO

FINLEY

After work, I send an SOS to the group and discover they're at River's house. All of them. Meeting without me. Come over. The door's unlocked, River writes back.

When I walk into the house, River's mom, Lila, is in the kitchen. "Hi, butterfly," she says, drifting over to hug me. "River said you came by when I was napping. We're so happy you and your mom are home."

I flush to my toes because this woman should hate my family, but it's also hard to believe what she says. If she's happy, why hasn't she called my mom or stopped by? "Thanks," I say.

River's mom has the same liquid eyes and sad lips as her son. She wears a long, flowing wrap over loose jeans and a cotton shirt with flowers embroidered on the front. Her pupils are dilated to an unnatural size. "The gang is in his room. You know the way."

"Yeah, I do." A short, dark hallway leads to River's bedroom. His cheap, hollow door still sports a hole in it from one of Bart's punches. It doesn't appear anyone has fixed anything around here since the shooting. I press my ear to the wood and overhear Mya and Eli talking while River plucks away at his guitar.

"River's right. That dude must have nine lives," says Eli.

"You told me it wasn't likely he survived," says Mya.

River plays louder. "Stop talking about it."

I enter the bedroom and slam the door behind me. My friends glance at one another—looking as guilty as hell. I confront Mya, breathing faster. "You told me Jason walked away. You said he was fine, so why are you shocked he's alive?"

Her mouth opens, but no words come out.

I snap my eyes to River. "You said she doesn't tell you everything, but I think you know more than I do."

"Fin—"

I throw out my hand. "No more lies, no more secrets. We're in big trouble."

Eli blinks at me. "You were as happy as a pig in shit last night, Finny. What happened?"

I drop to the brown shag carpet and cross my legs. A powerful feeling of déjà vu swarms me. Nothing in River's bedroom has changed since his father's murder. Same posters, same twin bed, same chair in the corner. The Madden family has not moved on or even begun to heal from Bart's death. It's clear they can't handle another tragedy. I release a breath. "The guy who came into the restaurant isn't Jason Walker. His name is Brady and he's Jason's identical twin."

River strums a sour note. I thrust the missing person

flyer at Mya. She snatches it, and the others gather around to read it.

Eli points to the sentence about Jason's illness. "Told you he smelled sick."

I rehash my encounter with Brady and the details he shared about his brother asking for help getting clean and then not showing up at the library. I take the flyer from Mya. "I . . . I think Jason's dead. And I think you already knew that."

She rears to her feet. "Do you know how many people say they want to get clean and then keep getting high? Jason changed his mind. That's why he didn't show up. Don't accuse me because you feel guilty."

I shove the flyer into my pocket. "But *we* know there's more to it. We know he wandered into a storm with a head injury." My voice throttles on the edge of hysteria. "Jason didn't show up at the library because he *couldn't* show up. Brady filed a report with the police. He's scared."

Mya covers her eyes. "This is . . . not good."

"I saw two sets of footprints leading into the woods, Mya. One set had blood. You just admitted you thought he was dead. Did you or Eli follow Jason's footprints and find his body? Did you hide it?"

"Jesus, Fin, we're not criminals. He was gone when we got there. I promise." Mya's eyes tighten. "This is your fault, your guilt. Grow up and stop blaming me for everything."

"Whoa, Mya, chill," says Eli.

River buries his head in his hands. "Please stop fighting," he whispers.

I'm not sure which one of us he's talking to, but I let out

my breath. "I think we should tell the twin brother what happened."

"No," says Eli flatly. "We promised we wouldn't."

Frustration bites at me. "But we can explain it was an accident."

Eli releases Mya and strides toward me, eye to eye. "Mopping up his brother's blood wasn't an *accident,* and this isn't your decision. Leave it alone."

"But . . ."

Mya touches Eli's shoulder, and he backs off. She looks at me. "You truly believe Jason is dead?"

"I do."

"And you want to admit you pushed him down the stairs?"

Panic slithers through my veins. I wanted to hurt Jason and now we're all paying the consequence, but Brady has a right to know. "I won't mention you guys. I'll take the blame," I say.

Mya tosses a helpless gaze at River and Eli, then looks back at me. Her tone grows calm. "If you admit you injured the guy at the Chateau, the police will get more involved than they already are. They'll examine the model home, local CCTV, your phone, everything. If they find Jason and he's dead, they'll investigate you for murder or manslaughter charges. And they will figure out the rest of us were involved. They have ways, Fin. You can't keep us or Northwood Estates out of this, and my mom will be pissed. Your mom will lose her job."

The air sucks from my lungs. "But if we explain . . ."

Her eyes bulge from her moon-pale face. "Explain that

we cleaned up his blood and said nothing for two weeks? You think that will set his twin or the police at ease?" She leans against River's door, trapping me in the bedroom. "If Jason's alive, great, he'll turn up. If he's dead, telling on ourselves won't change that."

Tears spill down my cheeks. "How can you be so cold? River, help me."

He stares at his lap. "I'm not neutral, Fin."

"What?"

"I'd rather not put my mom through more stress, and Mya's right; it's not like we can help Jason now. He either made it, or he didn't. The time for telling has passed."

Shock dries my tears. I can't believe this. I can't believe River is taking Mya's side.

He raises his head, his eyes pleading. Gone are the confident smile and sexy wink from when I first arrived. He looks . . . broken, or like he's breaking. River is backsliding.

"We made a pact, and you agreed to it," says Eli. "You can't change your mind, Finny."

Mya nods. "And my mom's houses have started selling again. She can't have police crawling around Northwood Estates. Remember how I said my parents were fighting? They aren't anymore. Please don't say anything."

The room shrinks and my chest tightens. "Let me out of here." I shove past Mya, yank open the bedroom door, and stagger through the house.

Lila stands up as I pass through the family room. "Butterfly, what happened?"

The kindness in her voice stops me cold. Her eyes search mine, big and brown, gentle and vacant. She's drugged up because she can't deal with her murdered husband. How would she handle an investigation involving her son and his friends?

My body goes stiff. "Nothing happened," I say to her. "Just a fight."

She smiles. "They love you, butterfly, but they haven't changed. Still as wild as a pack of wolves. But you—you've grown up, haven't you?"

"I don't know."

"I think you have. You're a young lady, no longer a wolf pup."

A memory surfaces of my friends and me howling at the midnight sun on a camping trip. I shake it off. "Bye, Lila." I make it to my car and pull for air. I'm no longer a wolf pup, but my friends still are, and they've dragged me into their den. This—this thing we did, that we're *hiding*—is a bond thicker than water.

I drive away feeling more alone than if I had *no* friends.

TWENTY-THREE

MYA

Eli drives Mya home from River's house and parks in her driveway. "Should we tell Finny the truth?" His truck idles, rumbling beneath them. His eyes skip across hers.

She shakes her head. "It won't help. It'll make things worse." She sucks her lip between her teeth, lets it go, and leans back against the truck window. "When Fin first said she saw the guy at the restaurant, I thought he made it somehow."

Eli holds her hand. "You knew that was unlikely."

Tears skid down Mya's cheeks as she balks against the terror building inside her. "We are bad, bad people."

"Stop it. We aren't bad. Shhh." He kisses her mouth, then her cheeks, then her eyelids.

"I'm worried about my mom. If she finds out . . . God. She'll be so angry."

"That we covered it up?" he asks.

Mya crushes her hands between her knees. "That we

didn't cover it up *better*. I shouldn't have let Finley take his stuff to that shelter. River said she found a sad poem in his backpack. She's attached to this guy because he's suffered like she has. Meeting his twin brother didn't help. It's just adding to her guilt."

"A hundred percent," says Eli. He withdraws his embrace. "Look, I gotta go. Chores."

"Oh." Mya slides away from him, unused to being dismissed by Eli. It's usually the other way around.

"Hey, don't be like that," he says, grabbing for her waist.

Mya dodges him, slams the car door, and retreats into her giant, empty home.

• • •

A few days later she visits Finley during her Wednesday after-school shift. Mya is worried her friend will break down and confess to someone. Finley has no idea the awfulness that would unleash. The restaurant is quiet as Mya slides unnoticed onto a wooden counter seat and watches Finley chat with the cooks. When an order comes up, Fin places it in front of a customer at the other end of the counter, then snatches a menu and approaches Mya. Their eyes meet and Finley's widen. "Mya," she rasps. "Are you . . . eating here?"

"I am. I'll get the veggie burger, moose fries, and a root beer." Fin scribbles the order, tucks it onto the order wheel, and fills a glass with root beer. She doesn't say anything more, and Mya's stomach twists. "So, how's it going?"

"Fine." Finley wipes down Mya's menu and places it beneath the counter.

"Do you make good money here? I'm looking for a job."

"Yeah, it's good, but they're not hiring."

"Oh, okay." Mya can't believe she and Finley are making small talk. It's strained and awkward, and ordering was a bad idea because now she's stuck here. Her eyes wander to the front door and settle on the Antler Rack bulletin board and the missing person flyer. Finley follows her gaze, and the silence grows thicker. Outside, fresh snow falls. So spotless, so bright, covering everything in a clean, innocent layer.

Mya's throat tightens. Finley has no idea what her friends have done to protect her. She hasn't thanked them or asked how they're doing. She doesn't care about their feelings at all. Of course, Mya doesn't deserve Finley's gratitude—she lied about Jason Walker, and she lied about the shooting four years ago—but Finley doesn't know that. "I think I should get my food to go," says Mya.

The bell over the door jingles and a customer enters the restaurant.

Finley touches Mya's hand. "No, stay. Sorry I got so mad yesterday. I thought this whole thing was over."

The customer approaches them and sits next to Mya. She shoots him a glance and gasps. It's the man Finley shoved. No, it's his ghost. No, his twin. Mya can't move.

Finley wraps her arms around her chest. "Hello again, Mr. Walker."

Brady slaps a piece of paper on the counter. It's a photocopy of a time-stamped photo. The image is grainy, but Mya recognizes the person pictured—it's Finley, looking up at a security camera. Her stomach shrinks. Whatever this is, it can't be good.

Brady points at the image and says to Finley, "Is that you?" He ignores Mya. Several customers glance toward them, including the freckle-faced Irish owner.

Finley studies the paper. "Where is this from?" she asks as Mya's heart *thump-thumps* in her chest.

"The homeless shelter Safe Spaces," Brady growls. "I asked the director to review his surveillance footage to see who returned my brother's things. He pulled this image for me yesterday, and I've been waiting for you to come back." He lifts the paper and holds it closer to Finley's face. "This is the person who returned my brother's things. This is *you*."

Finley's eyebrows lift. Her lips quiver.

Clodagh bustles over to them. "Sir, may I help you?"

He ignores her and looms closer to Finley. "You are a liar."

Finley's eyes fill with tears. Her lashes flutter.

Mya rockets to her feet. "Hey, stop harassing her. She turned some stuff in to lost and found, so what's the problem? She did a good thing."

Clodagh nods and her loose jowls shake. "Do not raise your voice in my establishment, mister. I won't have it."

Brady steps back, his eyes locked on Finley's. "Where's my brother? Tell me he's okay."

Clodagh draws Fin closer to her imposing body, and several regulars stand up, ready to intervene. "I kindly ask you to leave, mister. You're scaring this lass." Clodagh leads Fin away without looking back.

Brady clenches and unclenches his fists. His gaze turns to Mya and he pulls a flyer out of his jacket. "Have you seen this man? He's my twin. He looks like me."

She pretends to examine the photo. "No, sir. I'm sorry."

He stuffs it back in his pocket. "You tell your friend I'm going to the police with her picture. She knows something. I feel it." A male customer glides closer and Brady waves him off. "I'm leaving, I'm leaving." He zips his jacket and rushes out the restaurant door, making the bell jingle again.

Mya watches him go, her heart fluttering. *We are so fucked,* she thinks. A cook walks out of the kitchen with her meal on a plate. Mya eyeballs the greasy bun and salty, cheese-covered moose fries. "Can I get it to go?"

The young cook winks and boxes up the food. "Thank you." She clutches the bag and heads to the back room, where she finds Finley sitting on a chair with her head between her knees. Crash position.

Clodagh is with her. "Finley doesn't feel well. Can you sit with her, lass?"

Mya nods, and Clodagh returns to her customers after giving Fin the rest of the afternoon off. Mya squats beside Finley. "Are you okay?"

Her head shoots up. Her blue eyes water and her nose is red. "God, no, did you see his face? He's so . . . mad."

"He's worried, not mad."

"He's both," Finley sputters.

Mya rocks back on her heels and lowers her voice. "What exactly did you tell the people at the shelter?"

"Nothing. I mean, I told the worker I found Jason's stuff at the Flattop Mountain trailhead."

"Why there?"

Finley's voice rises. "Because you made me promise not to tell the truth. I had to make something up."

Mya's quiet a moment, deciding how hard to push Finley. "Please stop blaming me for this." They stare at each other, and Finley looks away first. Mya breaks the news that Brady is going to the police with her photo.

"I'm gonna be sick," says Fin.

Mya grips her friend's hands in hers. "Stick to your story if the police question you. I don't think this'll go any further anyway."

"What do you mean?"

Mya lowers her voice. "Brady can't prove his brother is missing. Jason has no address, job, or responsibilities. Aren't all homeless people technically *missing*?" Mya is on shaky ground and cannot risk losing Finley's trust. She bites the inside of her lip. "Look, I'm worried about Jason too, but he walked away from that house on his own two feet, and we didn't cause his problems." Real tears brim in Mya's eyes. Fin has no idea how bad she feels. She shoves her own guilt deep, deep down.

"How do you know that?" Finley asks. "Did you see him walk away?"

"No, but he was gone. He didn't fly." Mya's sarcasm lands with a thud. "Sorry. This is . . . stressful."

"Tell me about it."

Dead or alive, Jason Walker is a threat. Finley pushing him was the least of their crimes that night. A full-body shudder rocks Mya. She must stay strong. "I'm trying to protect you and all of us because there is literally nothing we can do to help him."

Fin exhales a long breath. "But we know his last location. If we tell, it will narrow down their search."

Mya shakes her head. The last known location was her mother's housing development. Northwood Estates cannot end up in the news again, and not for Jason Walker's disappearance. The city asked her mom to add affordable housing units and she refused. Bad press about a homeless man going missing there will hurt sales and get her mother canceled. They'll lose the three million dollars her mom invested. Her parents' relationship will devolve back toward divorce.

Mya attempts to explain this, but Finley struggles to accept it. "We need to search the woods ourselves," Finley says, wiping strands of blond hair out of her eyes.

"I thought you already did that."

"No, it was storming and I was scared. We should go together on Friday. All of us."

Before Mya can change her mind, she agrees. "Sure, as long as we stay out of sight of Northwood Estates. I'll talk to the boys. Are we good?"

Finley glares at her but nods.

It's tenuous, but Finley remains on Mya's side. For now.

TWENTY-FOUR

FINLEY

The sick feeling that invaded my stomach after Brady showed me the Safe Spaces surveillance photo yesterday hasn't left. He told Mya he was going to the police with it. I sit through my classes, chewing my nails and not hearing a word anyone says. We're prepping for the AP history exam, and I'm not ready. I'm either going to fail or pass it with a three, and not all colleges accept a three.

I'm most stressed about River. I don't like that he met the others without me, but I understand. I've been back for a month and I'm hurting him again. Plus, I snapped at him in his bedroom. Of the four of us, he's the most innocent. River wasn't there when Mya, Eli, and I returned to the Chateau, but he was at the Valentine's party. If this goes further with the police, he's too involved to remain unscathed. Misery encases me like ice.

My next class is leadership, and the room is set up with

large work tables, sofas, and comfortable chairs. I sit beside Josie on a sofa. "You look tired," she whispers.

I lift my eyebrows.

"I'm not saying you look bad, just tired."

"I heard you the first time."

Josie smiles, but her gaze takes in the circles beneath my eyes, my rushed makeup application, the stray hairs falling out of my Viking braids, and my mismatched socks. Alaskan mornings are dark, but not *that* dark. I'm tired. I don't sleep. I have nightmares about storms and freezing to death, and sometimes I imagine Jason in my bedroom. He spits blood in my face. He yells at me to *get out*. I believe it's his ghost.

Other nights I dream about my father, and he's covered in Bart's blood. I wonder if my dad felt angry or afraid or both when he pulled the trigger. I bet he would have regretted his choice if he'd lived. I regret pushing Jason.

As confused as I am, I've decided to trust Mya. It's not fair for me to project my guilt onto my friends and accuse them of violence when I'm the violent one. Besides that, Mya agreed to look for Jason after school on Friday. She wouldn't do that if she was guilty.

"Finley?" says the teacher.

My right leg jerks. "Huh?"

"We're discussing ways to model good behavior in the community. Do you have anything to add?"

I read the list on the smartboard—*show kindness, pay it forward, look for opportunities to help, speak against bullying, recycle, shove unsheltered men down staircases*. No, no, that last one isn't written there. "Tell the truth," I offer. Murmurs of approval erupt around me and hysteria bubbles inside my chest.

"I like that," says the teacher, adding it to the list. "Lying is easy, but telling the truth can be difficult. We want to inspire others and—"

A knock at the door interrupts her and an Anchorage police officer enters leadership class, looking like a soldier—clean-cut, dark blue uniform, and a holstered gun. He whispers with my teacher and then faces the students. A massive shudder rolls through me. Ms. Turner finds my face. "Finley, will you come here, please?"

Josie and the other students swivel their heads while I smile as if everything is fine. I stuff my papers and laptop into my backpack, and shuffle to the front of the room. "You don't need your things," says the teacher, but it's too late. I have packed as if this officer is arresting me and taking me to prison. Whispering voices trail my steps:

What did she do?

Maybe there's been an accident.

Look at that dude's gun!

"Let's talk in the hallway," the officer says to me.

The teacher frowns. "Should Finley call a parent?"

He shakes his head. "No, ma'am, she's not in trouble."

"All right." The teacher dismisses us.

The officer leads me to a woman in a suit who stands outside the classroom door, chewing a piece of gum. "Hello, Finley. I'm Detective Perez." She pulls a paper pad and a pen from her shirt pocket and nods toward her male partner. "This is Officer Hardin. You've been identified as the woman in this security camera footage." She shows me the same time-stamped photo Brady showed me. "Did you turn a backpack, a camp stove, and a small food bag over to Safe Spaces on February fifteenth?"

I swallow hard. "Yes, ma'am, that was me."

"Can you tell us where you found the items?"

Time stops at Bartlett High as I stand at a crossroads: tell the truth or lie. I know what I *should* do—I've been harassing my friends to do it—but telling the truth feels suddenly . . . hard. A primal desire for self-preservation invades me, and my stomach loosens. Right and wrong is for fairy tales; it's the luxury of heroes. Real life is about survival, and standing here, facing a real-life detective, all I want is for her to go away.

I double down on my original story. "I found them at the Flattop Mountain trailhead." My legs go weak beneath me, and I feel as if I leaped off a cliff. My teacher was a hundred percent wrong—lying is *not* easy, but lying has always saved my ass. I am a coward.

The gum-chewing detective writes on her pad. "Uh-huh. Where, exactly?"

"By the map." My mouth tightens. Is there a map posted at the trailhead? I haven't been there in years.

Perez crosses her arms and cocks her head. "Did it occur to you that the owner of the items might be near?"

My cheeks burn hotter. "I looked around and didn't see anyone. With—with the storm coming that night, I figured the stuff would get buried by snow." My brain screams: *Stop lying!* But to come clean now is to disappoint my mother, my teachers, these cops, and River. My bad decisions—from not calling an ambulance to lying to Panuk when I returned Jason's stuff—have piled too high. I could be in real legal trouble. I squeeze my hands into fists.

Detective Perez knocks her pen on her pad. "So you had no contact with anyone at the trailhead?"

"Nope."

"Why did you take the items to a homeless shelter? A backpack and camping stove would indicate a hiker in the area, perhaps someone in trouble. Did you think to report it?"

I can't tell if Perez is curious or accusing me. Sweat erupts on my brow and under my arms. I give a simple shrug. "I lived in LA for four years. Most people who camp are homeless. It was my first thought." I turn my eyes to the male officer, who is less interested in questioning a high school student than the detective is. "I'm sorry if I did the wrong thing."

Officer Hardin expels his breath and smiles. "No, not wrong at all, Finley. You did fine."

Perez switches her gum to the other side of her mouth. "We're asking because the owner of the belongings has been reported missing by his twin brother. We're trying to confirm if the man is truly missing. He's transient, which complicates things." Her partner nods. "We're just about done, Finley. What day and time did you find the items?"

"Huh? Oh, um, it was Friday after school."

"Valentine's Day?"

"Yes."

Officer Hardin frowns. "The weather wasn't great that day. Were you hiking?"

Crap. Why was I there? Another lie forms on my lips. "N—no. I just moved back to Alaska. I've been visiting my childhood stomping grounds."

Hardin smiles. "From LA to Anchorage? Is that a culture shock?"

"Not for me. I grew up here, but I like seeing how things have changed."

"Have they?" He rocks back on his heels, more interested in this conversation than the one about Jason Walker.

"It's colder than I remember."

Hardin laughs, and Perez clears her throat. "This has been helpful, Finley. Do you have your driver's license on you?"

"Sure." I slide it out of my phone wallet and hand it to her.

"You turned eighteen in September," she says, noting my birthday and license number and handing it back. "You're an adult."

I don't like the way she said *adult*. I want this chat over with. I pocket my license and glance at my phone screen.

Perez closes her pad. "That's all we need for now, Finley. You did the right thing by turning in what you found, but you should have left your name with the shelter worker. We had to tap into the city's CCTV to get your plate number so we could locate you. That wasn't helpful. Why didn't you leave your name?"

"I—I don't know."

Perez snaps her gum. "All right, then. We'll check out your story and be in touch with any further questions."

Check out my story? My stomach slides to the floor. "Okay."

The officers depart the school, chatting about where they should eat lunch while I gaze at my classroom door. No way can I go back in there. I shoulder my backpack and hide in the girls' restroom until the passing break. I text River: the police just talked to me!

His response is quick: are you at school?

Yeah. The girls' bathroom by the gym.

Moments later, the door opens and River is in the bathroom with me. I rush into his arms and tell him everything that happened. "I lied to the police. I'm so scared."

"Shhh," he says, kissing my cheeks. "Please don't cry." He holds me until my sobs subside. "I won't let anything bad happen to you."

"I'm so sorry I ruined everything." My voice echoes in the tiled room.

"Ah, Fin," he says, groaning. "You didn't do anything wrong. Seriously. And covering it up was not your idea, but at least the evidence is gone. You're fine. I wish—I wish I could make you see that."

River's words soak into me like medicine. My breathing calms. My heart slows. I feel safe in his arms. "Okay," I say, exhaling a shallow breath.

"Good. I have to get back to class. Call me later."

"Are you working this weekend?"

"Yeah, I am, but I can hang out any day after school."

After he leaves, I splash cold water on my face and look in the mirror. My makeup is streaked and my hair sweaty.

River said there're no evidence, but that word, *evidence,* jams in my skull. Does anything link me to Jason Walker? My mind crawls over that night and the morning after. Then a memory takes shape and rattles me. "Oh no." I skip the rest of my classes and race to my car.

Now that I've committed to my lies, I have evidence to conceal.

TWENTY-FIVE

FINLEY

I slide open my closet door, tug loose the shopping bag in the back, and draw out my bloody Valentine's dress. I had forgotten about stashing it here, and tears prick my eyes. I hid this dress *on purpose*. It's as if I knew what was coming. Jesus, I'm a born criminal.

"No, no," I say. "You're good. You made a mistake."

My closet mirror says otherwise. It reflects a pretty idiot sitting on her floor with a bloody sequined dress in her arms. She doesn't look *good,* she looks guilty. My anger at Mya returns full force. If she'd just let me call 911, this wouldn't have escalated.

I open my phone and double-check that I've deleted all my texts and photos since I moved to Alaska. Then I clear out the "recently deleted" album and erase my cloud backup. There, a clean slate. What else might tie me to Jason? There could be CCTV footage of my car driving to or from Northwood Estates, but the police think I found his stuff at Flattop

Mountain, which is in the opposite direction. I doubt they'll check every camera in Anchorage. Jason's fingernail marks on my forearms are still visible, but there's no way the police can prove they're his.

Unless...

Unless they find his body. No doubt my DNA is all over Jason and beneath his nails.

As I contemplate Mya's secrecy since Valentine's Day, I return to believing she lied to me. A story unfolds in my mind: she told Eli to follow Jason's footprints into the woods. What Eli did to the man or his body next, I don't want to imagine, but Mya's been covering up for us since preschool. She thinks I'm weak, and she's right. I am weak. We have fallen into our old ways, except instead of vandalism and shoplifting, she's hiding an assault and maybe a death.

Saliva instantly fills my mouth, and I hold very still until the nausea passes. It was not my choice to cover this up, but I've been silent for over two weeks. Jason either made it or he didn't. Like River said, the time for telling has passed. All that's left is damage control.

The giant trash dumpster at the edge of my complex looms in the afternoon shadows. The light above the dumpster burned out months ago, and the whole complex is upset about it. Except me. I toss the shopping bag into the trash bin. There—evidence concealed. There is no going back now.

. . .

Mom drops her purse and keys on the entry table when she gets home and rushes into the family room. "The school called and told me you talked to the police. What happened?"

I set down my laptop. I've showered and eaten and I'm catching up on homework. "Nothing. It's no big deal."

She rubs the back of her neck. "That's what you kids always say, *it's no big deal.* Then why did the police talk to you? It seems like a big deal, Fin."

I explain to her what happened. "I turned in someone's lost stuff, and everyone's making a federal case of it. I did the right thing." My hands tremble, but I get what I want. Mom backs off.

Upstairs in my bedroom, I flop onto my bed. My life is unraveling, and I vow to be the good person I became in LA. I'll be nice, generous, and helpful. I'll speak out against bullying. I'll vote and recycle.

My phone explodes with messages and calls from Josie. She's worried about what the police wanted at school. To shut her up, I call her back and give the simple answer I gave my mom, that I returned someone's lost things.

But Josie hammers me with questions and squeezes out a few more details—like how the owner is homeless and missing. "You did a good deed," she says, her voice brightening. "We should ask the shelter if they need volunteers. This could be a great leadership project."

"Turning stuff in to a lost and found isn't a good deed. Don't tell anyone, okay? It's not worth it."

"But—"

"Dinner's ready, I have to go." We say goodbye.

Dinner is not ready, and I call Mya next. Unless River or someone from my class told her, she doesn't know about my visit with the cops, and I don't mention it. I jump straight to our search party plans. "Don't forget we're looking for Jason after school tomorrow. It won't be snowing."

"Aren't you going to say hello?"

"Did you hear me?" I ask.

"Yes, we're searching the woods for a trespassing drug addict. Got it. What are friends for?"

We hang up and I drop my head into my hands. I didn't know friends were for *this*.

TWENTY-SIX

MYA

On the day they are supposed to search the woods for Jason Walker, it's Mya's turn to read her work in class. The assignment was to write a parable. Mya wrote about a goose that migrates south, stays too long, and sheds all her down. When she returns to the cold north, she joins her old friends floating on a pond. The reunion is short. Without her warm down, the bird freezes to death and sinks to the bottom. It's called "The Parable of the Foolish Goose," and it's not about Finley Dunn, no matter how much it appears to be.

When Mya finishes reading her story, everyone stares at her. Whispers erupt. They smell blood in the water regarding her friendship with Finley. Many students are from nomadic military families and don't know the two girls have a history. They just know that the cute California blonde got snatched up quick by Mya's group. Now they sense a fracture, which means Finley Dunn could soon be available.

Mya snorts. What no one, not even Finley, understands is that Mya will never let her go.

Tingles sweep up the back of her neck when she realizes her peers are whispering about her parable and laughing. It's creative writing—you can't do it *wrong*. She's about to tell the class to fuck off when the teacher receives a phone call and makes a relieved noise. "You're wanted in the office, Mya. Bring your things with you. We'll discuss your . . . parable later."

Mya shoves the typed pages into her backpack and storms out of class.

She spies her mother through the glass wall as she approaches the school office. "Shit, shit." Her mom is dressed in her "establishment attire"—a pantsuit and jewelry, her brown hair pinned up in a chignon. Her cheeks are an angry shade of pissed off. Mya enters the office just as her mother finishes signing the campus release form with undue flourish.

"There you are, Mya. Follow me." Cookie hobbles out of the school because she's unused to wearing heels.

"Is this about Brittany?" Mya asks. Her sister's much older boyfriend ditched her last night, and Brittany got so drunk she had to Uber home.

"What about Brittany?"

"Never mind."

"This is about you," Cookie says, snapping her fingers. "Get in the car."

Mya climbs into her mom's old Lexus and shoves papers and debris off the seat and onto the messy floor. "Do you drive clients in this mess?"

"Don't change the subject."

"I don't know what the subject is."

"The subject is you are grounded for the rest of your life if you don't tell me the truth." The car starts and off they go. Cookie's attempt to look like a conforming businesswoman is already failing. Two of her fake nails have fallen off, her pancake makeup doesn't blend with her neck, and each time her right sleeve creeps up, her tattoos become visible. Her mother's wealth dates back to the Alaskan gold rush, but she's not refined. Old Alaskan money is not the same as old money from Outside. As Cookie likes to say: "Refining is for oil, not for people."

Mya shrinks in her seat. "Truth about what?"

Cookie steers onto the snowplowed road leading to Northwood Estates. "The police are at the Chateau. They pinged a homeless man's phone, and they believe he's been sleeping there. They claim they've found 'evidence' of a crime." She puts the word *evidence* in air quotes because she doesn't trust any arm of the local or federal government. "Trespassing is the crime, I said to the cop."

Mya's leg twitches. She doesn't like where this conversation is headed and starts buttering up her mother. "You look nice."

"Shut the fuck up." When Mya flinches, Cookie rephrases. "Shut the fuck up, *please.* Did you bring your friends to the Chateau, Mya? The police mentioned Finley's name."

Mya groans and her mom shakes her head. "Yep, that's what I thought."

Cookie turns into Northwood Estates and spots police cars lined up in front of the model home. "Well, shit. Isn't this festive?" Yellow tape cordons off the property.

Mya's stomach lurches.

Cookie parks the car and twists to face her daughter. "Listen up, Mya. Do not speak to the cops."

"I—"

"Just listen. Please. Did you and your friends party here after you swore not to? You tell me the truth, Mya, not them." She waves toward the police. "You say nothing to them."

Mya swallows. "Yeah, we had a party here."

"Blast it, Mya. Is it true a homeless man has been sleeping in the house? Did you see him?"

A tear rolls down Mya's cheek. "He scared us, Mom." She explains to her mother about the fight upstairs, Finley's push, and Jason's disastrous tumble down the stairs. "I cleaned everything up. You said it's okay to make mistakes as long as I fix them." She doesn't tell her mom the rest. No one needs to know the rest.

Cookie taps her remaining fake nails on her leather steering wheel and peers hard at her daughter. "Were all four of you there?"

Mya clamps her mouth shut.

"Doesn't matter." Cookie's bun comes loose as she shakes her head. "Come on, let's find out what this kerfuffle is all about."

Mother and daughter approach the model home. A female investigator stops them. "Are you Cookie Green?"

Mya's mom crosses her arms. "In the flesh, and this is my daughter Mya. What's going on here? I have a real estate showing scheduled for tomorrow."

"I'm Detective Perez, and that won't be possible, ma'am.

This is a potential crime scene, and we can't release the property until we finish processing it."

Cookie almost topples over. "That's not gonna work. I have buyers flying in from LA at this moment, and they're bringing their designer with them. I need the property in the morning."

A frown appears on Perez's lined face. "We won't be finished by tomorrow, and we're organizing search parties to leave here at dawn."

"Search parties?"

"As I stated on the phone, a man named Jason Walker has been living here. His last phone call was made from this location."

"Living here?" Cookie screeches. "I don't remember signing a lease agreement." She squints at the cop but fails to intimidate her. "This is private property. You cannot commandeer it to look for a squatter."

Cookie rolls her eyes. "Let me see your warrant."

Perez shows Cookie the paperwork, and Cookie peruses it, then hands it back. "You can't find this man because he doesn't want to be found. He's a wanderer. You don't need to be a detective to figure that out."

Perez's voice turns crisp. "There's more, Mrs. Green. Let us show you what we found."

Cookie waves her arm as if she has any control over this. "Be my guest."

As they walk to the Chateau's porch, the officer glances at Mya. "Shouldn't you be in school?"

"Don't speak to her," says Cookie.

Perez grunts but obeys. She escorts Mya and her mom through the yellow tape to the front porch and stops them there. "No farther," she says. "Watch."

Officials wearing plain clothes push open the front door. The home's interior is dim, and the curtains are still drawn from the night of the party. "Turn on the light," says Perez.

One of the officials, who is wearing gloves and a protective suit, lifts an object that looks like a large flashlight. "Ready?"

"Ready," says Perez.

Mya holds her breath. Something awful is about to happen.

The detective shines the light on the white marble foyer, and a luminescent blue stain in the shape of a puddle appears. "What is that?" Cookie asks.

"Blood," says Perez.

TWENTY-SEVEN

MYA

"Someone attempted to scrub the scene," says the detective as Cookie and Mya gape at the luminescent stain. "The size of this puddle indicates severe injury."

"Or a coffee spill," says Cookie. "That can't be blood."

"I didn't know you held a forensics degree," says Perez.

"If it is blood," Cookie says through gritted teeth, "it's from one of my contractor's workers. When they get hurt, they bleed all over the place."

"I thought of that and already called your contractor. No injuries were reported in the past two months. I also contacted your cleaning company, and they have no knowledge of this stain."

Cookie circles her jaw. "Why are you so concerned about this intruder? Is he dangerous?"

"No, he's missing. We weren't concerned until his belongings showed up at a shelter without him. Brady Walker, Jason's twin brother, insisted we access Jason's phone activity. GPS data shows that he made a call here during the window of time he disappeared. The teen girl who found his phone and backpack claims they were lost at Flattop Mountain, but Jason's GPS data contradicts that. It's suspicious."

Perez points to the side of the house. "There's a broken basement window there, which we believe was Jason's point of entry. We found fingerprints and fibers stuck to the broken glass, and we'll run that evidence through our databases. Due to a prior offense, Mr. Walker's fingerprints and DNA are on file. We'll know very soon if the evidence matches to him. If so, the quantity of blood, the clumsy attempt to hide it, and the teen's false statement elevate our concern for his well-being."

Mya stares at the ground, her heart hammering. Finley's "good deed" is going to land them in prison.

"What kind of prior offense?" Cookie asks. "I have a right to know the criminal status of the man you admit broke into my property."

Perez shifts her gaze away. "It was for assault, a bar fight."

"Aha," Cookie spouts. "Not dangerous, my ass. When you find this Jason Walker, I'm pressing charges for breaking and entering."

"That's your right, Mrs. Green."

Mya turns hot from embarrassment. Her mother sounds heartless, but what Jason did is illegal. Her anger at him rebounds. Finley had every reason to defend herself, and if Mya hadn't been high that night, she might have had the guy arrested.

Detective Perez nods toward the massive bloodstain. "Until we find the missing man, we're treating this as a potential crime scene. Something violent happened here, Mrs. Green. That amount of blood loss indicates a critical injury that requires immediate attention. To top it off, unsheltered people don't abandon their food and belongings as Mr. Walker did. Also, we don't believe he was alone in this house. Because of that, we suspect foul play." Detective Perez angles her head toward Mya. "You're friends with Finley Dunn, is that correct?"

Mya nods, hesitant.

"Was Finley at this house on Valentine's evening or the day following?"

Cookie turns crimson. "Stop right there, Detective. You don't have permission to question my daughter. She's seventeen years old."

Perez smirks but backs off. "I understand you have a security guard and cameras."

Cookie crosses her arms. "The cameras are a pain in the ass. The batteries are dead, and I haven't changed them." This is not a lie, but Mya can tell Detective Perez doesn't believe it.

"That's convenient," says the cop. "Do you have alarms on the house?"

"Not activated. There were too many false alerts. That's why I pay a security company to send a guard through twice a day. A company I will fire as soon as we're done here."

Perez writes this on her pad of paper. "The name of the company?"

Cookie blows out a breath and gives the information. "I can save you some time right now. They didn't report a disturbance or intruders that night."

"Not very observant, are they?" says Perez.

"We're leaving," says Cookie. She snatches Mya's hand and ushers her to their car. She curses as she pulls away from the curb. "They're going after Finley next."

Mya's mouth pops open. "The detective didn't say that." But she messages her friends and calls off their search for Jason after school: Need to cancel our special plans today. Tell you why later.

Cookie rips the clip out of her bun and her hair falls loose. "The police will find out about your little party, Mya. Tell me any shit you left out of your story. Now. Then I'm calling a lawyer. I'm not taking you back to school today."

Mya releases a few more details about their Valentine's Day get-together, but not everything. A new fear plucks at her nerves. Jason has an arrest record, which is no surprise to Mya, but what if he and his twin are dangerous? Brady Walker knows where Finley works, and he already suspects her of being involved with his brother's disappearance. Mya recalls his anger when he confronted Finley at Mama Moose's. When he finds out about this bloodstain, he's going to lose his shit.

Things with him could get much, much worse. Mya needs to warn Finley.

TWENTY-EIGHT

FINLEY

My phone rings with a call from Mya as I walk between classes. It's unusual because she prefers messaging. "Hey. Why are you calling?"

Mya rushes her words. "Mom picked me up from school. The police are at Northwood Estates."

"Why?"

"They got GPS from Jason's phone, and it led them to the Chateau. They found the bloodstain and they know you lied."

"Oh my God." I halt and lean against a locker as students walk by in groups. This isn't what I expected her to say.

Mya continues. "My mom hired an attorney, her name is Ms. Chen. If the police try to talk to you, don't say a word. Call Ms. Chen!" Then she explains why she canceled our search. "The woods are crawling with cops, and there's one more thing, Fin. Watch out for Jason's brother. He's going to be pissed when he finds out you lied. He's already suspicious of you. Be careful, okay? I gotta go."

She ends the call, and I can't believe my lie backfired so fast. If this isn't enough, Josie told the *entire high school* what I told her in confidence—that I returned a homeless man's things to a shelter and that the police think he's missing. They're making me into some kind of hero.

My leadership teacher nicknamed me "the Good Samaritan," and a school journalism student contacted me for an interview. He's writing an article about homelessness in Anchorage, and he's curious about the shelter and why the police believe the man is missing. He congratulated me for "helping" with the investigation.

I dive back into the swarm of students with my head down. With each pat on the back my guilt seeps deeper into my skin, and terror sits like a cold stone in my stomach. If the truth that I lied to the police gets out, I will topple off this stupid pedestal I've landed on. Colleges could deny my applications on moral grounds. Everyone will be disappointed in me, Mom will have to deal with another family member on the wrong side of the law, and River could be implicated too. I can't expect him to forgive me a second time.

Avoiding River and everyone else, I scurry out of Bartlett High, waving off calls from the cheerleaders who ask me to join their competition squad. Their captain skips to keep up with me. "We could use another flyer. Two of ours have concussions. Can you do a roundoff?"

"Um, I don't know. Can I get back to you?" I make it to

my car and lock myself inside. As the windows defog, the hairs on my neck lift. Someone is watching me.

It takes a minute before I spot him, an adult man standing on the public sidewalk. He's wearing a hoodie beneath a green army jacket. The hood is pulled tight, but his straight nose and lightly bearded jaw are familiar.

It's Brady Walker.

Sweat beads on my forehead. He hasn't shaved since I last saw him, so he looks more like his twin than ever. Brady's hands are jammed into his pockets. He knows where I work, and now he knows where I go to school. Mya warned me to watch out for him. She was right.

Heart hammering, I slide my car into reverse and slam my foot on the pedal. The Volvo lurches backward. A student honks his truck horn. "Watch where you're going, fuckhead!"

I crack my window and wave an apology.

The football player recognizes me. "Shit, sorry, Finley. Ladies first." He flashes a cute grin.

I edge out of my spot and drive toward the front of the school, toward Brady. My stomach roils. I fumble for my sunglasses and slide them on despite the gray sky.

As I drive past, Brady withdraws something shiny from his pocket: a pen. He squats and writes on his hand.

"No, no!" He's copying down my license plate number. What does he want? Tears slip from my eyes and another horn blares. I veer onto the main road and a massive brown body appears in my windshield. I slam on my brakes and fishtail toward a huge cow moose—Princess Fiona. She holds her ground with her head lowered. I squeeze my eyes closed and brace for impact, but the Volvo halts a few inches from her body. "God, Fiona!" My hot breath fogs the window.

The moose blinks at me, unalarmed and unaware of how close she came to death. With a shake of her massive shoulders, Princess Fiona resumes her stroll across the street.

"Focus, Finley." I place my trembling hands at ten and two and study the road, driving extra careful and alert. Alaskan fog rolls across the asphalt and black ice slicks the road. *Thin ice, fog, darkness*—my AP English class would appreciate the metaphorical parallels to my fucked-up life. Just as my frozen car warms up, I pull into the townhome complex. I want my mom, my bedroom, and my warm bed.

Except there is no safety here. Swirling lights greet me. Four police cars are parked in our driveway. Neighbors stand on their porches and balconies, bundled against the cold and watching as uniformed and plainclothes officers crawl through the complex trash dumpster and parade in and out of my house.

No, not the trash dumpster! I tossed my bloody Valentine's Day outfit in there, and our collection day isn't until tomorrow. I never imagined things could go sideways this fast.

Bumps erupt across my skin. I slam my brakes and skid several feet. An officer I don't recognize spots me, and it's not difficult to read his lips. "There's her car." My first idea is to shift into reverse and get the hell out of here, drive east to Canada. Instead, I swallow and wait.

The officer and his partner approach my Volvo with

their hands resting on their belts. As they get closer, they shield their eyes against my shining headlights. One raps on my closed window with his gloved knuckles. "Finley Dunn?"

I depress the button and the icy window slides down. Cold air invades my vehicle as the police officer speaks to me. "You can park over there." He points to the last vacant parking spot on this side of the complex. "Our detective will be right with you."

He waves me forward, and I drive past him and park. My mother rushes out of the house and meets me at the parking space. "What's going on?" she asks.

"I don't know—I just pulled up."

She puffs her cheeks and exhales. "You're eighteen, so they won't tell me anything, and they have a search warrant. Your bedroom is taped off, you can't go in there." Panic shadows Mom's face. "Finley, I'm scared. This . . . this . . ."

She doesn't have to finish the sentence because I know this reminds her of when Dad shot Bart. The police searched our house, computers, cars, and garbage, looking for any sort of correspondence between the men—any evidence of disagreements that might speak to my dad's state of mind, anything that might indicate a motive for murder.

But it didn't matter in the end because my dad died in the hospital. They couldn't try him, so they closed the case.

The woman detective I met at school appears at my car. "Finley, we need to have a little chat. You weren't completely honest with me, were you?"

My scalp tightens. My lips close.

"We pulled GPS data off Jason Walker's phone," she says, and my nerves coil tighter.

"A phone's data is like a trail of breadcrumbs," says Detective Perez. "Jason's crumbs begin at a model home in Northwood Estates. The Green family owns it. Their daughter Mya happens to be your known acquaintance and your mother works for the family. Guess what we found there."

I decline to answer, and Mom wraps her arms around me as we stand in the cold.

"We found a large bloodstain, but where the crumbs lead next is more interesting. Care to guess?"

I shake my head, but I know where this is going.

The detective watches me. "They don't lead to Flattop Mountain, I can tell you that. The GPS data leads straight to your townhome."

I cough as the air leaves my lungs. Jason's cell was in his backpack when I brought his things to my house. When I charged and powered-on his phone, it must have left a digital trail. Mya will kill me for this.

"Who is Jason Walker?" Mom asks.

I can't focus on Mom right now and Perez ignores her too. "Finley, hand over your phone and car keys. Here is a copy of the search warrant."

I take the paper and read it. It grants the Anchorage Police Department the right to confiscate my phone, DNA, car, and computer and permission to search my home. The probable cause portion of the warrant states that police believe the search will reveal evidence as to Jason Walker's location and well-being. My hand flies to my mouth. "I—I don't know where he is. I told you that."

"Hand over your backpack," says Perez.

I hand over my phone, keys, and backpack, and she passes them to the cop standing next to her. I'm grateful I deleted the past few weeks of messages and photos off my phone and the cloud. God, senior year is supposed to be the beginning of my life, not the end.

Perez grabs my attention. "Finley Dunn, I have questions for you, but you aren't under arrest. Not yet."

Mom wrings her hands. "Is this about the stuff she found? She turned it in."

Perez ignores her. "Since we've confirmed that Jason Walker's phone was not where you stated you found it, I'd like to know why you lied, Finley."

"I—"

Mom interrupts. "My daughter and I need a minute."

"She can answer a simple question," says Perez. "We are very curious how Mr. Walker's phone ended up at your house in the wee hours of February fifteenth and where he is now. We believe your daughter knows more than she's let on."

Desperate, I try to deflect. "His brother was at my school today. He's following me."

Perez frowns. "Jason's twin? Are you sure it was him?"

"Yes. He wrote down my license number."

Perez unclips a radio from her belt and orders a squad car to the school. "We'll check it out," she says.

Mom grips my arm tighter. "What do you think she's done, ma'am? Finley's a straight-A student. She doesn't . . . lie. She's a good kid." Mom's head jerks toward me and I watch as the penny drops—she understands that my childhood friends are somehow behind this. Regret rises in her eyes. She blames herself for not making it in LA and now she's blaming herself for this.

I want to scream *It isn't your fault!* "Mom," I start, but then I'm crying.

"Let's talk at the station," says Perez. "It's too dang cold out here. Ms. Dunn, you may follow along, but your daughter is eighteen. You won't be allowed to sit with her in the interrogation room. You may hire an attorney for that purpose."

"You said she's not under arrest."

"She's not, but if she refuses to answer my questions, I'll be back with a warrant."

Mom shudders. "I'll call an attorney."

When Mya and I talked, she told me to call her mom's lawyer. "I have an attorney, Mom. Her name is Ms. Chen."

"You have an attorney?" Mom sputters.

Perez smirks. "I believe there is much about your daughter you don't know, Ms. Dunn."

TWENTY-NINE

FINLEY

"Your father killed a man four years ago," says Detective Perez in a casual tone. We're at the police station in an interrogation room. I'm waiting for Cookie Green's lawyer to arrive, Mom is in the lobby, and Perez is perusing a file about my family.

My voice abandons me. Bringing up my father is the equivalent of slamming a police baton into my gut.

"I worked on your father's case," says Perez.

I hadn't put two and two together, but now the last name rings a bell. The detective who questioned my mother years ago was named Perez, but I never saw her face. I tuck my hands under my legs to keep from fidgeting.

"Can I get you a Coke, a cup of coffee, a bottle of water? Pick your poison."

My answer rasps from my throat. "I don't want anything."

"All right, then let's chat while we wait."

"No . . ."

"Okay, I'll chat. You listen." Perez slides a piece of paper toward me. "This is a printout showing Jason Walker's phone activity." She points to the GPS data and then at the attached map of Anchorage. "Jason called his brother at twelve-fifty-two in the afternoon on February fourteenth from Northwood Estates. He indicated he was very sick and needed help. Because of the storm that night, his brother, Brady, couldn't fly down from Fairbanks. They agreed to meet at the public library the following day at noon. Jason didn't make it."

Heat whirs from the vents, but chills trickle through my body. I am not a person who ends up in an interrogation room. It's like being on a scary ride that I can't get off.

Perez glances at the wall clock and then continues. "Jason's phone remains at the model home until one-eighteen on the morning of February fifteenth, when the battery dies. Guess where it turns on again at three-twenty-three in the morning?" Her eyebrows slide up and down like dark wings.

"I'm waiting for Ms. Chen," I remind her.

"Fair," says Perez. "I won't make you guess because you already know—the phone powers on at your townhome in Anchorage."

Blood rushes to my cheeks, and my right leg starts to bounce.

Perez smiles. "After about five minutes, the phone powers off again. At three-thirty in the afternoon on that same day, you turn it in to Safe Spaces along with Jason's other belongings."

The detective leans back in her chair and tosses a fresh piece of gum into her mouth. She offers me one, but I decline. "There's much we don't understand, Finley. Did Jason travel to your home with his phone, or had he already become separated from it? Because it wasn't at the Flattop Mountain trailhead as you suggested. Had you told us the truth, I doubt you'd be here right now."

I stare at my lap, furious and frustrated.

"We don't understand why you lied to us, unless you're involved in foul play. Did your friend Mya tell you we discovered a considerable bloodstain at the Northwood Estates model home? She is your friend, isn't she? You were both at the party where your father murdered Bart Madden four years ago."

My mouth goes dry.

Perez inclines her head. "Bart's murder was a strange case. Things didn't quite add up, but I was a junior detective then. Now I'm the boss." She smiles. "This is a strange case too. Somebody sustained a possible fatal injury where Jason went missing."

My eyes flit to the interrogation room door. What does Perez mean about Bart's death being a *strange* case? "Where is Ms. Chen?" I ask.

"I'll fill your lawyer in when she gets here," says Perez. "Our forensics team will review your phone activity and search your vehicle, home, and computer. Whether you tell me or not, we'll determine how and when you and Mr. Walker crossed paths." Perez taps the table. "Look at me, Finley."

I let out a quiet breath. Because of the salmon poaching, the pot growing, and Cookie's distrust of all things government, our parents drilled it into us kids to never talk to the police. My distrust runs deep and it conflicts with the girl I've become since moving away—the girl who wants to be good and obey authority. I do as Perez asks and look at her.

The detective settles deeper into her plastic chair. "I know you and your mother are friends with the Green family. Your mom works for Cookie, right?" She continues without pausing for an answer. "I believe your GPS history will place you at Northwood Estates during the hours Jason went missing. Does your mother have a key to the model home?"

"No," I answer before I can stop myself.

Perez makes a note and tilts her head. "I talked to your boss, Clodagh O'Brien. She said you showed up to work on the fifteenth with a fresh bruise on your face, and you have human scratches on your arms." She points at them. "Those are fingernail marks."

I flip my arms over to hide the faint red welts.

Perez leans forward, feeling out a new idea. "Did Jason Walker force you into that house, Finley? Did he try to hurt you and you fought back?"

I shake my head.

"Victims generally don't scrub their own crime scenes, but they might if they felt afraid or embarrassed. It's a theory."

The door flies open and a well-coiffed woman in a bronze suit enters the room and extends her hand. "I'm Tiffany Chen, Finley Dunn's attorney. Are you questioning my client?"

Perez slides her arms behind her head. "Nope, just talking to myself. She's been quiet."

Chen nods toward the camera on the wall. "I want the recording of this session."

"You shall have it."

"Have you arrested Miss Dunn? Cautioned her?"

"She came of her own accord," says Perez. "As to the former, I believe we'll gather enough evidence to charge her in the near future." She turns to me. "Perhaps Jason assaulted you, perhaps you assaulted him, but someone bled hard on that white marble floor. Giving false information to a peace officer is a crime you've already committed, Finley. At best, you're getting charged with that. Obstruction of justice is next."

Ms. Chen's perfectly painted lips quirk. "Miss Dunn can't obstruct justice if there is no victim and thus no crime."

Perez's smug expression dissipates. "We're processing the evidence, but if that blood belongs to Mr. Walker, we'll have much more to discuss, including how a missing person's phone ended up at your client's townhome and why she lied about it. Now that you're here, let's begin with some easier questions."

"Not gonna happen," says Chen. "This child has school tomorrow, and I'm invoking her right to remain silent. Come, Finley." Ms. Chen pats my shoulder, encouraging me to stand.

Perez stands too. "Per the search warrant, she needs to leave a DNA sample with my deputy on the way out."

Chen nods. "Send her file and the interview recording to my office." She drops her card on the table. "From now on, all communication will go through me. Good night, Detective."

"She's not a child!" Perez shouts after us.

Ms. Chen ignores that. On our way out a deputy swabs my cheek, and then we meet my worried mother in the lobby. "What happened?" she asks.

"Nothing yet," says Chen. "Finley, I will handle everything from here, all right?"

I nod, but my entire body has clenched since hearing the word *arrest*.

Mom's blue eyes bulge. She's cried off all her makeup and looks even closer to my age. Her voice dips lower as we exit the police station. "How did that man's phone end up at our house, Finley? Did you try to help him? Did he hurt you?"

My head throbs. "Mom, no—"

She waves her arms at the surrounding police station. "*Something* happened. Tell us."

I open my mouth, dying to confess.

Chen stops me. "Not here and not now, Finley. Look, I know you want to spill your guts, and there is nothing I would enjoy more—besides a hot cup of coffee—but I won't let you tell me what happened. My options are reduced if you say something that incriminates you. All that matters is the evidence, which currently amounts to very little. We'll see what the search warrant produces. Go home and get some rest. We'll talk later."

The search of my complex's dumpster is going to produce a bloody Valentine's dress, I am positive of that.

When we arrive home the police are gone, but the crime scene tape is not. "Finley," Mom starts.

"Mom, can I go to bed? Please. I'm so tired."

She sighs but agrees. I trudge to my bedroom. The police ransacked my closet and drawers, and my things are strewn across the floor. They took my phone and computer, so I can't message River or Olivia or Imani.

Ignoring the mess, I drop onto my bed and pass out until Mom wakes me for dinner.

THIRTY

MYA

Towering triangular windows reveal the white wilderness beyond. It's Saturday morning, and Mya is lounging on her sofa. She can't get out of the house or away from her mother until the snowplows arrive. Ever since Detective Perez showed her the bloodstain in the foyer, Cookie has been in hurricane mode. Then Mya heard that Finley's house, phone, and car are being searched. This worries her. She doesn't know anyone as desperate to tell on herself as Finley Dunn.

She left Mya a voice message the other night: *Jason's twin came to my school and watched me. He wrote down my license plate number. I'm scared.* This is what Mya feared— that Brady is dangerous.

Cookie's voice erupts across the cavernous, wood-beamed great room. "Once they pin this on Finley, we're next."

Mya swings around. "God, Mom, you scared me."

"You should be scared. Where's your father?"

"I don't know. Why are we next?"

Cookie arches her brows. "Do you know why that man's bloodstain was detectable at the Chateau? I'll tell you why. Because you and your friends used organic fucking cleaner. Christ. You need hydrogen peroxide to dissolve blood."

"Organic is all we had," Mya says in a small voice.

Cookie snorts. "You can blame your vegan father for that. The point is you made a mistake, probably more than one, but until there's a bona fide victim, Chen says not to worry."

Cookie hefts an iron fireplace poker and stabs at the blazing wood, sending sparks up the chimney. Mya's mother knows a lot, but not everything. She has no idea about the driver's license Mya burned in their outdoor firepit or what happened to Jason after she and Eli returned to the model home and discovered he was still alive. If he survived what happened next, he has a big fat court settlement coming his way. Mya's stomach lurches. This will end with someone going to prison—she is sure of it.

Cookie pokes harder at the fire. "The search parties will draw news crews. Maybe the attention on Northwood Estates will sell more homes, who knows? There's no such thing as bad press."

"Silver linings," says Mya. Cookie grunts and retreats upstairs. Moments later, Mya hears the shower running.

She pops the tab on the Coke she grabbed earlier and guzzles the chilled sweetness. Last night Mya texted Eli to come over. I want to talk, she wrote. Instead, they tore off each other's clothes and dived under her covers. A smile plays on her lips as she remembers his eager kisses and smooth, muscled body. The way he tilted her hips and breathed her name. The way they melted into each other afterward. She can no longer deny it: Eli is growing on her.

Mya's sister enters the family room and throws a pillow at her. Mya's Coke spills on the fabric. "Hey, why'd you do that?"

Brittany crosses her arms. "I heard you with your boy toy last night. I hope you used protection."

Mya wipes up the spill with the edge of a throw blanket and glares at her sister. "Why can't you leave me alone? What's wrong with you?"

"You and your fucked-up friends are wrong with me. Mom's on the warpath, Dad's sleeping in the den again, and we're going broke. What did Finley do to that homeless guy? Mom told me the police searched her house. Did he, like, rape Finley or something? Did she knife him? Mom said the bloodstain at the Chateau is massive."

"Jesus, Brit, let it go. Chen will fix it."

Brittany laughs. "Wow. Okay. Maybe Mom should call a psychiatrist next time there's trouble instead of a lawyer. This family is fucked. I mean that literally."

Mya's face turns hot.

Brittany plunges ahead. "If Mom and Dad divorce, Dad's leaving Alaska and I'm going with him. What's your exit plan when we lose this house? Hang with Mom at the hunting cabin? Online college?"

"Dad won't leave Alaska."

Brittany nods. "That's cute. Keep thinking that, little bunny. He hates Alaska. He can't wait to leave."

"Why are you being such a bitch?"

Brittany folds her arms over her stomach as heaviness settles between them. "Because . . . I don't want them to divorce."

"Oh." Mya sets her Coke on the coffee table. "I don't either."

"Why is Mom so mean?" Brittany whispers, her eyes sparkling.

Mya doesn't know how to answer that, but she tries. "I think she's scared. She doesn't want to lose everything her family gave her."

"Yeah, I get that, but what about us?" Brittany wipes her face. "Whatever Finley did, please don't let it get out of control."

"I won't," Mya promises. Her sister plods to the kitchen with her furred flipflop slippers smacking the wooden floor.

Mya contemplates the past few weeks. This is all happening because Finley Dunn moved to LA, grew a conscience, and then moved back. She didn't use to scare so easily or be such a rule-follower. The old Finley scooped roe out of salmon bellies and ate it raw. She skipped school on sunny days, kept secrets like a vault, and swore to have Mya's back forever.

There's no way around it—LA ruined Finley Dunn. Mya isn't about to let Finley ruin her, too.

THIRTY-ONE

FINLEY

Mom wakes me with a cup of chamomile tea and honey. I crashed after we returned from the police station, and now it's evening. We sit across from each other in identical positions, legs crossed, hands cupping our hot mugs, our blond hair loose around our shoulders.

"I want the truth. All of it," says Mom.

Relief gushes through me that I finally get to speak. I confess about the Valentine's party—about everything we did, including the drugs—and how we promised not to tell anyone what happened. "We were high and didn't want to get in trouble," I say. It's that simple in the end—we exchanged a stranger's survival for our own.

Mom's eyelids flutter as I finish. She is quiet for several minutes. Tears pool in her blue eyes, but she doesn't let them fall. She sets down her tea and exhales a long breath. "What were you thinking, Finley? You know what it's like to be down and out. Remember when we slept in the car and that man tried to get in? You remember the terror?" Her tears overfill and slide down her cheeks. "That's how Mr. Walker must have felt. It sounds like you surprised him in the bathroom."

"But he's the one who broke into the house, Mom. We didn't expect him to be there. He scared us. He yelled at us to get out." I don't mention the anger I felt when I shoved him.

She nods. "It must have been confusing, but after you pushed him you said he was unconscious and bleeding. How could you leave him there without calling an ambulance?"

I want to tell her that Mya told me not to call, but it sounds like an excuse. It *is* an excuse. Mya says I'm weak-minded and she's right. I'm not the leader I pretend to be in class. I can't say any of this out loud, so I state the facts: Jason threatened us with a pocketknife and Mya promised to go back later and call the police if he was still there. He wasn't.

"Do you believe Jason left the model home on his own?" she asks.

I have to believe it's true. "Yes," I tell her.

Mom holds my gaze. "Why didn't you report the incident once you were safe, and why did you lie to the detective about where you found his stuff? It doesn't add up, Finley. You know better."

I grip my cup to keep my hands from trembling. "I told you I'm sorry." My heart cracks and I slide to the floor. She slides down too, and collects me in her arms. I release all my stress and worries into her embrace, sobbing and sniffling. *Why didn't I call* her? I wonder. I'm eighteen, but she's my mother; she'll always be my mother—the one I can trust the most, the one who will do anything to help me. "Mom, don't hate me."

"Shhh," she says, stroking my hair. "I could never hate you, Fin. I love you."

She's crying too, and I see my future self in her face: a few wrinkles, less freckles, still pretty. Will I be in jail or living free when I reach her age? This is a real concern, but my breathing slows and my tears begin to dry as she holds me tight. I'm spent and exhausted, but my mom doesn't hate me and that feels good. I release a weighty sigh. "What's going to happen next?"

"I don't know." We wipe our eyes and return to our chairs to finish our tea. "I'll call Cookie tomorrow. It concerns me that she hired a lawyer and is paying your bill. She insisted, by the way."

"I think it's because it happened on her property." I have avoided Cookie since we moved back and I'm not sure why. Like Mya, Cookie is protective of me, but I've always felt it was for her own good, not mine, like she's a cat and I'm a mouse and I'm only safe until she tires of playing with me.

Mom's big eyes narrow. "You and your friends did not handle this well. Cleaning up blood makes everyone look guilty."

I start crying again. I'm miserable and sick to my stomach; my heart flutters, making me dizzy. I reach for my tea, miss the cup, and spill the liquid on the floor.

"I've got it," Mom says, waving her hand over the spill. "Why don't you go back to bed and call in sick tomorrow?"

"Okay, but should I tell the police what I told you? I don't want to make things worse."

She frowns. "The police know Jason is injured and where he was last seen. You don't have anything new to add. Let them do their job and find Jason. We have time to think about this and consult with Ms. Chen. Detective Perez is not on your side, Fin, just like she wasn't on your father's side. They were quick to condemn him." Mom's still bitter that the police called the shooting an execution-style killing. It made Dad sound like a monster. Dad should not have killed his best friend, true, but he did it to protect River.

"The detective said Dad's case was strange. What did she mean?" I ask.

Mom is quiet a moment. "I think she's talking about the motive. The police couldn't prove the theory that the shooting was over their HVAC business and I wasn't about to tell them the real reason. It would have sealed their case against your dad had he survived." Mom sweeps my hair to the side, looking as exhausted as I feel. "The goal—my goal—is to ensure you start college in the fall. Let's hope Jason's okay and the police let this go. I'm serious about you staying home from work tomorrow. Okay?"

"Okay." I drag myself upstairs and tackle the mess the police left behind. I thought I was cried out, but I was wrong. I want to talk to River. He promised me I would be okay, and I need to hear him say it again. I need to feel his strong arms around me and his kisses on my cheeks. He's the one person who doesn't think I'm weak or stupid or reckless, but the police took my phone and computer, and I'm too tired to drive to his house.

I give up on the mess in my bedroom, cuddle with the one stuffed animal I never got rid of, and weep myself to sleep. Memories of what Bart did to River four years ago plague my dreams. It started with a kiss.

THIRTY-TWO

FINLEY, THEN

River crosses his arms. "Five bucks says you miss."

"You don't have five bucks," says Mya.

We're fourteen and playing cornhole at River's house while our parents sit around the firepit and drink. It's the summer after eighth grade. School is over, and the sun will be up most of the night. The music is loud because there are no neighbors for miles, and the older siblings have slipped off to smoke weed. My mom and dad sit side by side, holding hands. Mosquitoes feed off us and bald eagles hunt overhead.

As Mya takes her turn, my focus is on River. Each time our eyes meet, my stomach lifts and floats. Dad took me to the Midtown Mall last weekend and let me buy new shorts and a light pink crop top, which I'm wearing now. I braided my long hair while it was wet and slept on it. This morning I unraveled the braids and my hair fell in perfect waves down my back, shining almost white in the sun. Eli's older brothers noticed me for the first time ever, but River is the one I want looking.

Mya tosses the cornhole beanbag and it falls through the black opening in the board. She pounces on River and reaches inside his pockets. "You owe me five bucks."

He allows her to ransack his outfit, but the search produces nothing.

Mya huffs. "I knew you were a liar, River Madden. You don't have any money."

He shrugs. "I didn't think you'd make the shot."

"I'm hungry," says Eli.

"Me too," says Mya. We gaze at the food table in dismay. The wasps have gotten to the chicken wings, and flies crawl over the potato salad. Our parents are wasted, and no one thought to carry the food inside.

"I'm not eating that." A mosquito latches onto my skin and I smash it.

River peers at me from beneath his floppy bangs. "Want to help me get the s'mores?"

My heart stutters. "Okay."

Mya and Eli begin a game of darts as I follow River into his cabin. The curtains are drawn, and the wood paneling is dark brown. The orange countertops are chipped. I trip over a laundry basket on the cluttered floor. "Careful," River says. He flings open the kitchen cupboards and piles marshmallows, chocolate bars, and graham crackers on the counter. Then he stops. "I caught a lizard. Want to see him?"

"I guess so." I don't care about the lizard, but I follow River down the hallway to his bedroom, which is a disaster. The two things not on the floor are his lizard cage and his guitar, which rests on a stand. River lifts the lizard out of its aquarium cage. "He's pretty tame. You can pet him."

The creature's hide is spotted and he has dragon-like eyes. He looks like he could run fast. "No thanks. What's his name?"

"I call him Bob."

I plop onto River's bed. "Bob is a dumb name. What about Eragon?"

"He's used to Bob." River replaces the lizard and the silence between us grows wide and deep, like a canyon. Outside his window, we hear Mya and Eli arguing over the darts.

I start to squirm. "We should get back."

"Wait. I'm writing a new song." He picks up his guitar and plays a few bars. "Do you like it?"

"It's catchy."

River lays the instrument down and crawls across the carpet toward me. Behind his glasses, his eyes glitter in the evening sunshine, honey brown and shot with flecks of gold. The sun has bronzed his skin and lightened his hair. He's grown taller than me. "Have you ever kissed anyone?" he asks.

I shake my head.

"Do you want to try it?"

I laugh, nervous. "Yeah. Someday."

He scoots closer, and my stomach tingles. "I think we should practice for high school in case anyone wants to kiss us." His eyes drop to my lips, and the tingles spread throughout my body.

I give a small nod and tilt my head.

He tilts his head the same way. We laugh. We reposition.

Our eyes meet, and that makes us laugh harder. He places his warm hands on my shoulders. His breath is warm and scented by the candies he ate earlier. Raspberry.

When our lips touch, our noses bump. We burst into giggles. "Sorry," he says.

Before I can readjust, River lunges and kisses me for real. His hands wrap around my head, he slides off his glasses, and his weight presses me against the wall. His lips are softer than I expected.

Blood rushes through my head, clearing it of everything. Time slows, and the room fills with the sound of our breathing and the squelch of our lips. I peek. His eyes are closed, and his eyebrows are knit together. His kisses are hungry but gentle. Something beautiful sprouts inside my chest.

Thud!

River's bedroom door flies open. His father stands in the doorway. River and I break apart. "D-Dad," River says.

Bart sways on his feet, his eyes half-closed and bloodshot, his breathing heavy. His long brown hair frizzes around his face. Everyone loves Bart, but not when he's drunk. "What the fuck is this?" he slurs.

I wipe my lips dry and blush to my toes.

Bart looms over his son. "Get your ass outside. Your friends are raising hell." His eyes slant toward me, then back to River. "Keep the door open when you got a girl in here."

River's eyelids twitch.

"You hear me?" Bart slaps his son across the face.

The blow terrifies me, and I reel backward into the wall. Instant tears wet my eyes.

River absorbs the fear on my face and does something I've never witnessed before. He talks back. "Get out of my room."

Bart's eyes widen. He backhands River's other cheek. "Don't tell me what to do in my house."

"Stop, please! It's my fault." Tears stream down my cheeks.

Bart's face turns redder. His eyes gleam. He lifts River with both hands and hurls him across the room. River's back strikes the corner of his dresser with such force that the dresser topples over. I stifle a scream as his head slams into the thin wall, leaving a crumpled dent in the Sheetrock. River slides to the floor, gasping and groaning. He cups his injured back with one hand and his head with the other. His body curls into a ball.

"Stop crying." Bart drags his son to his feet. "Get outside. Both of you."

River lurches up and out of his bedroom.

Bart follows, and I take up the rear. Bart cuffs River one last time. "Don't be a baby in front of Finley."

On the way out, I grab the s'more ingredients. Bart returns to the firepit with the rest of the parents. They're drinking and getting friendly with each other. My dad catches my eye and raises an eyebrow. I take River's hand in mine. "I'm telling my dad."

"No!" he barks. "You'll make it worse."

"But—"

"Promise me you won't." His eyes plead with me.

I don't promise, but I agree not to tell for now. I smile to soothe my father. River and I catch up to where Eli and Mya are playing darts. One look at River's face and they huddle around us. "What happened?" asks Mya.

"Bart," I whisper.

"Your dad's a piece of shit," says Eli.

"I gotta piss," says River. "Stay here." A sheen of sweat glistens on his face. He staggers into the wilderness and disappears into the brush.

"Motherfucking Bart," says Eli.

A few minutes later a strangled shriek comes from River's direction.

My pulse speeds. "Bear?" We race toward River.

There's a thump, like a body hitting the dirt.

We run faster.

THIRTY-THREE

MYA

Mya's mom prepares a rare family dinner while search parties hunt for Jason Walker in the woods. It's been snowing all day, and Mya sits at the kitchen island, scrolling on her phone. She hopes the dinner is an olive branch to her father, who has begun sleeping in the den, but it could just be that Cookie needs a distraction.

"My LA buyers drove by Northwood Estates this morning," Cookie says as she pulls ingredients out of the refrigerator. "I tried to stall them, but they're only here for the weekend. Apparently, police tape and a search party are not the 'welcome home' they're looking for. They asked their agent to show them other properties."

"They're searching for Jason in the snow?" Mya asks.

"*Jason*—I am tired of hearing that name. And yes, I believe the bad weather adds to the urgency, but that's not the point. The point is that I lost the buyer for a one-point-three-million-dollar property."

"I'm sorry, Mom."

Cookie shrugs. "You have a legal right to party in a house that we own. It's that man's fault."

Mya lets out a breath. For once, they agree.

Dad pops out of the downstairs den, groggy and disheveled from a power nap, which is part of his new health craze. When he spots Mya, he blushes. "Hi, bunny."

"Hi, Dad."

"I better start dinner," he says.

"I've got it," Cookie tells him. His eyes widen, but he doesn't comment.

Mya shifts in her seat, unsure what to do. If she stays, her parents won't fight. If she goes, they might talk things out, but the dinner ingredients could end up hurled onto the floor. Mya stays.

To quell the awkwardness, Cookie turns on the television and scrolls to the local news, then returns to browning the beef she thawed. Mya's dad doesn't eat meat, but he is bent on keeping the peace and says nothing.

Mya's mom brings up work again. "Those LA people were skimping on the upgrades anyway. Why buy a house in Northwood Estates if you don't want it to pop?"

"Because they can't afford the upgrades?" her dad posits.

"Of course they can. They're from California," says Cookie. "I loathe cheap people, but good riddance. They would have been nonstop pains in the ass."

"It's too bad locals can't afford your homes," says Mya's dad.

"Are you trying to piss me off?"

"No," he says, and he's genuine. One reason Mya's parents fight so much is because her dad can't read a room.

Cookie narrows her eyes and stirs the beef. "It's not my responsibility to ensure every human being owns a home."

Mya tunes them out to watch the TV over the fireplace. A reporter talks about a new tax law proposed by the Alaska House of Representatives. "Not gonna pass," says Cookie as her meat begins to steam.

"Back to our breaking story about an Anchorage man who was reported missing by his twin brother on February fifteenth," says the local news anchor. "Authorities have reason to believe that Jason Walker was the victim of a violent assault at a stalled housing development called Northwood Estates."

Cookie slams down her spatula and looks at the ceiling. "You've got to be kidding me."

"Amber Towkie is on the scene with more," says the reporter.

The camera switches to a dark-haired woman wearing a faux fur–lined ski jacket. She stands before the police-taped model home, huddled against the wind. Floodlights illuminate the property, and the moon adds a silver glow to the fallen snow. Uniformed officers and search volunteers gather in the background, everyone bundled against the cold. The reporter nods to cover the video delay and then speaks. "Thank you, Dan, and good evening. As you can see behind me, there is a lot of activity at this uninhabited model home in the Northwood Estates housing development."

She glances at the notes on her phone. "Concern for the missing man escalated when an anonymous citizen turned over his belongings, including his phone, to Safe Spaces, a downtown homeless shelter. Detective Perez with the Anchorage police department tells us they obtained GPS data from Jason Walker's phone that led authorities to this location."

The camera switches to drone footage of the housing development that was filmed during daylight hours. Mya's father puts on his glasses to better view the TV, and Cookie stands ramrod straight at the stove.

"After obtaining search warrants, forensic investigators inspected the model home and discovered a large bloodstain in the foyer. There is evidence that someone attempted to hide the stain by washing the floors with cleanser."

"Organic cleanser," Cookie huffs.

The on-site reporter wipes a lock of windblown, ice-crusted hair off her face. "After collecting a blood sample and entering it into the DNA database maintained by the Alaska Department of Public Safety, Detective Perez received a verified match to Jason Daniel Walker, the Anchorage man reported missing by his twin. The size of the bloodstain is significant, Dan, leading police to believe Mr. Walker sustained a serious injury at this location. Walker has been experiencing homelessness in Anchorage for the past two years and may have entered the empty home to get warm."

Amber Towkie glances again at her phone screen. "Important questions remain—who cleaned up the blood, and why didn't they seek medical care for the unhoused man?

Police are treating this as a crime scene, and a desperate search is on to locate Jason Walker, who is considered a missing and endangered person. Police are also checking area hospitals, shelters, dreg rehab facilities, and homeless encampments for information about his whereabouts. Jason's twin, Brady Walker, is very concerned. Local advocates for the homeless are picketing city hall this morning, once again demanding affordable housing over large-scale, expensive developments like Northwood Estates."

The newsroom anchor asks a question. "Do the police have any suspects in this alleged assault?"

Amber grimaces. "They identified a person of interest, Dan, but they haven't made their identity public. There have been no arrests in Mr. Walker's case."

"Mr. Walker," mutters Cookie.

Mya lets out a breath. So far, police aren't identifying Finley. That's good.

The newsman furrows his eyebrows. "How about motive, Amber? Have police suggested whether this attack was random or a planned assault against a vulnerable person? A hate crime, perhaps?"

"They have not identified a motive, Dan. The ironic aspect of this case is that the owner of the development where Mr. Walker sought shelter fought against building affordable housing here."

"You're blaming me?" Cookie yells at the TV. Mya sinks deeper into the sofa.

The anchorman nods, his expression grave. "Has the owner of development been questioned?"

"Detective Perez indicated that the owner is cooperating."

"Well, shit," says Cookie. "Like I had a choice."

Amber finishes by providing the police tip line and information about how to join the search.

Cookie shuts off the TV, and Mya's parents stare at her. "What?" she says.

Her mother wipes her brow. "I'm going to ask you one more time, Mya. If you know where that man is, tell me right now."

"You said Mya's not involved," says her father.

His wife and daughter ignore him. "I don't know where he is," says Mya.

"Is there anything you're *not* telling me?"

"Mom, stop. I told you everything."

Cookie's wrinkles smooth as her face goes flat with rage. "You chew your lip when you lie. It's called a *tell*. I recognize it because I'm your mother. Come on, spill it."

There's a part of Mya that would love to confess, but she's afraid if she does, it won't stop with Jason Walker. Once she opens her mouth, she'll spew *everything,* all the way back to Bart's shooting. She'll tell her dad and the whole world what really happened that summer. The best way to keep a secret is to remain silent. She concentrates on not chewing her lip.

"I see," says Cookie. She peers out her giant picture windows and Mya follows her gaze.

Outside, the snow has stopped falling and a pale blue moon peeks through the clouds, the same moon that shines on everyone in the world, including Jason Walker. Wherever he is.

THIRTY-FOUR

FINLEY

Saturday morning I use Mom's phone to call in sick and spend the day flipping through the local news channels, watching stories about the search for Jason. The police have identified a "person of interest," but they haven't released my name. Not yet. A reporter digs up Jason's prior assault charge. It turns out he punched a man who was harassing a woman at a bar. *Great*. He's an everyday hero and not a violent criminal. This information adds to my guilt and misery.

It's the weekend, and River said he's crabbing with his cousin again. I don't care to see Mya or Eli and they haven't invited me to hang out anyway. Josie wants to catch a movie, and I use illness as an excuse to avoid her and my job.

"The sun's shining, Finley. You should go outside," says Mom. Her purse is slung over her shoulder and her car keys jingle in her hand.

"And do what?" I ask. "Ride my bike? The police have my car, I can't go anywhere."

"How about go outside and synthesize some vitamin D? You've barely seen the sun since we moved here. It's not healthy. Cabin fever is real."

My eyes are glued to the TV. "I'm fine. I just need my phone and my car."

Mom blocks my view of the screen. "Finley?"

"Could you move, please?" I peer around her.

"Finley Marie Dunn, I am on your side. Don't get short with me for trying to help." Her hands jam onto her hips and her mouth presses tight. She's wearing my mukluks over a pair of skinny jeans, and her blond hair is swept up in a high ponytail.

She looks like me and it pulls a smile from my lips. "You're cute when you're mad."

Mom's expression ripples, then settles into a deflated smile. "Thank you. I'm getting an oil change and a bagel. Want to come with?"

"No, but will you bring me back a breakfast bagel?"

"Sure." She moves away from the TV. "Don't watch the news. It's upsetting. I'll be back in an hour or so." She departs, leaving me alone in the townhome.

I can't wait an hour to eat, so I slide off the sofa and hunt for a snack in the kitchen. I settle on toast, peanut butter, and an energy drink. I'm still wearing last night's T-shirt and sweats and haven't showered yet. A faint odor wafts from my armpits. I don't care.

Returning to my nest of throw blankets and pillows, I curl up on the sofa to eat and watch more news. The program cuts to the affordable housing protests occurring at city hall and at Northwood Estates. "Not good," I mutter. The backlash of this could bankrupt Mya's family.

Mom and I have a meeting with Ms. Chen after school on Monday, so this weekend there isn't much to do except chew my nails and make sure the doors and windows remain locked. Brady Walker has shown up twice at Mama Moose's and once at my school, and now he has my license plate number. I'm worried he'll use the number to find out where I live.

After a while, I tire of watching TV, snap it off, and stare at the white walls. Mom and I need to paint this place and get rid of Gran's wallpaper in the bathrooms. We need to make it *ours*.

Then I remember that my mom has a computer tablet. I can use it to message my friends in LA. I throw off my covers and ransack her bedroom. The tablet is in her nightstand and I tap out a message to my group chat with Olivia and Imani: I miss you guys!

A few minutes later, Olivia responds. Is my girl homesick? Even though this is a written message, I can hear her Valley drawl.

I type back: Technically, I am home

If home is where your heart is, then LA is home 💜 We love you and miss you too. Imani is here, bugging the shit out of me. She says to say hi. Her phone died

I laugh because nothing has changed. Imani has been saving for a new phone for months because of her old battery. I write: Hi Imani 👋. I imagine them sitting on Olivia's bed, eating Takis and debating lip plumpers. My Lower Forty-eight pals have never fished, hunted, or howled at the midnight sun, but Olivia wins essay contests and Imani plays a mean game of chess. As I get closer to college, these skills feel more valuable than drilling ice holes in three seconds flat.

Can I call you later, writes Olivia. We're seeing Hamilton at Pantages. Again!

My throat tightens. No, that's ok. I have plans with my mom. Have fun!

I can't do this. I can't think about LA. I need to fix my mess so I can go to college with my friends. Imani, Olivia, and I applied to USC and Irvine among other schools, but I'll need a massive financial aid package now that I'm out of state. It's depressing.

I watch people's stories for a while, thinking about Brady Walker. If he's stalking me, maybe I can stalk him right back. I do some searching, discover he has social media, and spend an hour scrolling through his posts. It turns out he's a software developer for virtual educational products. He's divorced. His ex-wife and kids also live in Fairbanks. Most of his posts are about fishing, hanging out with friends, and playing with his kids. He doesn't appear to be a criminal, but that doesn't mean he's not dangerous when he's angry.

As I scroll back in time, there are photos that include his twin brother, Jason—the two of them in matching ugly Christmas sweaters, camping, and attending family events. The brothers seem close. Sometimes they're dressed alike, sometimes not. They're a good-looking pair, with nice teeth, translucent green eyes, and wavy brown hair. They're lean and muscular.

Things change after a post about Jason's snow machine accident five years ago. He drove off a mountainside and the machine landed on top of him. It broke his leg in six places, fractured his neck and ribs, and injured his brain. According to Brady's posts, Jason spent weeks in the hospital and months recovering.

Over the following year, several pictures depict Jason losing weight. His skin turns pallid. His smile becomes taut. Then he disappears from family photos altogether. The single clue as to why is a post from two years ago. Brady attends a mud run event to raise money and awareness for opioid addiction. His caption is simple: *For Jason.*

Brady's most recent post is a graphic of his brother's missing person flyer.

I set down Mom's tablet with trembling fingers. Jason has been hard on his luck since his accident. I'm more certain than ever that at the model house he was delirious from a fever, high on opioids, or both. I relive the moment, reimagining it so that I call for help instead of push him. In my fantasy, I receive a thankful hug from Brady and praise from my teachers. I am a *real* hero.

With a sigh, I turn the TV back on. A news crew is at Northwood Estates, interviewing protestors. The signs read:

JUSTICE FOR JASON

HOUSING IS A HUMAN RIGHT

LIKE SNOW? TRY SLEEPING ON IT!

BOYCOTT NORTHWOOD ESTATES

My mouth goes dry. This is for sure going to keep Cookie's home buyers away.

Meanwhile police and volunteers continue to comb the woods. Three volunteers have been treated for frostbite and one for dehydration. The terrain is difficult—wooded and steep. A newscaster mentions that search and rescue dogs will join the effort tomorrow. The story is starting to catch on with the national media.

I walk into the kitchen and open the refrigerator for another drink. A square of leftover congealed lasagna turns my stomach. I grip the edge of the sink to steady myself and spot a male figure through the kitchen window, his face hidden by a hoodie. He's lurking on my porch, reaching for my doorknob.

Oh my God! I duck down, heart racing. We don't have a landline, and Mom isn't here. I have no way to call for help.

Bang. Bang. Bang. The man pounds on my front door and tremors roll through me. What if it's Brady Walker?

"Finley, open up!"

I know that voice. It's Eli. I open the front door, shaken and annoyed. "What are you—"

He pushes past me and strides into my living room. I follow him, confused. He whirls, and his large body looms over my much smaller one. "Are we alone?"

My mouth hangs open.

Eli drags me deeper into the living room. "Is your mom here, Finny?"

His use of my nickname loosens my tongue. "She's out."

"Good. Sit down." Eli pushes me onto the sofa and squats in front of me. He's wearing a thick leather jacket and a black corded necklace. His big hands squeeze my arms.

Ice encases my stomach, and my voice rasps from my throat. "You're hurting me." I've witnessed Eli's anger before, but never up close.

He squeezes me harder. He doesn't care if it hurts. "What did you say at the police station?"

"Nothing!"

He glares at me, his brown eyes simmering. "I need to make sure you get it. We're in big trouble, all of us. The police are going to grill you hard, Finny. You can't cave. You got that? You can't say a word."

I try to pull away from him. "I know. Everyone keeps saying that. Did Mya send you? Are you her henchman now?"

"Henchman?" A familiar smirk flickers across his lips. "LA totally Disneyfied you, bro. I think for myself."

I haven't seen it, but I don't say this out loud.

He loosens his grip but doesn't let me go. "You have no idea what we've done for you, Finny. Mya won't tell you, but it's way more serious than pushing a guy down the stairs." His jaw circles. "She won't tell you this either, but if you drop a dime on us, it will be your word against ours."

My scalp tingles. "What did you do for me, Eli? Tell me."

He is unflinching, shameless. "The less you know, the better."

A sob catches in my throat. I break away and scoot back, afraid of Eli for the first time in my life. "You got rid of his body, didn't you? Mya doesn't have to admit it, I see it in your eyes. Was Jason dead when you got there, or did you kill him yourself?"

Emotions scrawl across his face and then vanish, leaving his features smooth. "You refuse to face it, but you know who killed him, Finny."

I draw a ragged gasp. My eyelids flutter. "No, I don't."

He shakes me. "Yes, you do. Who killed Jason Walker? Say it, Finny. Say it!"

"M-me?" I stammer.

Eli nods.

Huge tears drip from my eyes. "But Mya said he walked away."

Eli lifts a hand. "No details. I told you—the less you know, the better, and Mya wants to keep it that way. She lives in the same fairy-tale land that you do, Disney-fucking-land, the place where Jason is alive and well and dancing a jig. I don't live in that place, Finny. I live in the real world, where we go to prison for eight to ten years, okay? I'm looking out for *all* of us."

I wipe my eyes with my sleeves and nod.

Eli pulls my limp body into a hug. "We are your *best* friends, Finny. Stay loyal to us and we'll stay loyal to you . . . to the fucking death. We love you. Don't betray us, and don't tell Mya or River I was here. This talk is between you and me, and it's for your own good."

"Are you . . . threatening me?"

Eli's eyes widen, and he clucks his tongue. "You don't

get it. *You're* the threat, Finny. *You* are." Eli rises to his full six feet four inches, and his good-natured smile returns. "Good talk." He departs as quickly as he came.

I'm left breathless and wondering what the fuck just happened.

THIRTY-FIVE

MYA

Mya applies for jobs from her four-thousand-dollar laptop computer—the movie theater, Nordstrom Rack, REI, and Home Depot. If the police get a search warrant for Mya's phone like they did for Finley's, her GPS history places her at the model home when Jason went missing. She needs a new phone, which means she needs money. And since her mom cut her off, that means getting a J.O.B. She messages Eli and River and tells them to buy new phones too.

She presses the submit button on her most recent job application, then messages Eli: what are you doing?

nothing

Want to hang out?

No response.

She DMs him a few more times. Nothing. Mya's nose twitches. Something is wrong. She calls him and he doesn't answer his phone. It's not like him to ignore her. She grabs her key fob, slides on her boots, and drives to his house.

"He's in his room," says his mother as she lets Mya inside, then stops her. "Wait. Do you know what's going on with that homeless guy? Your mom's not answering my calls. The news said something happened to him at her housing development."

Mya maintains a blank expression. "I haven't heard anything that's not on TV."

Eli's mom tilts her head. "It sounds like he broke in and hurt himself. I don't understand why protestors are going after Cookie. She's not the bad guy here."

"Yeah, it's wild," Mya says. She slides past Eli's mom and enters his bedroom without knocking. Music blares from a Bluetooth speaker, and Eli's bent over his laundry basket, tossing clothes out of it, looking for something. He's shirtless, fresh from the shower, and his muscles ripple down his back. Mya swallows. "Hey."

He jolts upright and sweeps his hands through his hair. "Shit, you scared me."

His underarm hair flashes, dark and springy, reminding Mya of . . . other things. He catches her look but hangs back. "Why are you here?"

"Wow. Hostile much?"

"I'm having a bad fucking day, Mya."

"You haven't answered any of my messages."

"That's what people do when they're having a bad day. Read the handbook." He's annoyed but his gaze softens the longer he looks at her face. "I thought you didn't like me."

"I don't like you."

They continue staring until Eli breaks into a smile. He snatches Mya and scoops her into his arms. "Who knew you were the cure for a bad mood?" He licks her neck and kisses her mouth. "Is this a conjugal visit?"

Heat floods her groin. "It isn't supposed to be."

Eli sets Mya on his bed and leans his bare chest over her body. His musky scent fills her nostrils, and his deep-set eyes gleam. She wonders how you can know someone most of your life and feel like you're just getting to know him.

He traces his fingers down her neck to her stomach. Then a deep shudder rolls through him. Eli unfolds on top of Mya and starts to cry.

Shocked, she strokes his shower-damp hair. "Baby, what's wrong?"

He buries his head deeper into her shoulder. "I don't trust Finley to stay quiet. I'm scared. I don't want to go to prison."

Mya sits up, bringing him with her, and tries to sound more certain than she feels. "She's fine. She can't tell on us without telling on herself, and leaving a homeless guy for dead doesn't fit her perfect prep-school image."

"Yeah, she's changed, hasn't she?" Eli lifts his head. "Her leadership pals will shit their pants if she gets arrested. You're the only one I trust, Mya."

A lump forms in her throat. "I trust you too." Safe in his arms, Mya releases a breath. "We let this go way too far."

Eli kisses her eyelids. "We're not the first people on Earth to make a mistake."

"Is that what we're calling it? A mistake?"

He shrugs. "Yeah. We're not bad people, Mya."

A slimy feeling crawls through her. "I'm not sure about

that. Look, I should go. I'm trying to find a job. Get a new phone, okay?" Mya kisses him and departs his bedroom.

They *are* bad people, and admitting it is its own kind of punishment, but one Mya can accept. What she can't accept is getting caught.

She climbs into her car and exhales. "I am a bad person." Saying it out loud makes her feel better than she should, and she returns home.

THIRTY-SIX

FINLEY

Sunday morning, I drag myself to work in Mom's car, grateful for the distraction. Eli's visit rattled me. Without saying it, he confirmed that Jason died because of me, and it's too much to bear. I imagine the stranger lying dead on the marble floor when Mya arrived. Instead of turning me in, she and Eli carried him into the woods and let the snow cover him. The two sets of footprints belonged to *them*. They don't have to admit it. *No details. The less you know, the better.* I vacillate between shame and rage. I did not ask them to do this for me, and now our futures are intertwined. I cannot tell the truth without bringing them down too.

I wonder if River knows what they did. Did Mya confess at their secret meeting? I can't imagine her not telling River everything. He must be terrified this will come back on him, and it's my fault. I've ruined any chance we had to get back together.

Clodagh greets me when I bluster into the restaurant. A concerned smile lines her ruddy, freckled cheeks. "Ay, lass. Can you believe the man you helped is still missing?"

The man I *helped* or the man I *murdered*? I can add Clodagh to the list of people who will be disappointed if the truth comes out. "I hope they find him," I say as I tie on my apron. I have no energy, no pep at all. Customers dot the tables, but my countertop is empty. I stare at it, exhausted.

"I think you have cabin fever, lass. You'll adjust." She winks and moves on to take an order.

Josie sidles up to grab the coffeepot. "Are you still sick?" she asks, referring to my excuse for missing work yesterday. She's pulled her turquoise hair into a tight ballerina bun that accents her dark eyes.

I stare at her for what feels like a full minute. She told everyone at school what I told her in confidence and disguised the gossip as bragging. I saw her posts: Finley's the one who found that missing man's stuff. She should get the thousand-dollar reward! I get a sinking feeling she's not a real friend and force a smile. "I feel better," I say.

She rests one hand on the coffeepot handle and her face brightens. "Did you hear about the bloodstain at Northwood Estates? My friend Scotty thinks Mya's mom shot the guy for trespassing and then got rid of his body."

I suck in my breath. "Seriously?"

"Well, yeah, it's Cookie Green. She brought a gun to a town council meeting once. I think you were in LA then."

I wince, but I'm not surprised. "Cookie takes her gun everywhere."

Josie shrugs. "I've seen her on the news in the past; she's not a nice lady. It wouldn't surprise me if she shot him."

I take in her wide-eyed excitement, eagerness to talk about everyone else's business, and passive-aggressive digs at my appearance. My chin juts. "You know what, Josie, for someone who claims she's not a gossip, you're always spilling tea."

Her hand flies to her chest. Her eyes narrow. "How can you—"

A voice interrupts us. "I need to talk to you."

I whirl and come face to face with Brady Walker. His face is pinched, his eyes shadowed, and he's wearing a baseball cap. I leap back and bump into a chair, sending it sliding. A few customers glance up at me.

Josie rushes away with the coffeepot. I don't bother handing Brady a menu. He's not here to eat. "Are you following me?" I ask.

He snorts. "I talked to Detective Perez. She tracked my brother's phone to *your* house. You want to explain how that happened?"

My stomach rolls over. His gaze is a tractor beam that holds me in place. He hasn't shaved and looks more like his twin than ever. "I saw you watching me at school," I say. "I told the police."

Brady glances around. No one is paying attention to us. The customers have returned to their meals. Clodagh gestures and smirks as she jokes with a table of regulars. Brady lowers his ball cap. "I'm following you because you have information about my brother you're not sharing."

My heart *tap-taps*.

His eyes sweep my body and then my face. His expression crumples as he changes tack. "Jason isn't dangerous, but the drugs have changed him. Did—did he force you into that empty house? If he hurt you, Finley, I will kill him myself. I just need to know the truth. I understand if you had to fight your way out. I wouldn't blame you for that."

His words stun me. Noises fill in the silence—human chatter, forks clinking against plates, and the cooks joking with one another—but I can't speak. My cheeks burn under his gaze.

Brady wipes his face. "I got a bad feeling about this. We're twins, and I know when Jason is in trouble. I won't be mad if you had to hurt him. I promise. Where is he?"

My grip on my pen softens. Brady's not stalking me to hurt me. He just wants answers. "He didn't force me anywhere," I say and then repeat Mya's story because it's the only one I have. "He left the Chateau on his own two feet. I don't know where he went."

"But why were you two together?"

I shut my mouth. I've said too much already.

His eyes search mine, then he exhales and tugs on the brim of his baseball cap. "Do you know why I wear this hat, Finley? It's to disguise myself. Jason's flyers are all over town, and people keep mistaking me for him and calling the tip line with false leads. You have no idea what this is doing to me. I love my brother. Whatever he's done, he'll pay for it. I just want him safe." A single tear rolls down his cheek and he brushes it away.

I scream inside my head: *Tell him. Tell him you pushed his brother down the stairs!* But the truth will send me and my friends to jail. Eli pretty much confirmed Jason is dead and that he and Mya hid his body. There is no way out of this mess that doesn't drag everyone, including River and my family, through the mud. And for some crazy reason, I don't want Brady to hate me. I'm a bona fide coward. This horrid truth burns deep.

Brady grips my wrist hard. "I can tell you know something, Finley."

A bell jingles. The diner door opens and a customer steps inside. Brady shifts his head and locks eyes with the newcomer. It's River.

"Let her go," River growls. He advances in two quick strides, his eyes glimmering.

Brady drops my wrist and holds up his hands. "I let her go." Then he drags a piece of paper out of his pocket and hands it to me. "That's my number again if you decide to talk." He slides past River and out the door.

My feelings cascade and tears flood my eyes. I cannot break down in front of Clodagh and her customers. I flee toward the bathrooms. River chases me, and Clodagh frowns as we rush past her. Josie pulls out her phone and starts texting, no doubt sharing the drama with her friends.

River corners me in the restroom hallway and blocks my escape as I sob into my hands. "That was Brady, wasn't it? Jesus, they *are* identical."

I nod, my body shaking.

"Did you tell him anything?"

I cover my face. "I can't! I don't know anything." I lift my eyes. "Do you?"

He shakes his head and tries to wrap me in his arms, but he's safer *away* from me. "Why are you here? I thought you were on the boat."

"I got the day off. I've been calling you, but Mya said the police have your phone. I want to talk." He rubs his jaw. "Are you mad at me?"

"No! Never." I grasp his hand to reassure him. "Are you mad at me?"

River startles. "Why would you think that?"

"I don't know. Mya was stupid to believe we could hide this. It's blowing up. I—I don't want you to get in trouble."

"I won't. Look, Fin, the more I learn about Jason Walker, the better I feel about what happened. He's been arrested for assault and drug use in the past. We defended ourselves. We did the right thing." His shoulders slump as he sighs. "It's going to be okay."

"He's not a bad guy," I retort. "He defended someone in a bar, and you can't promise that anything will be okay."

River sets his chin. "Yes, I can. I've made a decision. If the police try to charge you, I'll say I pushed Jason and cleaned up the blood. I won't let you, Mya, or Eli go down for this. You have nothing to worry about."

My eyelashes flutter. "River, that's crazy. They'll find out you're lying. It won't work."

He shakes his head. "It will work. You're worth saving, Finley Dunn."

I bend over, breathing faster. My father destroyed River's

family, and River's willing to sacrifice himself for *me*. The past storms up out of nowhere and swirls between us. I squeeze his hand. "I don't deserve you—"

"Holy Mother of God, what are you two doin'?" screeches Clodagh. "You've got customers, lass."

My heart rate kicks into overdrive. "I'm sorry! We were just talking."

"Mmm. Are you staying to eat?" she asks River.

He flashes his dimples. "Yes, ma'am."

THIRTY-SEVEN

FINLEY

Mom picks me up Monday after school, and we meet my attorney, Ms. Chen, at her downtown Anchorage office. Her assistant offers a selection of beverages and then leads us to a conference space that overlooks the city. It's a dazzling oval room with floor-to-ceiling glass windows, a long, polished blond wood table, a smart screen, white leather and platinum metal chairs, and a white marble floor. The marble brings to mind Jason's spilled blood in the foyer, and my stomach churns.

"Ms. Chen will be in shortly," says her assistant.

Mom and I sit beside each other with the glass windows and the view of Anchorage's city skyline at our backs. Mom runs her fingers along the gleaming table. "How can Cookie afford this with her financial problems? I think you're right, Fin, she's trying to protect her housing development." Mom rubs her forehead. "I just want to protect you. Ah, here she is."

Tiffany Chen enters the conference room at a brisk walk, wearing a hot pink suit and a warm smile. "Good afternoon, ladies, thanks for coming downtown. Don't forget to have my assistant validate your parking before you leave." She shakes our hands and sits across from us. The clouded light filtering in from the windows highlights her brown eyes.

Mom murmurs a greeting. We're nervous, and this woman holds my fate in her small, manicured hands, but she exudes a confidence that is reassuring.

"I had an interesting, if frustrating, conversation with Detective Perez," she says, opening a file. Her next words toss all my composure out the window.

"The police are preparing to arrest you, Finley."

Mom's hand flies to her mouth. "Why?"

Tiffany Chen peruses a sheet of paper. "She indicated they found incriminating evidence during their search of Finley's car, bedroom, complex dumpster, and phone, but they aren't ready to reveal it. They are likely waiting for lab results and other forensic data. The idea is to pressure you, Finley, but without a victim they can't prove assault or wrongful death."

"Jesus," Mom says.

Chen's expression softens. "Either way, she's signaled arrest, and I know Ms. Perez. She wouldn't do that if it weren't forthcoming."

I grip the table with all my strength. My desire to confess has increased rather than decreased since I lied to the police at school. I can't live with this guilt. It's hell. I am in hell. "Ms. Chen—"

She holds up a hand. "Let me ask you a few questions, Finley, and you answer yes or no, okay? This is good practice if the case advances."

I nod, but I'd rather fly out the window and never return.

Chen poises her pen. "Has Jason Walker ever entered your home or bedroom?"

"No!"

"Remain calm," Chen says. "Getting excited won't help you."

"Okay. No, he hasn't entered my house."

"Just say yes or no," she instructs. "Did Jason ride inside or obtain access to the trunk of your 2012 Volvo?"

Mom looks at me funny, and my upset stomach begins to fizz. "No. Why the trunk?"

Chen shakes her head. "Don't ask questions. Just answer yes or no. Did you at any time lay hands on Jason Walker?"

The hairs on my scalp dance. "Yes."

The attorney's right eyebrow lifts higher. "Did he lay hands on you?"

"Yes," I whisper.

"Did this happen inside your bedroom or your vehicle?"

"No."

Chen records this on her pad of paper. "Did this touching happen at the model home in Northwood Estates when Jason went missing?"

I squirm at her word choice. "Yes," I answer.

"This is my last question for now. Other than Jason Walker, were you alone at the model home?"

My mouth snaps shut. My heart thuds. I'm responsible

for Jason's injuries. There's no need to involve my fucked-up friends any more than I already have.

Chen sees I'm not going to answer. "Let's pause here," she says. "Detective Perez doesn't have enough evidence to request warrants for alternative suspects unless you name them, Finley, and you don't have to. You can skip that question for now."

Chen sips her water. "I expect we'll have an arrest affidavit later this week. Mr. Walker's case is becoming high profile. Community stakeholders and safe housing advocates are upset, but for different reasons. The policies in place to support or not support unsheltered people are under intense scrutiny. Northwood Estates and the State of Alaska are under fire. The media is leaning into Jason Walker as a victim, and any suspects will be vilified."

"He terrorized my daughter," Mom blurts out.

Chen tilts her head. "The media attention will complicate things for Finley, and I want you to be prepared."

"But she's a student, they can't release her name."

"She's eighteen and an adult in the eyes of the law," says Chen, "but Finley is small, and she has the girl-next-door look. No one is going to believe she got the upper hand with Jason. His prior assault charge will also muddy the waters, but the new press photos his brother provided are game changers. Jason Walker is getting a media makeover. His new photos depict a handsome, beloved twin brother who fell into opioid addiction after a severe accident. He's a poster child for the evils of Big Pharma and the Anchorage housing crisis."

"But it's possible he's fine and on a bender, right?" Mom asks.

Chen glances at me, then shuffles her papers. "Due to the excessive amount of Jason's blood at the model home, no one believes he's fine, Ms. Dunn."

Mom's voice clogs in her throat. "Do the police think Finley . . . killed him?"

"Mom—" I start.

Chen interrupts. "That's a moot question until they find Jason or his body. Finley turned in his things, refused to leave her name, and lied about where she found them. I believe the search of her phone, vehicle, dumpster, and bedroom has revealed proof that she and Jason had an interaction, and Finley has admitted as much to me, but the evidence is circumstantial as far as I can tell." She presses her hands on the table. "You two need to be prepared for what happens next. When they arrest you, Finley, this story will explode. Online speculation will be divided. It's imperative we win over the media, even more so if this goes to trial."

My face grows hot. "But it was—"

Chen stops me. "I will ask for your story after I've seen an arrest affidavit, Finley. There's no point in going over it until we know the charges and review the evidence. While we wait, I want you to think hard about what happened. If you remember that Jason Walker assaulted you first, that would be helpful."

I gape at her. Is Ms. Chen trying to tell me what to say? Jason did attack first, but it's not as simple as that, and it doesn't explain why Mya and Eli cleaned up his blood or why I lied to the police.

"Sleep on your story before we chat next," says Chen. "Your arrest is imminent, so be prepared, but don't worry. I will take care of you. Detective Perez believes Jason Walker is dead. Do you understand what that means, Finley?"

"A—a murder charge," I whisper.

Chen frowns. "It means he can't dispute your story."

THIRTY-EIGHT

FINLEY

Friday, River drives me home. "Can you stop there?" I say, indicating a snow-covered city park. The lot is empty and he guides his Bronco into a spot facing the frozen playground.

He turns to me. "What—"

I dive into his arms and kiss him hard. This! I've wanted this for weeks. To forget. To wrap myself in someone else's strength. To feel loved.

A heartbeat, a blink, the flutter of an eyelash and then River's on top of me. His warm lips and hot hands light fires inside me. "Finley," he gasps. He kisses my cheeks, neck, and chest. His hands slide down my waist and cup my ass, shifting me beneath him. His back muscles quiver and flex as I stroke them. We kiss and touch for what feels like hours. He pulls back for air. "You're so beautiful. So perfect."

I drag him back down. I don't want to talk or think. I want him to devour me and my problems. I want to obliterate the last few weeks, and I pull off my top. Words abandon

River—good—and then he yanks off his T-shirt and we're chest to chest, writhing to get comfortable. A seatbelt receptor digs into my back. His body is crumpled to fit lengthwise in the car, he bumps his head on the ceiling. The windows steam and drip.

I slide down his zipper and feel inside his pants. He's excited, ready. Pleasure seeps to my innermost core. I unsnap my jeans.

River grabs my hand and stops me. "Not here."

I gape at him.

He pulls up his zipper and swipes his hands through his hair, catching his breath. "I'm sorry."

It's as if I've been bucked off a galloping horse. I inch upright, confused, my pulse racing. "My mom's not home. We could go there," I say.

He attempts a smile and fails. "I guess I'm saying not yet."

"Oh."

River admitted to being a virgin during the truth or dare game. Maybe he's not ready or I'm going too fast. God, I'm an asshole. I expected him to drop his pants on demand. "I can wait," I say, my face flushing. Maybe he doesn't want me at all. "I—I should go home."

River draws a breath, choosing his words. "It's not you . . . ," he starts.

"It's not you, it's me?" Our eyes lock and then we burst out laughing.

"You're my best friend," he says. "I want to go slow. That's all."

"Okay, I understand." River is sincere, and I decide to be flattered instead of humiliated. Despite my legal troubles, happiness blooms inside me. River is the best part of returning to Alaska.

. . .

At home that afternoon, I craft a latte in my kitchen. I enjoy one sip before reality crashes in on me in the form of a police cruiser. It glides into my complex and parks in my driveway.

No lights. No sirens.

I set down my cup before I spill it. This is it. I'm getting arrested. Soon everyone at school will find out what I did. Detective Perez and two officers approach my porch, hunched against the cold. The setting Alaskan sun reflects off their badges.

"Shit, shit." My breathing ratchets higher as I open the front door. They aren't smiling. Officer Hardin, the cop I met at school, fingers his handcuffs.

My knees give out, and I collapse in the doorway. "No," I say, shaking my head. "No."

Perez lifts me to my feet. Her grip strangles my upper arm. "Finley Dunn, you are under arrest for the murder of Jason Walker." She recites my rights while spinning me around so my back is to her and the officers. "For your safety and ours, we're going to handcuff you."

Tears squeeze from my eyes. A deep chill settles in my bones. "You found him?"

Perez scowls at me. "We'll talk at the station."

Officer Hardin tugs my hands behind my back and handcuffs my wrists together. I struggle against him. "Relax, Finley. Do you have anything in your pockets that could cut or poke us?"

I shake my head. Everything happens in slow motion as my thoughts churn like sludge. Hardin leans me against the cruiser, and the female officer pats down my pockets and slides her hands over my body. They've brought out my new backpack. I watch as they shuffle through it, taking out my keys, and putting the pack and the keys in a larger bag. The bag goes into the police car.

"Am I going to jail?"

"Yes, you are," says Officer Hardin.

My knees wobble. When I lived in Los Angeles, getting arrested never crossed my mind. The worst thing I did there was sneak candy into the movies. I followed the rules. I was good.

The police usher me into their cruiser and drive away with Perez following. A four-year-old neighbor boy waves at the police cars from his window. "Did you call my mom?" I ask.

Officer Hardin answers. "We don't call people's parents when we arrest them, Finley. Not when they're adults."

I stare at the metal cage that separates me from the police, and the truth hits me—I'm alone. My mom can't fix this. I'm in handcuffs and my freedom is gone. I am under arrest for taking the life of a fellow human being. Whatever happens next, it won't be up to me. My fate is out of my hands.

I shut my mouth and lean back.

• • •

"She's shorter than I thought she'd be," says a small, frizzy-haired woman when Officer Hardin marches me into the city jail. She sits back with a scowl on her face. The booking area is constructed of concrete and glass, and it's cold.

Perez enters behind us. "Once you're booked, you can call your lawyer or your mom."

Officer Hardin speaks to the woman behind the desk. "Hi, Tammy, this is Finley Dunn. She's been cautioned and searched."

The frizzy-haired woman grimaces. "I know who she is. I got a cousin experiencing homelessness. People think they can mess with them without consequence."

Hardin releases a gust of air. "No need to get personal. Let's start. I don't want to be here all afternoon." He hands her the bag that holds my possessions.

With that, Tammy asks me to remove my necklace, earrings, and rings. She places those items with my backpack and keys and seals them into a bag, assuring me I'll get them back if I'm released on bail.

I sit at the desk while Tammy asks me a series of personal demographic questions and enters my answers into her database. After that, another staff member photographs me from the front and the side, takes my fingerprints, and attempts to collect my DNA. I twist my head away from the long cotton swab. "I already gave a sample. I want my mom and my lawyer."

"It's standard procedure, and you don't have the right

to refuse it," says Hardin, who is standing by. "Open your mouth."

Afterward a nurse collects me. A series of medical questions ensue, including an exam, a Covid test, and a lice check.

"She's ready," the nurse says into a wall phone. Two female guards approach and lead me to a private room. They command me to strip, and then body-search me as I battle back tears. Do they really think I'd put something *there*?

They walk me to a shower and watch as I bathe myself in a tiny white stall. "Put these on." The shorter guard hands me jail-issued clothing and a pair of slippers. They chat with each other as I cover my body:

"He asked me to the movies again tonight."

"Already?"

"That's what I said."

Once I'm dressed and slippered, I'm allowed to use a phone. My mother answers on the second ring, still at work. She doesn't recognize the number. "Hello, Terry Dunn speaking."

"Mom!" Sobs overtake me, and it's several minutes before I can collect myself.

"Where are you?"

"J-jail."

"Finley!" she cries. "Oh my God. Did the detective arrest you?"

"Yes. For murder." I crumple, reliving in my mind the horrible booking procedure. "Call Ms. Chen."

Mom is quiet for a moment. "Did they find Jason?"

"They didn't say," I cry.

"Okay, okay. I'll call Ms. Chen right now. I can't believe they arrested you without letting me know."

"I'm eighteen, Mom." I wanted this so much—to become an adult and make my own decisions. How many times did I use *I'm eighteen* against my mom? Well, now it's being used against me.

"I love you," Mom says in a fierce voice. "I know you didn't kill anyone. Stay strong, honey."

"But he—"

"Shhh, don't say anything on the phone."

After the call, the guards escort me to a holding cell. "Dinner is at seven," says the older guard. They slam the metal door and lock it.

My cell is a tiny concrete room with a thin mattress, no sheet or pillowcase, and one wool blanket. There is a metal toilet. No mirror. No window. I fall back on the bed and stare at the ceiling. I've been arrested for *murder*. I touch the cold wall, thinking of my father. He didn't have to face this. He died in the hospital, and now it seems like a mercy. If my father had lived, he wouldn't be home with Mom and me like I've always imagined. He'd be in prison or awaiting the death penalty.

A sob builds in my chest as I think about my dad and about Jason. The indignities I faced minutes ago pale in comparison to Jason succumbing to his wounds and bleeding out in the foyer, then Mya and Eli carrying his bloody body into the woods, if that's what happened next. *You have no idea what we've done for you, Finny,* Eli said. My friends are my *accomplices.*

I curl beneath the thin blanket. I believed I became a good person in LA, but it was a mirage. I'm a reckless woman, a liar, and a coward. Soon everyone will know the bad thing I did.

I deserve this cell.

THIRTY-NINE

MYA

Mya's phone pings while doing her math homework. She's the only senior in her Algebra II class, and it's her second time taking it, and she still doesn't understand the material. She slams her laptop closed. She will never use this crap in real life.

Her phone shows her six missed messages from River. The last message reads: where are you? Finley got arrested. It's on the news

Her chest tightens. Arrested? God, did they find Jason's body? Mya reopens her laptop and types "Finley Dunn, Anchorage" into the search bar. Articles and videos, some just minutes old, populate her screen. She reads a headline from the *Alaska Daily*:

ARREST MADE IN CASE
OF MISSING ANCHORAGE MAN

The article identifies Finley Dunn as the "person of interest" in Jason's case and says she was taken into custody earlier this evening and charged with giving false information to a peace officer, tampering with evidence, obstruction of justice, and murder in the third degree.

Mya's heart seizes at the word *murder*.

The article states that her arrest affidavit will be released before her arraignment hearing, which is scheduled for four in the afternoon on Monday.

The shocking piece is that Jason's body remains at large. A reporter explains the murder charge. "A judge agreed that blood and other forensic evidence provided by the Anchorage Police Department indicated probable cause to arrest Dunn for murder in the third degree against a vulnerable victim. Police allege that Jason Walker received life-ending injuries and Finley Dunn covered up the crime. Detectives believe Ms. Dunn had assistance and are looking for information regarding possible accomplices. If they discover evidence of premeditation, the charge will be elevated to murder in the first degree." The article appeals to the public for their help.

Mya groans because Finley was right—they should have called 911 right away. The punishment for getting high, partying at the Chateau, and assaulting a trespasser is nothing compared to what's coming.

She shuts her laptop again and leans against her headboard. What will the media say when they connect the final dots and realize that Finley is the daughter of a murderer? They're going to go nuts. Mya's heart thumps in erratic beats.

Her bedroom door squeaks open and Brittany enters. Her sister slumps against the threshold and crosses her arms, wearing a green facial mask and a long white T-shirt. She slides her jaw back and forth. "Finley is on the news. Did she kill that squatter?"

Mya bites hard on her lip. "It's a mistake. Finley wouldn't hurt a fly."

Brittany picks at her fingernail polish. "Then why did she clean up the blood?"

"I told you it's a mistake."

Her sister uncrosses her arms and touches her mask to test if it's ready to come off. "I know you all were together when that guy went missing. You're the accomplices, aren't you?"

Mya wipes her face. "You can go away now."

Her sister's voice rises. "I am legit worried about you, Mya. Your friends are losers, and this is destroying Mom's business. You better figure it out." Brittany slinks out of the bedroom and back to her own.

Mya opens her laptop a third time and types into the search engine: *Can you be tried for murder if there isn't a body?*

The answer is quick and shocking. Yes—a person can be convicted of murder if there is enough circumstantial and forensic evidence to infer that the victim is dead and the defendant is guilty.

Her head drops into her hands. The search parties won't find Jason in the woods behind Northwood Estates. She could tell the police they're wasting their time and offer them a better location. She has the power to end this.

Mya lifts her covers and slides into bed. If she were a religious person, she'd cut bait and confess. It might be worth it to avoid an afterlife in hell. One of her mother's sayings comes to mind: *Never make a big decision when you're tired, hungry, or horny.* Mya is tired, and she doesn't believe in eternal damnation.

She goes to sleep.

FORTY

FINLEY

Popularity in high school does not equate to popularity in jail. The inmate who delivers my meals explains it to me. "Chicks in here been homeless, some of 'em. And you come from a good home, you good at school. You fucked with one a' their own. They hate you. Why you think the warden won't let you out?"

Being alone with my thoughts all weekend is unpleasant. I'm a pariah and a disappointment even among criminals. It's like falling into a bottomless pit that is filled not with fire or brimstone or demons but nothing at all. Ostracism is hell. *Ostracism* also happens to be an SAT word. As I stare at the concrete walls, my college dreams evaporate.

"Dunn. Get up."

"What?"

"Your mom and your lawyer are here." The guard leads me to a small holding room. Mom rushes to me, but the guard holds her back. "No touching."

235

Mom bursts into tears, while Tiffany Chen remains seated. "Are you all right?" Mom asks.

"Yes. They kept me by myself." Some primal instinct keeps me calm. The stakes are too high to break down.

"Your arraignment is at four," says Chen. "Here's a copy of Detective Perez's arrest affidavit. Read it. Then we'll talk."

Chen slides the document across the table. It's a sworn statement written by Detective Perez, and it sends me reeling. It mentions that the search of my home, trash dumpster, and Volvo uncovered Jason's blood in the trunk of my car and on my pink dress. It states that GPS data and forensic evidence indicate that Jason and I were at the model home together and that his phone pinged at my townhome later the following morning. CCTV shows my Volvo leaving Northwood Estates in the dark, early morning hours.

The affidavit also details Jason's blood in the model home foyer and the botched attempt to clean it up. A few of my hairs were discovered in the main bedroom's rumpled king-sized bed, along with Jason's hairs and unidentified hairs, which I know belong to River. To top it off, the report includes my Safe Spaces surveillance photo, detailed photographs of my Volvo and its trunk, Jason's luminol-enhanced bloodstain, and my blood-splattered pink-sequined dress.

Due to the evidence listed in the affidavit and my lie to the police, the judge granted Perez permission to arrest me. I set the papers aside. "I can explain—"

Chen lifts her hand in a halting gesture. "I'll start," she says. "If Jason had a job or a home, I'd be worried. But I dare the prosecutor to try you for murder when the victim has no known daily routines and the body hasn't been recovered.

He's been a nomadic drug user for several years. I believe Perez put her cart before her horse. She's hoping you'll confess or that community members will come forward with incriminating information. She's applying pressure because of the media attention."

I nod as my thoughts ping-pong inside my head. Jason's blood in my trunk looks bad—but I set the bloody dress, not his *body,* in there.

Chen continues as if reading my mind. "The evidence is compelling—his DNA in your trunk and on the rumpled bedsheets—so we can't deny you two were together. However, my medical expert will rebut the state's expert and testify that the amount of blood loss in the foyer was survivable. I'm negotiating with the DA about the murder charge. The only witness to what happened that night is *you.* It's 'she said, she said' at this point, which is in our favor." Chen glances at my mom, who does not appear soothed by anything Chen has said.

"If they don't charge Finley with murder, will she go free at the arraignment hearing?" Mom asks.

Chen stacks her papers. "The lying to a peace officer and obstruction of justice charges will stick, and you'll plead guilty to both, Finley. They are class A misdemeanors, so yes, I expect her to go free if the DA agrees to dismiss the murder three charge. Tampering with evidence relates to the murder charge and I'm trying to get that dropped too." She aims her sharp chin at me. "I'm ready to hear more details about what happened that night. You may tell your story."

I peer around the jailhouse holding room, searching for

a camera or recording device. I trust Chen to be aware of that kind of thing anyway. I let out a breath and tell her what happened without mentioning my friends' names. I let her believe that Jason left on his own even though I no longer believe it myself. I decline to tell her I pushed him out of anger. That shame can stay buried.

Chen is stunned. "Had you contacted me that morning instead of running, we wouldn't be here right now. I could have argued self-defense."

"It didn't occur to me to call a lawyer," I say.

Chen nods. "Are the people who were with you willing to come forward as witnesses on your behalf? I can guess that one of them is Mya Green, but you don't need to confirm that."

I play with my hands. "Not unless they have to."

She scrawls on her notepad, unperturbed. "All right, that's okay for now. Know this, Finley: if Jason's body turns up, the murder charge can be reinstated and new charges can be levied. The best thing for you is that he stays missing."

I flinch and Chen catches my reaction. "I represent you, not him, Finley. This is about survival. It's about you pursuing your dreams at college and staying out of jail."

"What if . . ."

Chen anticipates me. "What if you come clean? Too late. This arrest affidavit is being published today. It's scintillating and scandalous—a pretty teenager and an arguably attractive male, alone in a house for five hours with evidence of rumpled sheets, a bloody Valentine's dress, and a giant bloodstain—public speculation will be rampant and salacious. Your father's history doesn't help. The media will be running with that later today."

"Dear God," says Mom, deflating.

Chen pats my hand, real sympathy in her eyes. "You're a beautiful and successful student, Finley. People will tune in to watch your arraignment hearing today. This story will be on the news tonight, and once the sordid details come out, it could make the national news and *Good Morning America*. If you confess now, I can't promise you an unbiased jury in the future."

My bones turn to rubber. Mom grips the table so hard her knuckles turn white.

Chen slides more papers out of her sleek briefcase. "The DA and I are speaking in an hour to discuss your charges and a plea deal, so more to come there. Let's go over what will happen at your arraignment hearing this afternoon, what you'll wear, what I'll wear, and how we'll interact. Your TV debut must be perfect and orchestrated to garner sympathy. Your mother and I spoke earlier, and she's brought an outfit for you. With the right tone and media image, we can turn the tide away from you and against the victim."

"That doesn't seem fair," I say in a quiet voice.

"Justice rarely is," says Chen.

FORTY-ONE

MYA

On Monday, reporters stand outside Bartlett High, bundled against the Arctic chill, interviewing students. Mya darts past them with her hood pulled over her head. The media has figured out Finley's past and, like sharks in the water, they ravage this piece of information with razor-sharp headlines.

**DAUGHTER OF 'BACKWOODS KILLER'
ARRESTED FOR MURDER**

THE DUNNS HAVE DONE IT AGAIN

LIKE FATHER, LIKE DAUGHTER

Mya, River, and Eli gather at their lunch table. Mya pulls the pickles out of her school lunch cheeseburger. "We should watch Fin's arraignment hearing together. Can you guys come over after school?"

"It's on TV? Cool," says Eli.

"Not cool," says Mya. "The story is blowing up."

River drops his sandwich back into his lunch sack. "I can't believe Finley's in jail. I haven't slept all weekend. I can't eat."

"She'll end up someone's girlfriend," says Eli.

River blinks at him. "Why would you say that?"

Eli bites into his burrito, talking with his mouth full. "'Cause she's hot, man."

"You should be in there with her, asshole." River's voice flows hot beneath the hum of lunchroom chatter.

Eli rests his arms on the table. "I'm just fucking around. I'm worried about her too. Finny's way too sweet for jail."

"She's hot *and* sweet?" Mya mutters.

Eli pauses mid-bite. "What?"

"It's not fair," River adds. He glares at the other students, his fists clenching and unclenching. "Did you know people call us the Cullens? Finley told me about it. They think we're weird."

"Who are the Cullens?" asks Eli.

"Dude, seriously?"

The floor tilts under Mya's feet. Is River implying that they are weird or that *she* is weird? She changes the subject. "One of Finley's charges is tampering with evidence. Do you know what that's about?" She looks at River. "Has she talked to you?"

He pokes through his lunch sack. "She can't. She's in jail."

"When are you going to admit you like her, man?" says Eli. "I know you two didn't go upstairs on Valentine's Day to talk. Is she a good kisser?"

River thrusts to his feet. "Shut up, Eli."

He laughs harder. "Jesus, man. Calm the fuck down."

"Stop arguing and sit," Mya hisses, glaring at them both.

River uncoils, joint by joint, and sinks onto the table bench. He rests his head on the engineered wood. "She wanted to help that guy, and we didn't let her."

Mya smacks his shoulder. "Shhh!"

"We don't talk about anything real anymore." River drags his eyes to Eli's. "Like how you and Mya are fucking."

"Dude, if I can't talk about your girlfriend . . ."

Mya's cheeks catch fire. "We aren't—"

River snatches his lunch and stands. "Stop lying! Both of you. What other secrets are you keeping?"

"Be quiet." Mya grabs her lip in her teeth. "We can't start fighting *now*. Are you guys coming over after school or what?"

"Fine," says River.

Eli winks at her. "Wouldn't miss it."

The boys take off, and Mya tosses her uneaten cheeseburger into the garbage. River is correct. There are secrets between them, creeping like termites. Secrets that can destroy them.

FORTY-TWO

MYA

Finley's mug shot appears on the news before the arraignment hearing. "Finny looks scared," says Eli.

River rubs his face. "This is so fucked up."

They're in Mya's home theater, reclining in the leather chairs, looking at Finley's traumatized mug shot photo on the big screen. Her swollen eyes bulge, and her eyelashes are spiked from crying. Her nose is red at the tip, and her lips are pale. The freckles that sprinkle the tops of her cheeks are darker against her pallid skin.

Police released her arrest affidavit and mug shot two hours ago. The details about Jason's DNA in Finley's vehicle and home, plus evidence that they may have shared a bed, have led to the full resurrection of Finley's past and rocketed her story into the national news.

MURDERER'S DAUGHTER LAST PERSON TO SEE MISSING MAN

'LARGE BLOODSTAIN' INDICATES UNHAPPY ENDING FOR MISSING ANCHORAGE RESIDENT

VALENTINE'S DAY RENDEZVOUS ENDS IN BLOODSHED

'WARM PLACE TO SLEEP' NOT SAFE FOR UNHOUSED MAN

BLOODY DRESS TELLS GRUESOME TALE

Talk show hosts, influencers, and activists take to the internet to either roast or defend Finley. Mya flips through YouTube clips on the large screen while they wait for the arraignment hearing to begin. They listen to snippets from various sources:

> Finley Dunn looks sweet, but can you judge a book by its cover? —*Alaska Daily Network Commentator*

> Violence against the homeless is rising. Is it so far off to believe a teenager lured that unfortunate man into the home and tortured him for sport? Perhaps involving her friends as well? —*CNN*

> Jason Walker pled guilty to assault and battery just a few years ago. It's possible he abducted

the girl and Finley Dunn is the victim here.
—*KTUU-TV*

She lied to the police and scrubbed the
bloodstain. Those are the actions of a guilty
woman. —*KTBY Commentator*

Mya mutes the most recent video feed, and Eli rubs his face.

"We have to come forward," says River.

Mya shakes her head. "Mom's lawyer says this is a publicity stunt. They're going to release Finley at the hearing with a slap on the wrist." She studies River for signs of emotional cracks and notices he won't look at her at all. "This is bigger than us now, River. Look at how the story is exploding. We don't need that kind of attention on us or our parents."

"It's not fair to Finley," he says.

"Don't forget who pushed him," Mya snaps.

"How do they *not* know we were there?" says Eli. "We must have left fingerprints and DNA behind."

Mya rereads the affidavit. "The report mentions unidentified hairs and prints, but we're not in the police database, so they can't match them to us. And without probable cause, they can't get our samples. We're safe."

River's head snaps toward her. "Safe? Fuck you. If this gets any worse, I'm taking the blame. I'll keep you two out of it."

Mya's heart flaps inside her chest. She and Eli can withstand the heat, but River cannot. When he's around Finley, he pretends to be fine. He plays the strong, supportive friend. But when she's not around, he spirals inside his fragile brain. She must keep him calm and grounded. "I told you they're releasing Finley after this hearing. It's over, River." Unless someone finds Jason's body, Mya thinks, but doesn't say it out loud.

"Look—there she is." Eli unmutes the speakers. The three of them settle into their reclining chairs and face the screen.

Finley enters the courtroom, escorted by her lawyer and a bailiff. She's dressed in a pale pink blouse, khakis, and ballerina flats. Her hair is pinned into a conservative bun. Her makeup is simple and fresh. Beside her, Tiffany Chen and her all-female team of colleagues wear dark suits and high heels, reducing Finley to a child-sized and delicate apparition beside them.

It's over in ten minutes. Finley pleads guilty to lying to the police and obstructing justice, and the judge slaps her with community service hours. The District Attorney's office dismisses the tampering with evidence and murder in the third degree charges, and Finley is free to go. Detective Perez seethes from her seat in the courtroom. The DA did not have her back on this one, and Mya smiles.

"That was quick," says Eli.

River is transfixed. "Did you see her? She was shaking."

As Finley exits the courthouse, Mya is proud of her. She's doing what she's supposed to do—keeping her mouth shut.

Tiffany Chen and her team lead Finley to the courthouse lobby, where Chen gives a short statement to the local press while Finley stands beside her. "I won't be taking questions," says Chen. "My client made a mistake, and she has accepted the consequences handed to her by the judge. She does not know Jason Walker's location. We are as concerned as anyone about his well-being and hope he is found safe."

Chen wraps her arm around Finley's shoulder. "Ms. Dunn is a dedicated high school student with a bright future ahead of her, and we ask that you respect her privacy going forward." Chen leads Finley away as media personnel shout questions and aim their cameras at Finley.

Mya lets out a breath. "See? It's over." River nods but looks away.

Eli pushes against his seat and stretches his arms. "We went through a lot of shit because of that Jason Walker."

"But we made it through. *She* made it through," says Mya. "The truth stays with us."

River grumbles something unintelligible. His lips are pressed tight, and Mya grips his arm. "Stay strong, River. We're at the end of this."

He smiles without humor and yanks his arm away.

FORTY-THREE

FINLEY

My townhome might need updating, but it's cozier than jail. I'm so happy to be home. Mom's lavender candle scent lingers in the living room and her flowered wall prints are cheerful. Even the drive home was comforting. The Chugach Mountains loomed over us, protecting Mom and me like they protect Anchorage, and we spotted Princess Fiona at the downtown bakery, admiring herself in the glass as pedestrians crossed the street to avoid her.

"Something is wrong with that moose," said Mom. "She's not afraid of people."

Now we enter our townhome through the attached garage and Mom hands me a brand-new phone. Her blue eyes are pale, her expression haggard. "This is not a reward. You need a phone . . . but it comes with conditions."

"Anything you want, Mom."

"Enable the tracking so I can watch you. Your new curfew is eleven, and I want you to take a break from your friends."

I hand the phone back to her. "I can't do that."

She drops into a chair at the kitchen table, exasperated. "Look at the mess they dragged you into."

I crash down beside her, still smelling like jail cell. "No, I dragged *them* into it. I told you I'm the one who pushed him."

"I think there's more to it, Fin. I don't understand why the rescue dogs haven't found him if he wandered off like your friends said." She lifts her chin. "I think Jason died and your friends moved him."

I grab the clip in my hair and yank it out. "Can we not talk about this? I need a shower."

"They've always been liars, Finley. It wasn't a big deal when you were little, but your friends and their parents haven't outgrown it. Have you noticed that I don't hang out with the old gang anymore? I overheard Cookie lying to a potential buyer the other day, and she was quick to lawyer you up, wasn't she? When Dad and I were younger, I didn't question this idea of *us against the establishment.* Our group believed laws were stupid. We were not good people, Fin, but you and I have changed."

I wipe my palms on my khakis. I am exhausted, but I won't back down. "If my friends hid a body, they did it for me. You don't want to believe it, but I'm the bad one."

Tears shine in Mom's eyes. "This wouldn't have happened in LA."

I shut her down with one cruel sentence. "It's your fault we moved."

Mom narrows her eyes. "You're blaming me?"

The stress from the weekend unravels. "I'm sorry. I didn't mean that."

She stands up. "I won't make you decide between me and your friends, Finley. As you enjoy pointing out, you're eighteen. Whatever trouble you get into from now on, you will pay the price. The full adult price." She hands me the new phone. "Keep the tracking on, pick up when I call you, and be home by eleven. I'm taking a nap. For a year." She strides out of the dining area and up the stairs.

My voice follows her. "I said I'm sorry." She doesn't answer.

I shower and dress in cotton pajamas and a soft chenille wrap. I power up the new phone and charge it. There are congratulatory messages from Mya and Eli regarding the charges that were dropped. I don't know what to say back. *Thanks* feels trite, so I ignore them.

Chen said my car, computer, and old phone should be returned to me in the next few days. I guess Mom couldn't wait until then to start tracking me.

I never finished cleaning up my bedroom after the search, so I tackle it the way Mya tackled that bloodstain, with gloves and cleansers, except mine are not organic. My cleansers are high-powered and full of harmful chemicals. I want the police presence *annihilated.*

Olivia and Imani left me a voicemail. "Finley, oh my God, we saw you on the news! What's going on? Are you okay? Call us!" Ocean waves crash in the background. They're at the beach.

I don't have the energy to explain, so I message that I'm okay and will talk to them later.

I check out my social media feed. Mistake. Comments about my case flood my most recent post. The bad ones blare the loudest:

> Instead of Missing White Girl Syndrome can we start Killer White Girl Syndrome? Finley Dunn isn't the story. Jason Walker is.

> She fucked that dude for college money

> She's a killer like her daddy. The apple didn't fall far from the tree

> Rich bitch

> If we find out Jason raped her y'all going to feel like shit

With each horrible remark, I tumble farther off my pedestal. One news outlet reported that I own a townhome outright, so now I'm not just a potential killer, I'm a *privileged* potential killer. Everyone hates me.

I text Clodagh. She's heard about my arrest if she watches the news. Should I come to work on Saturday? I write.

Her answer is immediate. Of course, poor lass. Come to work.

My heart clutches and I burst into tears. My boss believes in me, and she shouldn't. Thank you, I write back.

I fall onto my pillows and stare at my ceiling. I will never live this down at school. People think I either slept with Jason or that he raped me, and I pled guilty to lying to the police. I can never go to my leadership class again, not after saying that telling the truth models good behavior. I am such a hypocrite. River's messages pile up on my phone, but he doesn't deserve a girl like me and I leave them unanswered.

"I want to go home," I whisper, and I have no idea what that means—home to before Dad died or home to LA. My empty stomach squeezes. My nerves jangle. I cry so hard I dry-heave into the toilet.

After falling asleep for a few hours, I wake up with a fresh perspective. If everyone thinks I'm bad, I no longer have to try to be perfect. I can be myself, whoever that is. Feeling lighter, I ransack the kitchen for food.

It's ten in the evening and the moon is a round nickel in the sky. I gaze out the back window as I eat leftover enchiladas. Stars poke glittering holes in the blackness, and the lagoon glows silver. Walking trails surround the frozen water and cut across it like arteries to other places.

Yellow flames catch my eye. They lick out of a garbage can on the lake. Several people surround it, warming themselves. There is a small homeless encampment in the woods near the lagoon, and I suspect the people by the fire are residents of the camp. Families ice-skate on weekend evenings, but later, at night, unsheltered people drift out of the woods and onto the frozen water to enjoy a change of scenery and a fire.

Mom keeps binoculars in a side table drawer for looking at moose, beavers, and birds. I slide them out and focus on the people by the fire—six men and a woman. They huddle in a circle, wearing mismatched clothes and rubbing their bare hands together, chatting and fidgeting. Glimpses of their colored tents and smaller campfires peek through the pine needles. The locals get very upset about the campfires, which can cause wildfires. Many of them have picketed city hall to have the homeless encampments removed. People want affordable housing, but not this way.

I'm about to set the binoculars down when one of the men dances a jig, making his friends laugh. He slips on the ice and falls. The man nearest him lifts him back to his feet. Another brushes ice crust off his pants for him. Their kindness to one another is like a slap in my face. Did this community watch out for Jason too? If so, why did he abandon them? Was it to get clean on his own?

I squint harder at the people below. The police questioned groups like this, but I remember from my brief stay at a shelter that many unhoused people don't trust the police, and they might not have shared information with them. If there is anything about Jason the police don't know, no matter how small, these people might have it.

My nerves hum with an idea. Finding Jason, dead or alive, is the best way to redeem myself and earn back my self-respect. If River loves me, maybe he'll help me.

I call him and he answers on the first ring, sounding panicked. "Finley? Are you okay? Are you still with your lawyers?"

"No. I got home a little bit ago and I'm fine. I promise."

"It's not fair—"

I cut him off. "Will you come over and do something crazy with me?"

He exhales. "I'm on my way."

FORTY-FOUR

FINLEY

I meet River on my front porch, bundled head to toe in my Mount Everest outfit. "Hi," I whisper as I close the door. "We're going to the lagoon behind my house."

His eyes crinkle with a confused smile. "When you said crazy, I had something... sexier in mind. It's almost eleven. Why the lagoon?"

"Because there're homeless people on the ice. We're going to question them about Jason."

His face falls. "Finley..."

"I'm going with or without you, and I'm bringing money."

"That makes no sense."

"It's to lube their wheels, you know? They have no reason to trust me." I stuffed all the tip money I've been saving into my jacket pocket. I also grabbed Jason's missing person flyer out of the kitchen drawer.

"Lube their wheels?" River shakes his head. "The last time you tried to help, you ended up on a security camera and then in a jail cell. This isn't smart, Fin."

"I don't care! I never went and looked for Jason like I should have. These people know him and they might have information they haven't shared. Even if he's dead, I need to know. People already think I'm bad and they have no idea I pushed him on purpose. You're the only one I've told. I—I owe it to Jason to try. No one should have to wait until the ice melts to get found." A guttural sob scrapes my throat. "You coming?"

The look River gives me is unreadable, but he agrees.

We cross the street to the lagoon. The garbage can surrounded by strangers is about fifty yards offshore.

Cold air stings my lungs, and the scent of smoke and snow mingles in my nose. I pull my beanie to my eyebrows and zip my jacket to my chin. My wool mittens do little to block the evening wind that sweeps across the frozen lagoon. River is wearing a sweatshirt. He shivers.

"Sorry, I should have warned you to dress for an excursion."

"I'll live," he says.

We approach the garbage-can fire with our bodies hunched for warmth. The lone woman in the group spots us first. The men follow her gaze, and a collective shudder runs through them at the sight of two approaching strangers, but they stand their ground.

The flames whip in the can, crazed by the wind, creating their own hissing energy. "Hello," I say.

They scan me up and down, then do the same to River, assessing if we're prying do-gooders or self-righteous citizens who want their space back.

I pull Jason Walker's flyer from my coat pocket. "Hello, we're wondering if you can you help us? We're trying to find this man. Do you know him?"

Their feet shift as they look at one another. Two of the men turn back to the fire, dismissing us. The woman eyeballs my warm jacket, and a gray-bearded man with large ears studies the photo on the flyer. "That's Pipey," he says.

"Is that a nickname?" River asks. The man nods.

I rub my arms. "Have you seen him?" My exhale produces a stream of vapor like dragon's breath.

The woman snatches the flyer from her friend and studies it. "Whaddya want with him?"

"We want to . . . help him."

She traces Jason's square jaw in the photo and snorts. "He's been on the TV at the shelter, and his twin came lookin' too. Pipey ran off to get clean by himself. Mistake."

I begin to shiver, but not from the cold. They've watched the news, which means they might have seen my arraignment hearing.

"Have you seen him recently?" River asks.

The woman points at the reward figure at the bottom of the flyer. "One thousand dollars says I haven't."

"For sure," says the man. "We'd 'ave called."

"Pipey prob'ly hittin' his pipe again and done wandered off," says the woman. "He's a good sort. He'll come back." The others smile and grunt in agreement. They're each over fifty years old, I'd guess. Elders in their community.

I dance from foot to foot, feeling the cold in my toes. "But have you seen him since Valentine's Day?"

The oldest man, a Native Alaskan, turns away from the fire and peers at me. "Pipey slept where he shouldn't have slept. A white girl killed him. Saw it on the news."

River flinches, and my heart dives toward my feet. We take a step back.

"The reporter didn't say she killed him," says the gray-bearded man.

"They found his blood in the trunk of her car. What do you think that means?"

The woman sucks air through her teeth. "That's not true, is it?"

He tugs on his beard with chapped bare hands. "It's true. The police let the girl go. Damn fools."

The group grumbles about the police. River tries to lead me away, his eyes casting a warning, but the old man closes the space between us. He tilts his head and a spark lights his dark eyes. "You look like her—the blondie on TV."

His words deepen the chill inside my body. My feet freeze in place.

"Yeah, yeah, you are her." His voice skids across the ice. "This girl killed Pipey."

"No, she didn't," says River, taking my hand.

The group gathers closer together. "You're the angel-faced killer," one says, referring to one of the inflammatory news headlines about me.

The woman's face creases into a frown. "The devil was an angel once."

I stumble backward. "I didn't kill . . ." I can't finish the statement. I can't lie to them. I hurt Jason. I might have caused his death. "Here." I reach into my pocket for my tip money. It's not much, but I want to help, to leave them with something.

"You gonna kill us, too?" says a smaller man who hasn't spoken yet. The group bursts into laughter.

I hold out the tip money but don't have a good grip on it. The money flies out of my hands and swirls around us like leaves.

"You expect us to dance for it?" asks the Native man, his gray eyebrows pinched together.

"No. I'm sorry." River pulls harder on my arm, but I haven't gotten what I came for. "I'm trying to help. I promise."

"Help yourself off our ice."

"Let's go," says River.

The group ignores the money I dropped, and my offering looks ridiculous against the backdrop of their shoreline encampment. Their needs are too great for a little cash to fulfill. Someone throws Jason's flyer into the can, and his image turns to ashes. Tears stab my eyes. "I'm sorry."

River leads me away. We're almost to the shore when I slip, fall, and bang my head on the ice.

"Finley!" He drops to my side.

"Leave me alone. Please." I push him away. River rises off the ice and stands over me like a sentinel.

I lie there, stunned, and my eyes claw at the sky for answers about who I am and what I've done. I *feel* like an angel who has been cast down from the stars. It's actions that make us who we are, and I have done bad, bad things. It doesn't matter whether I get caught. I know what I did.

I weep for what I've lost—my integrity, my self-respect, my innocence.

Moments later, the sky begins to glow. I swallow my tears, watching and shivering. The northern lights wisp overhead like undulating ribbons dyed in green and pink hues.

"Look at that," says River.

My heart lifts and I raise my hand toward the magical glow.

He snatches my arm and hisses, *"Never wave at the lights."*

There are many legends about the aurora borealis: that it's the dead playing soccer, or spirits of hunted animals, or demons, or the dance of angry souls seeking revenge. If the last legend is true, these lights could contain the souls of River's father and maybe Jason Walker—two men who are dead because of me.

"I forgot," I say. Head down, I push myself up and shuffle with River across the lagoon toward my townhome, afraid that one of those dead men will see me. *God, please help us find Jason. Please reveal his location.*

It feels too late to pray, but it works.

Three days later, Jason Walker is found.

FORTY-FIVE

FINLEY, THEN

A few minutes after River takes off to pee in the woods, my friends and I hear him yelp and fall. We race toward the sound of his groaning. "Watch for bears!" I shout. Eli snatches up a thick branch as a weapon. Mya does the same. We burst into a clearing to discover River lying flat on his back, his eyes closed. His blood splatters the brush and soaks the front of his pants. Mya skids to a halt and drops her branch.

"Oh my God!" she cries.

I glance around for animal tracks or a bear. There's nothing. "Why is he bleeding?"

"Hey, man, what happened?" Eli drops to his best friend's side. "River? Wake up."

His features twist. "Leave me alone."

"It looks like he peed blood," I say. Worried about internal injuries, I slide up his T-shirt and the three of us gasp. A rotten-looking bruise has spread across River's lower back where it hit the dresser. We swam in his pond yesterday, and that bruise was not there.

"Bart should be in jail," Mya says.

River vomits onto the dirt. Tears squeeze from his eyes, and fresh blood stains his jeans.

"Shit, guys. He *is* pissing blood," says Eli. "That's not normal. It might be his kidney."

River curls into a ball and shudders in deep, violent waves. Tears wash my eyes, and Mya's lips tighten. "Pick him up; he needs help."

We ease River off the ground and hold him upright. "I'm fine," he says, groaning.

"Stop it. You're not fine." I peer at my friends. "Can he die from this?"

Mya gulps. "No. No way."

"Hurry," says Eli as we start back together.

River's body shakes as we half walk, half carry him toward his house. "Why did Bart hit him this time?" Mya asks in a ragged voice.

My cheeks warm. "We were in River's bedroom with the door closed."

Her thick eyebrows draw together. "You know Bart doesn't like us in his house unsupervised."

"His rules change every day," I snap.

"Stop fighting," says Eli.

"We're not fighting," we say at the same time. "I'm not blaming you," Mya adds under her breath.

We're almost in sight of the house when we hear gunshots and drop to the ground, covering our heads. *Pop. Pop. Pop.*

"Target practice?" Eli asks. *Pop. Pop.* More gunfire pierces the sunny evening, followed by adult laughter. Eli releases a breath and stands. "I think they're shooting over by the shop."

"I hate it when they shoot drunk," I say.

"They're stupid," says Mya. "Come on, let's set him on the bench."

Mya and Eli throw River's arms over their shoulders, walk him to the dilapidated gazebo, and set him on the mossy, rotted bench.

"I'll get my dad," I say.

River snatches my hand. "You promised not to tell. You'll make it worse."

I said I wouldn't tell, but I didn't promise. "My parents will know what to do, River."

"Finley, don't . . ."

"I won't let you die." I run away before he can change my mind, skirt the backyard firepit and the shooting range, and find my dad returning from the range with his rifle strap slung over his shoulder. "River's hurt," I say.

Dad frowns. "Okay, where is he?"

"The gazebo."

He follows me, and we choose a path that isn't in view of the firepit or the distant shop. Pine needles carpet the trail, crunching beneath our feet. Sunlight dapples the trees and Dad slides on his sunglasses. It's midnight.

When we get to the gazebo, Eli is there alone.

"Where's River?" I ask.

"He and Mya took off."

My dad notices droplets of blood leading into the wilderness. "Does River need a doctor?"

"Yes," I whisper. "His dad whooped him good. He's peeing blood."

A string of curses flows from my father's mouth. "You two get help. I'll find River and his dad."

Eli and I race back toward the party.

FORTY-SIX

MYA

"Tiffany Chen is a genius," Mya says.

Eli rolls over in her bed. His mouth is red and raw from kissing her, his hair is rumpled, and his eyes are half-closed. He rests his heavy arm across her stomach and traces a vein in her hip with his finger. "Do you tan? I mean, can you tan?"

"Shut up."

He blinks, and she likes how his eyelashes are thick and curled. "I'm not being mean, baby. I want to road-trip with you after we graduate. I'm trying to imagine you in a bikini on the beach."

Mya strokes his dark hair, enjoying the familiar shape of his head. "I might be able to achieve a darker shade of white."

He nibbles her neck. "So tell me why Tiffany Chen is a fucking genius."

"Look at this." Mya shifts her laptop and Eli scoots closer to look. "Dressing Finley as a sad little church girl worked. The media has flipped."

She shows him clips, headlines, and articles. Finley's tearful, shocked mug shot photo has been replaced by her senior picture, a charming image taken on an LA beach last fall. She wears a white gauzy dress and no shoes. It's the golden hour, and sunlight plays on her yellow hair. The photographer caught a candid moment—Finley in the middle of a laugh, her white dress backlit and glowing, her body a dark, feminine shape beneath the fabric—a real-life angel.

The media has swapped out Jason's photo too. Gone is the handsome shot taken before his snow machine accident that Brady provided. Instead, the media displays his prior assault mug shot. Jason is unshaven and wild-eyed, his face emaciated.

"'Beauty and the Beast,'" Eli says, reading a news headline. "Fitting."

Many media outlets redraw Finley as an ill-fated victim—first of her father's horrific legacy and then of the hell she likely endured during her five-hour ordeal with Jason Walker. The theory that she was dragged into the model home and assaulted, but is too embarrassed to come forward, catches fire. Since Jason's body hasn't been found, speculation arises that he's alive and hiding from the police.

Influencers and talk show hosts slobber over the unknown details. Did he tie Finley up, beat her, drug her? He raped her for sure, no question about that. Poor girl. It's obvious the two battled—blood in the foyer, the scratches on

Finley's arms, the bruise on her face, her ruined dress—all of which are depicted in great detail in the arrest affidavit.

Speculation is rampant:

> He's in Russia. Mexico. Canada.
>
> Finley is pregnant.
>
> He stalked her.

All complete bullshit.

Mya is about to close her laptop when a breaking story catches her attention. Her heart seizes. She can't breathe.

"What is it?" Eli has moved on to licking her stomach.

Her fingers tremble as she opens the latest article. The headline is simple:

**BODY OF MISSING
ANCHORAGE MAN FOUND**

Heat flushes Mya's body. "They found him."

Eli cranks his head to read what she's reading, and his body goes still. "Holy fuck. I thought it would take longer." He rises naked from the bed, his muscles rippling. As he collects his clothing, he pauses to appraise himself in her mirror.

Mya throws her pillow at him. "Take this seriously, idiot." Eli is too fucking comfortable with death, with lies, with everything.

"Okay, sorry." He pulls on his jeans and rolls his T-shirt

down his chest. "I tan pretty easily, by the way. I get dark as shit."

"They *found* him, Eli. Let that sink into your stupid head. Please. We are in big trouble."

He can't stop smiling at her, and Mya starts to cry. She can add *poor judge of character* to her list of deficiencies— lousy liar, messy crime scene cleaner, embarrassing math student.

Eli zips his jeans and embraces her until she stops thrashing. "We knew they'd find him when the ice melted, if not sooner, baby. It's only serious if Finley cracks."

"I think Finley will crack. This will undo her."

Mya's phone pings with a text from her mother. Time to cut bait, Mya. The trespasser is dead. I've hired another attorney, Matt Haydon. He says he can get you an immunity deal if you turn on Finley. No one likes a rat, but I'm not letting that murderer drag you down with her. You have an appointment with Matt at four. I'll pick you up.

Mya tugs on Eli's arm. "Mom wants me to make an immunity deal with the police."

"You should take it, Mya."

"No! I can't and you know why."

He cups her face. "Stop protecting everyone else and protect yourself. You didn't do anything wrong."

"I literally cleaned up a crime scene, and then . . ."

"Hey, you cleaned up a spill, that's all. You should take the deal. Save yourself."

"A spill, Eli?"

"Yeah, a leak. His head sprang a leak."

"Jesus," says Mya.

Eli kisses the top of her head and his musky scent is as calming to her as aromatherapy. Is this why they work well together? Is it simple, mindless chemistry? Because when Eli is not around, all she sees are his flaws.

Her phone alerts again, this time with a DM from Brittany: Mom and dad had a massive fight. He went to a hotel! Fix this now!

Mya's heart clutches. "My dad went to a hotel, Eli. A hotel."

"This is Finny's fault. Maybe we need to, you know, take care of her?" He cracks his knuckles.

"What are you talking about?"

He shrugs. "Scare the shit out of her? We can't exactly cut out her tongue or bust her kneecaps. Can we?" He winks.

"That's some dark shit, Eli. You love Finny."

"Joking," he says, "but I'll tell you what is some darker shit—prison. We can't let her talk."

Mya furrows her brow and then nods. "I have an idea. Go home. I have to think . . . and talk to River and my mom. I'm not taking the deal."

He kisses her head again. "You're the brain."

"Compared to you."

. . .

Mya gazes at the purple walls of her bedroom after Eli leaves. She assumed Jason Walker was dead, but now that she knows for certain, sadness engulfs her in waves. It's not his fault he got addicted to pain medication and became homeless. But it is his fault he crawled into someone else's home and spooked an overreactive girl at the top of a staircase.

Mya hugs her knees to her chest. They shouldn't have covered it up. It's so obvious in hindsight that it's painful to think about.

But the police have Jason's body now, and someone is going to jail—it should be Finley. She left them four years ago and then came back and committed a fucking felony and hasn't apologized. "Finley Dunn, you ruined my life," she says into the mirror. But they each swore an oath of silence. Not telling was *Mya's* idea, and Finley has upheld her end of the covenant under great pressure.

Mya dials River for his opinion.

He answers on the first ring. "I saw the news. I don't want to talk about it."

"Don't disappear on me, River. Eli and I need you."

"Mya, I'm done. I'm fucking done."

Her chest heaves, and her stomach squeezes into a ball. "You—"

River hangs up on her.

"Oh my God." She throws herself on her bed and yells into her pillow. "Asshole! After everything I've done for you." Mya breaks into sobs.

Her door opens and closes and Brittany appears at her side. "Are those human tears?" she asks, poking at Mya, but her voice is gentle and concerned. "Who broke my sister?"

"It's not funny."

"Look at me."

Mya sits up and looks at Brittany. Her older sister is

wearing a kitten T-shirt, no makeup, and her hair in a messy bun, as if she's ten years old again. Her dark eyes are not derisive or bored, just concerned. "I'm sorry I've been such a bitch about all this," she says. "Is there anything I can do? Do you want to talk about it?"

Mya sniffles. "My friends are turning on me and I'm just trying to help them."

"I think you're in over your head this time, bunny."

"I think you're right." Mya's life is falling apart, her parents are fighting, and her friendships are ending. Her friends don't get it—*they* are the fuckups. Every bad thing Mya has done has been for them. They each swore to be loyal, but they aren't loyal to *her*. Except for Eli. Eli is her soldier.

She imagines Jason Walker's body at the county morgue, cold and alone. He'll never get married, have kids, or inhale another breath of Alaskan air so cold it burns your lungs. A shudder rolls through her, and tears blur her vision. "There's nothing you can do to help me," she says to Brittany. "It's too late."

"It's never too late. Mom's new lawyer will help. Please talk to him." Brittany wraps Mya in a tight hug. When the hug is over, she leaves her alone in her bedroom.

Mya tugs on her hair until pain washes out her guilt. After high school, she will find a better group of friends.

FORTY-SEVEN

FINLEY

"This has gone too far, Finley. You need to tell the police the things you told me. The man is dead." Mom is ashen, and her fingers entwine in an arthritic curl. Her blue eyes plead with me.

I hug my pillow and turn my eyes away. Yesterday, a traveler spotted Jason's bare hand sticking out of the snow in Girdwood, Alaska. He called the police, and a forensic team dug Jason's body out. Brady identified his brother—the story is on TV.

A tarp veils the site and the body from the drone footage. The location is a ditch close to the Alyeska Highway, about fifteen miles from the model home. It's too early for spring breakup, the season when the snow and ice start to melt, but a couple of sunny days and warm Chinook winds melted enough snow to reveal Jason's hand. When I close my eyes, I imagine the stiff hand reaching out of the ditch as if for help.

Texts and messages started blowing up my phone last night when the news was released, which is why I skipped school. I can't face anyone right now. As promised, Chen has turned the media tide in my favor and amplified Jason's prior assault. People like Clodagh believe *I'm* the victim. She and a few other people text me.

They found him!

Did you see the news?

He can't hurt you now.

I haven't received any messages from Mya, Eli, or River, and now Mom and I face off in my bedroom. "Confess," she says, grinding her teeth.

She has no idea how much I want to do that. "It's too late, Mom."

She rubs her swollen eyes. "You wanted to help that man, Finley, and your friends wouldn't let you. I was wrong to trust Cookie and her lawyer. It's time to speak up."

I grip the bedpost and pull myself upright. Everyone is about to discover I'm a coward and a liar, that I'm not the Good Samaritan or the innocent victim they want me to be. I accept it, I revel in it. There's relief in admitting you're a total fuckup, but I am the one who killed Jason Walker. "Stop blaming them!" I smack my chest. "I did this to myself. I could have called nine-one-one, but I didn't. I *let* my friends talk me out of it. Do you understand? I let them and do you know why?" A guttural sob fills my bedroom. "Because I *wanted* to hurt him, Mom. I did it on purpose. This is *my* fault." My chest deflates as I let out a huge breath.

Mom's body crumples until she's sitting on the bed. "Why did you want to hurt him, Finley?"

"Because he hurt River. I didn't want him to die, though. I swear it. I—I wasn't thinking."

"Did you put him in the ditch?"

"God, no." I shake my head and my eyes defocus.

Mom snaps her fingers at me. "Finley! This is your life. Jason didn't walk fifteen miles in a storm. One of your friends hid his body. You're all in serious trouble." She covers her mouth with her hand.

She hasn't been this frightened or horrified since Dad shot Bart. I shudder for breath. "Ms. Chen will tell me what to do."

"That's the other thing," says Mom. "I believe Cookie hired that lawyer to protect her business, not you, and now you're on the hook for this by yourself."

"Mom, stop. Please."

"The media won't be on your side for long. You're the only suspect, Finley. Cookie and Ms. Chen have counseled you straight to jail, and they've kept Mya out of it. You pushed him, and we can talk about that later, but it was in the heat of the moment. I believe you didn't mean to kill him, but hiding his body was calculated and cruel. Did you consider that Mya scrubbed the house to clean up *her* crime, not yours? That's how I see it."

Mom is voicing my thoughts, but I don't know what to do about it. I feel like I'm two moves behind everyone else.

She wrings her hands. "Perez told us she'd charge you with murder if that man's body turned up."

"That's not what she said."

"It's basically what she said." Mom uncurls her fingers and crosses her arms. "We need to hire our own attorney. Someone who isn't in Cookie's pocket."

I fold into a ball on my bed. "I feel sick."

"You should. A man is dead." Mom drops her head into her hands. "For God's sake."

My shoulders shake as I weep into my pillow. The truth that Jason Walker is dead and gone forever is too much to hold in my heart, and I cry harder. "I should have realized he was sick. I shouldn't have pushed him. Am I like Dad?"

She collects herself, scoots closer, and strokes my back. "Dad was drunk when he shot Bart."

"I was high." I lift my eyes to her face, but there's no hatred or disappointment there, just sadness. We're both very sad. "I'm sorry, Mom."

She hugs me. "You're a good person who made a mistake. That's what you are. You can make it better by telling the truth. It's time."

"I swore I wouldn't." I hold my stomach.

Mom presses her lips together, then sighs. "If you can't stand up for yourself, you'll never be able to stand up for anybody else. I'm getting you a new lawyer."

Misery presses on my chest. "We can't afford that."

"I'll figure it out. The police won't do anything until the autopsy is finished, so we have some time. Look, I have errands to run. Do you want to stay home or come with me?"

"I'll stay."

"Will you be okay by yourself?"

"Yes, Mom. I'll be fine." She leaves my door open a crack

like she did when I was little and drives away. Rare winter sunlight streams through my window, but another storm is coming. A big one. I let the sunbeams warm my skin and watch my ceiling fan spin around and around.

All there is to do is wait for the autopsy report. I message River. Did you hear they found him? My mom's not home. Please come over.

I heard and I can't come over.

Why not?

I have shit to deal with. I'm sorry.

But I need you.

No, Fin, you don't

What the hell does that mean? Is River mad at me? I call him, but his phone goes straight to voicemail. He promised I would be okay. He said he'd take the blame. I don't want him to do that, but he can't abandon me now.

I drop my phone and punch the wall, pounding it until I'm dizzy.

FORTY-EIGHT

FINLEY

New information leaks to the press in advance of the autopsy report and my reputation takes a nosedive. It leads to a fresh slew of damning headlines:

MISSING ANCHORAGE
MAN VICTIM OF ASSAULT

ARREST FORTHCOMING IN DEADLY
VALENTINE'S RENDEZVOUS

MISSING MAN LIKELY KILLED
AT NORTHWOOD ESTATES

I wait in dread. I can't eat. I stay home from school. Mom and I live each day on edge, waiting for the police to knock on our door. River, Mya, and Eli each abandon me. The media reminds everyone I lied to the police about where I found Jason's stuff. Olivia calls and yells at me. "Why don't you just explain what happened? It's like—it's like you killed him or something. Don't you care?" She starts crying and hangs up.

I try working a shift at Mama Moose's, but customers keep interrupting me to talk about Jason. Clodagh pulls me aside. "Why don't you take some time off? The job will be here once things settle down." She hugs me and adds extra money to my paycheck, but her kindness makes me feel worse, not better.

Then a truck hits Princess Fiona on Arctic Boulevard and animal control has to put her down. For some reason the loss of the moose sends me spiraling into bed for an entire afternoon.

Now I trudge into leadership class with my head down because Mom forced me to return to school. "You can't hide from this forever, and your grades are slipping," she said.

Students sprawl across the sofas, desks, and chairs. The room goes silent when I walk in late, then whispering erupts. Josie scoots closer to one of her friends and sets her backpack on the seat next to her so I can't sit beside her. Not that I want to.

I find a reclining chair in the back and sit by myself. I didn't bother with makeup today. I dragged a comb through my hair and brushed my teeth. I'm wearing my mukluks, leggings, and one of my dad's old sweatshirts. I feel closer to him than ever. We both lost our shit to protect River. Dad paid the price with his life. How will I pay it?

Ms. Turner stiffens at the sight of me. "Ms. Dunn, come here please." She leads me into the hallway. "Should you be here?"

A fat tear rolls down my cheek, and I swipe it off. "Are you kicking me out of your class?"

She moves closer. "No, Finley, of course not. I mean that you look exhausted. You have a lot on your plate right now. I can write you a note to visit the student adviser if you want to talk to someone. You've been through an ordeal, and you have a lot more coming your way."

My breath hitches.

"Would you like to talk to someone?"

I shrug.

She pats my arm. "I want you in my class, Finley, but it's an elective and it's okay with me if you take a break or sit in the library. It won't affect your grade."

Ms. Turner is not kicking me out, but I feel kicked out. "I'll go to the library."

She looks relieved. "I'll write you a pass. You will get through this, Finley."

I gaze at her scuffed shoes, clingy sweater, and outdated eyeglasses and wonder how in the hell she knows that. "Thanks," I muster. She gathers my things and hands me a hall pass. As the classroom door closes, the students erupt into a roar. I hear snippets:

"Finley looks terrible."

"Did you know her dad killed River's dad? Murder runs in their blood."

"I can't imagine Finley killing anyone."

The teacher tries to quiet them. "Remember, class, US

citizens are innocent until proven—" The door shuts all the way, cutting her off.

I wander the empty hallway alone until I reach the library. It's quiet. Several students work at the tables. The librarian doesn't look up. I turn away, crumple up the hall pass, and leave campus. I have only one class left anyway.

After driving around Anchorage, trying to work up the energy to shop or hang out at a cafe, I give up and go home. I arrive to Brady Walker sitting on my doorstep. My heart rate kicks up a notch, but for the first time, I'm not afraid of him. I deserve whatever he's about to do to me. I park and approach.

"I just want to talk," he says, holding up his hands.

I study Brady from the bottom of my stairs. Bags have appeared below his eyes, frost covers his light beard, and his nose is red from the cold. I bet he misses his kids in Fairbanks. I bet he wants to go home. He takes a long, deep breath. "Whether you admit it or not, the truth is gonna come out, Finley."

I nod once.

He sways on the top step. His green eyes scan my face. "Did you kill my brother?"

It's just him and me—no police, no lawyers. I nod a second time.

His chest quakes. "Jesus." Tears stream from his eyes, and he drops down. "Why?"

"It—it was an accident." My throat is dry, my voice hoarse.

"Why did you hide it?"

"I didn't want to get in trouble."

A guttural laugh emits from his throat. He stands back up, shaking his head. "Did my brother . . . suffer?"

I squeeze my eyes shut, remembering Jason's tumble down the stairs, the *crack* of his head hitting the door, the moaning. Of course he suffered. "I'm sorry," I whisper.

Brady trots down the porch stairs and stands inches from me. His jaw is tight, his eyebrows pinched. His eyes dart back and forth across mine. "I should— I want to . . ."

I close my eyes. "Go ahead."

"Fuck!" He turns and punches the side of my house. Minutes pass as he gets control of his breathing. Then he faces me again. His watering eyes are as shiny as emeralds. "You're young, and believe it or not I don't want this to ruin your life, Finley. I believe in second chances. My brother didn't get one, but your life isn't over yet. Do better. You hear me? Do fucking better."

"Yes," I croak. "I will."

"Good. I'm reporting this conversation to the detective."

"Okay."

Brady Walker walks to his car and drives away.

I enter my house and bawl until I can't produce another tear or make any noise at all, but Brady's words have given me something to focus on. *Do better.*

I can't change my past, but I can change my future. If I still have one.

FORTY-NINE

FINLEY

Eight days pass after Jason's body is found. If Brady reported our conversation, Perez hasn't said anything to me yet. Everyone is waiting for the evidence. On the ninth day, Tiffany Chen emails me a copy of his autopsy report, and the police release it to the public. The time of death is confirmed. Jason died sometime during an eight-hour window that includes the night and morning of the Valentine's party. The final words of the report swim in my mind: CAUSE OF DEATH: Homicide.

I read the explosive report again with trembling hands. Certain phrases blare at me as if they're in bold type:

```
Decedent identified by fingerprints and
visual inspection by family member.
```

```
Well-developed, undernourished white male
with antemortem lacerations of the face and
scalp and fractures of the calvarium.
```

Blood pooling indicates the decedent was **moved after death.**

Foreign DNA collected beneath fingernails. Foreign **blond hairs** entwined in fingers.

Blood positive for **fentanyl**. Elevated white blood cell count positive for **illness**.

MANNER OF DEATH: Cardiac arrest secondary to hemorrhagic shock, traumatic brain injury, fentanyl ingestion, and pneumococcal pneumonia.

CAUSE OF DEATH: **Homicide.**

I sink to my knees and close my eyes. *Murderer.* Just like Dad. It's official.

Mom bursts through the front door with grocery bags in her arms, her Saturday shopping. "Finley!" She drops the groceries, crosses the room, and crushes me to her chest. "Ms. Chen has been trying to call you all day. She—she emailed you the report. Did you see it?" Mom's eyes fall to my laptop. She snatches it up and skims the autopsy file. The last words drop her to the floor next to me. "It's true. Homicide." She gapes at me. "I can't protect you from this, Finley."

I let her hold me.

Mom's eyes dart around the townhome. "When we spoke, Ms. Chen said Perez is going to arrest you tonight. The DA is allowing the murder charge, and now we don't have time to hire a new lawyer. Why haven't you answered her calls?"

"I turned off my phone." My hands start to tremble. "Perez is arresting me *today*?"

"Yes. Chen accepted responsibility for your surrender. She and I will drive you." With Herculean effort, Mom collects herself. "We need to—to get your things in order. We have to deliver you to Perez by eight tonight. After dinner."

"What do I pack?"

Tears cascade down Mom's cheeks. "I'll call the lawyer. I don't know if you're allowed to bring anything."

Something unusual happens then. A seed of anger I didn't know existed blooms inside me. My back straightens. My eyes narrow to slits. I am sick and tired of being bossed around. "A lot of decisions are being made without me."

Mom tilts her head and sniffles.

I back away from her, my voice rising. "Why doesn't anyone ask what I want? You dragged me to LA and then dragged me back. Mya and Eli made Jason disappear. Chen promised the detective I would surrender after dinner. No one cares what *I* want."

"You don't have a choice." Mom's round eyes scan mine.

I grab my purse, jacket, and car keys. "I am done doing what other people tell me to do."

"Fin, stop. Where are you going?"

My lips draw into a snarl. "To get answers."

FIFTY

FINLEY

From my car, I turn on my phone. Missed calls and messages jam my notifications. I use Bluetooth to call Mya. "Did you hear about the autopsy report? What the fuck is going on?"

Her voice comes out strained. "I've been trying to call you. It's not what you think."

"Bullshit." I drive down the salted road, breathing like I've run and lost a race. "You let me believe Jason was gone when you got there. Why didn't you tell me you moved his body?"

"He *was* gone when we got there. We didn't touch him." Mya's voice deepens. "I promise."

"Stop lying to me!" My hands squeeze the steering wheel harder. "Did you carry him into the woods, kill him, and then move him? Or did you find him dead, drive him to Girdwood, and dump him in a ditch like a fucking animal? God." Sobs break inside my chest.

"Are you driving? Where are you going?"

"I'm getting arrested for murder tonight, Mya." I pound the steering wheel. "I want you to admit what you did, and then tell the police. We have to come clean."

A door shuts in her house. "Please calm down," Mya whispers.

"Was it you or Eli who moved him *after death,* because I don't believe Jason called an Uber."

She's quiet.

I give a short, derisive laugh. "Eli visited my house last week and threatened me. He said I had no idea what my friends had done for me. Now I know. You drove Jason's body to Girdwood." There is a long silence that I don't know how to interpret. "I'm telling the police what happened on Valentine's Day. No more lies, Mya."

She snorts. "You will not."

"What's that supposed to mean?"

Mya's voice shifts into a growl. "You're a coward. If you had the balls to tell the truth, you would've by now."

The breath leaves my lungs as my fury returns full force. It's true I let Mya's iron will bully me into silence, but a better friend wouldn't have bullied me *at all.* "Because of you, Mya! You made me promise not to say anything. You squeezed his blood onto my hand."

"God, do you hear yourself? That's like saying the devil made me do it. I'm seventeen years old, you don't have to do what I say."

Her words rip the entire fabric of the universe out from under me. My thoughts bang into each other like dominoes.

"You're not perfect, Finley. Embrace it. You'll feel better," says Mya.

I breathe hard into the phone. The streets blur past as I fight for solid ground. "You and Eli lied to me."

Mya gasps. "We *protected* you." Her tone sharpens. "You changed in LA. You haven't thanked us or shown any compassion for our stress. It's your turn to protect your friends. Stop thinking about yourself."

"I'm thinking about Jason Walker." There it is—the true wellspring of my anger. None of us have thought enough about *him*. I utter a humorless laugh. "You want to see balls? Watch what I do next."

I end the call and command my phone to text River, who is probably at work: I'm coming over. I'll wait at your house until you're done fishing.

I smash buttons on Gran's old Volvo, trying to turn on the defogger, and my aggressive moments cause the car to fishtail on a patch of ice. The car swerves into the oncoming lane. Headlights stream into my eyes. I yelp, jerk the wheel, find traction, and return to my side of the street.

Heart thudding, I slow down and drive five miles below the speed limit. A massive storm mounts in the western sky. Dark gray clouds pile in billowing clumps. A breeze rifts the air. I drive toward the storm. Toward River's house.

He's the only friend I trust.

FIFTY-ONE

MYA

Mya sends an SOS to the boys: Finley has lost it. Meet at River's.

It's cold. I don't wanna go out, Eli responds.

Jail is cold, Mya writes back. She's going to tell on us. Get to River's.

Thumbs-up emoji from Eli.

Finley texted me. She's on her way here, writes River.

Ok, I'm closer. We need to talk before she gets there, Mya returns.

On Mya's way out the door, her mother stops her. "Where are you going?"

Feelings converge on Mya like electrical pulses—anger, fear, loneliness. "Since when do you care?"

Cookie recoils but lifts her head. Her eyes focus on Mya. "Excuse me?"

Mya stomps toward her mother, hurling truths like poison darts. "You're never here, you don't check my grades, you treat Dad like shit. All you care about is money. You don't care what I do as long as I don't get caught."

Cookie's head retracts farther on her long neck. "Mya, this is uncalled-for."

Tears, real human tears, drip down Mya's face. She lets them. They feel good. Her ragged voice mimics her mother's. *"Don't trust the police, don't rat on your friends, hide your mistakes*—at what cost, Mom? At what *cost*?"

"Mya."

"You ruin lives. You've ruined mine and my friends'. You know what I'm talking about."

Cookie's skin turns ashen. "That is over and done with."

"Is it, Mom?" They glare at each other, mother and daughter, for a solid minute. Mya has rendered her mother speechless. She turns on her heel and walks out the door.

· · ·

Mya and Eli arrive at River's house at the same time. Lila Madden answers the door, wrapped in a Navajo-style blanket. Her pupils are as large and black as olives. She hasn't been sober too often since her husband was shot. River's mom floats around her house like a jetsam from a crash. She cups Mya's small face and smooths Eli's dark hair. "You two don't come over like you used to. I miss you, kids. You're so big, you're going to fly away." Her eyes water. "Everyone flies away."

"Not everyone," says Mya. "I'll visit more, I promise."

"Me too," says Eli. He hugs Lila. When he lets her go, she

retreats to Bart's old recliner and opens a book. "River's at the ice hut," she says.

They head outside and Mya gazes across the murky wilderness. The first snowflakes create a shimmering white curtain in the air. "Let's take the machines to the hut."

"Wait." Eli clasps her hand and tugs her closer.

"What are you doing?"

His perpetual smirk vanishes. "This could be our last day of freedom. Our last day together."

"You're being dramatic."

He shakes his head. "Listen, I want to say sorry for all the times I've been a dick. Not to other people, but to you."

She glances from him to the pond trail, then back. "We have to go. The lake is over a mile away, and we need to talk to River before Fin gets here. Tell me this later."

He kisses the top of her head. "I have . . . real feelings, Mya."

Her heart gives a magnetic tug in his direction, but she shakes her head. "Are you serious right now? Your timing sucks."

Eli sweeps her up and kisses her. Mya melts into his arms, and feelings fill her body like confetti.

"It's not just sex anymore," he says. "Admit you feel it too."

She kisses his cheek. "When hell freezes over."

"That soon?" They press their foreheads together and breathe each other's air.

Mya looks harder at Eli and it's like seeing him for the first time. Her world expands so fast that her legs go weak.

A portal opens and she allows Eli to pass through it, then it closes behind him, shutting them into her world together. She smiles. "Okay, I feel it too. A little bit. Let's go."

Mya powers up a snow machine and they ride double to the pond. Her heart glows. *Is this love?* she wonders as she drives the machine with Eli tucked close behind her. Love isn't screaming insults or threatening to hurt each other—it's being on the same team? If so, Mya likes it better than she thought she would. "It's warmed up the last few days," she says over her shoulder. "Is the pond safe to drive on?"

"If River's out there, it should be."

Eli rests his chin on her shoulder as the machine's runners glide across the snow. The temperatures dropped last night with winds sweeping down from the Arctic Circle. Dark clouds billow to the west, masking the setting sun. She turns on the headlights to brighten the trail even though she's ridden it a thousand times. A white hare bolts into the underbrush, and a crow returns to its nest, buffeted by the cold front that threatens to dump more snow on Anchorage.

The ride to the fishing hut is otherwise uneventful, but Mya drives onto the pond's ice with her heart hammering. It's mid-March, and that's when she starts to worry about slush, cracks, and thin patches. But the ice looks clear, which is a good sign. River's snow machine is outside the hut.

They park beside it and Eli pushes open the door. River doesn't look up. He strums his guitar, sitting beside the fire he built. "Beware the hole," he says.

Mya grips Eli's arm and jumps back after almost stepping into a wide wet fishing circle that is partially frozen over. "Why's it so big?"

"That's what she—"

Mya elbows Eli before he can finish his joke, and River shrugs. "I lost two fish because they didn't fit through, so I made it bigger. Got that sucker, though." He points to a large salmon, flopping in a bucket.

"Nice," says Eli. "Why didn't you whack it?"

River shrugs, and Mya gives the ice hole a wide berth. River sets his guitar down and gazes up at her. His facial muscles have gone slack, his movements are clumsy. He's spiraling into the bad place like he did after his dad died. She drops onto the bench and lets out a massive sigh. River is weakening, and she doesn't have the energy to rally him.

Eli notices too. He sits next to River and places a hand on his back. "You all right, man?"

River peers into empty space. "Lois's egg hatched last week."

Mya has no idea who Lois is and doesn't care. "We need to talk about Finley."

"We can't control her," says River.

"Yeah, I know. She's pissed at me and Eli and threatening to confess. Did you read the autopsy report? They posted it online."

"Yep. Homicide. Another murder." River's pupils grow larger. His left hand trembles.

Mya shakes her head. "Maybe not. Chen told my mom that homicide doesn't mean murder. People get the two

confused. *Homicide* means that a person's actions contributed to a death, but *criminal intent* has to be proven in
court."

River flicks his eyes toward her. "I don't understand
anything you just said."

Mya groans. River is half here. The other half is flying
with the birds. She holds his hand. "Finley wants to know
how Jason got in the ditch. If we don't explain it, she'll tell
on us, and that will give police the authority to collect our
phones, DNA, and cars." She waits for him to look at her.
"You need to manage her."

River's head jerks up. He squeezes her hand so hard she
gasps. "You said this wouldn't come back on us."

"Well, things have changed, and Finley's on her way
here. You know how to calm her down. She trusts you."

He scowls. "That was her very first mistake."

Mya yanks her hand away from him. "Get out of the past,
River. We need to deal with *now,* with Jason."

Eli stands over the small fire, rubbing his hands. "Hey, I
have an idea. If we tell police the truth *first,* we control the
story, right? I don't want Finny to get in trouble, but it's not
like we homicided the guy. She did that, and her credibility
is shot with the police." He gets no reaction from Mya or
River. "Someone is going down for this—why should it be
all of us?"

Mya chews her lip. "I'm trying to keep Finley *out* of
prison."

"But she's threatening us." He glances at River. "And
we're not exactly innocent."

Mya turns her attention back to River and jostles his leg.

"We can still get away with this if she keeps her mouth shut. Chen says the case is not as strong as it looks, and Finley has no motive to murder a homeless guy. They're arresting her *tonight*, River. This is our last chance." Mya pulls off her jacket. "Finley is going to ruin her life, and ours, and you're the only person who can stop her."

He glares at her. After a long, palpable beat, he exhales. "I'm sick of lying."

His words stab Mya. "Wh-what?"

He shoves his guitar aside with a sharp twang and stands up. "Lying makes everything *worse*."

"Are you bringing up the past again?" she hisses. "You're the one who's going to crack." Why are her friends hell-bent on driving their lives off a cliff?

"Fuck you," says River.

"No, fuck you!" Mya spins in a circle. "Why do I have to fix everything? I didn't ask for this." She glances at Eli for help.

He lifts his hands. "I'll do whatever you say. You know that."

She could hug him, her soldier, her last loyal friend. Mya squints at River's face. He looks . . . disgusted, and she wants to slap him.

He glares back, sensing her mood. "Fuck you both and what you're doing to Finley."

He tries to bolt from the hut, but Eli steps in front of the door. "What *we're* doing to her?" He laughs. "That's rich, man."

"Finley will be here any minute," says Mya. "You want to tell her everything, River? Fine. I'll tell her *everything*."

His eyes widen. "Not that, Mya. You swore you wouldn't."

"You're not the only one sick of lying, River. I'm done keeping your secrets." She blasts past both of them and starts walking to shore.

"Watch out!" hollers Eli.

Mya turns. River has a fish bat, and he's striding toward her, his eyes two empty pits. This is how he looked four years ago at the summer party.

Mya recognizes the devil when she sees him. She runs.

FIFTY-TWO

MYA, THEN

She catches up to River near a cluster of hemlock trees. Eli stayed at the gazebo and Finley went to tell her dad, but River doesn't want help. "You're hurt bad," she says, out of breath. "Eli thinks it's your kidney."

He leans against a tree and removes his glasses, wipes them with his shirt. "Go away." He groans as waves of pain flow through him.

"Your dad is going to kill you someday if you don't do something." River scowls at her, and Mya hugs him. He resists at first, then slumps into her arms. His hot tears wet her T-shirt. "Come back to the house," she says.

"No. Take me to my dad."

"Why?"

River pushes back his hair and straightens his glasses. "He feels bad after a fight. He'll fix me up. I—I don't feel good." His stomach heaves and he vomits again.

"Okay, let's hurry." Mya wraps an arm around him and helps River limp toward the firepit by the house. Finley's dad and Bart are absent.

"Let's check the shop," says Mya.

They stagger through the backwoods toward Bart's shop and shooting range. Mya bends under River's weight as they make their way. At the shop, they hear voices rising in anger.

"You can't be hitting your kid, man."

"Your nosy daughter needs to mind her own business," Bart growls.

"Shit," River groans. "I told Finley not to tell her dad."

The shop door is cracked open an inch, and Mya pushes on it. She watches Bart take a swig of something. The fathers stand, holding their rifles. They spot Mya and River.

Dusty Dunn swears at the sight of River's pinched and pale face. "Damn it, look at him." He rushes to River's side.

"He's peeing blood," says Mya. She lifts River's shirt to show Finley's dad the purple bruise over his kidney.

"I didn't do that," says Bart, unsteady on his feet.

"Finley saw you do it. You've gone too far," says Dusty.

Right then River's knees give out and he collapses. His mouth goes slack. "Am I gonna die?" he rasps.

Dusty yanks his phone out of his back pocket. "I'm calling the police."

"You self-righteous . . ." Bart chambers his gun. The sound is unmistakable.

Boom!

The rifle shot deafens all other sounds. A bullet strikes

Dusty's stomach. He spins a circle, and his phone and gun fly from his hands. He crashes to the floor, and his blood pools around him. Mya opens her mouth to scream but her breath is gone.

Dusty crawls toward his dropped rifle, cursing and crying. "What the hell, man! You shot me."

"I'll shoot you again if you don't get out of my business. River is *my* son."

Mya's heart thunders. Bart shot Finley's dad—she can't believe it. River rises to his hands and knees and starts crawling. Mya can't move at all. She's glad Finley's not here. She must have run back to the gazebo to look for River.

Bart snorts. "Put a Band-Aid on it and get another drink, Dusty."

"You're out of control." Dusty wheezes as he grabs his phone off the shop floor. A second gunshot rings in the shop. Bart's bullet strikes the ceiling, a warning shot. Dusty drops his phone and Bart kicks it out of his reach. "Your do-gooder wife can drive you and my son to a clinic."

Meanwhile, River drags himself toward Dusty's fallen rifle and picks it up.

"Don't!" cries Dusty.

Stop, Mya mouths.

River aims the rifle at his father's back and chambers the bullet. Bart taught him how to shoot, he knows what to do. Before his dad can turn around, River squeezes the trigger.

The bullet slams into Bart's back and tosses him onto his stomach. Stunned, he doesn't move at first, but then he rolls over. "What are you doing, kid?" Fear widens his eyes. Shock muddies his speech. The exit wound in his stomach is massive and weeping blood.

"Mya, go get help," says Dusty, but Mya can't move her legs.

River stands over his father. An animal noise rises from his chest. His eyes become dark, empty pits. He looks like the devil as he levels the barrel at his father's forehead.

"River, no!" shouts Dusty.

Bart flips over and tries to crawl away. River pulls the trigger. The second bullet enters the back of Bart's skull and exits his nose, demolishing half of his face. His body smacks the floor. One sightless eye remains open.

Full-body tremors assail Mya.

"I'll get help." Finley's dad lurches for the door and stumbles toward the main house and the other parents, a solid quarter mile away.

Mya rushes toward River. He's trembling and staring at his father. His face is slack. His mouth shut. Mya tugs him out of the shop and he follows, still holding the rifle. They catch up to Dusty outside.

Finley's dad has fallen on the trail. Mya squats and shakes him. "Mr. Dunn, Mr. Dunn!" His blood creates a large pool around his body. His eyes are closed, but he's breathing. "Come on, River, we need to get help. Put that gun down," says Mya.

River drops the gun and it lands next to Dusty's hand.

Finley appears with her mother, running down the trail. Mya's mom is right behind them. Finley must have told the other parents that River was injured and they called an ambulance. Mya hears sirens as two police cruisers and an ambulance drive onto the property toward them.

Finley's mom drops to her husband's side. Dusty is pale and losing consciousness. Dirt and leaves stick to the front of his shirt as blood pumps from the hole in his stomach. She holds him and sobs into his hair. "Who did this?"

"Bart . . . ," he gurgles, then passes out. Mya watches Finley fall to her knees. Her best friend is too shocked to cry. Her other best friend, River, sits cross-legged on the path and holds his head in his hands. It will be months before he speaks again.

Cookie snatches Mya, drags her into the woods, and leans her against a tree. "Tell me what happened."

Weeping, Mya tells her everything and Cookie absorbs the information. "River shot his dad in the back and in the head while he was down?"

"Y—yes," says Mya.

"That's not self-defense."

"Will they arrest him, Mom?"

"They sure as shit will, but River used Dusty's gun. It will look like Dusty did it. Mya—hear me now—let the police figure this out. Look at you, you're shaking. You don't know what you saw. If you blinked or turned your back, you could have missed something."

"But I did see."

Cookie shakes her head. "If you tell anyone, you can kiss River's freedom goodbye, and that boy doesn't deserve more pain. Neither does his mother. But Dusty . . . he's not going to make it, Mya, and it's his gun. It doesn't matter if the police think he did it."

"Oh." Mya closes her mouth.

"Good girl. Don't say a word. You can't trust the police anyway."

They exit the woods in time to watch Dusty Dunn being loaded into an ambulance, still unconscious. His wife and daughter climb in beside him. Detective Perez bags up the rifle that killed Bart, which rested at Dusty's side moments ago. His fingerprints are on it and he has gunshot residue on his hands from target shooting.

While Perez's partner tapes off the shop, the detective attempts to question River. Cookie interrupts. "He's the reason we called an ambulance. He fell out of a tree and needs help. Could you talk to him later?"

"Do you know what caused the fight between the men?" asks Perez.

"No idea," says Cookie. "They sometimes fight about their HVAC business."

Mya opens her mouth to correct her, but Cookie's look reminds her to stay quiet. When the detective questions Mya, she lowers her eyes and lies. "I didn't see anything."

Medics arrive in a second ambulance and whisk River away.

Dusty Dunn dies in the hospital two weeks later without regaining consciousness. His proximity to Bart, his discharged rifle, and the gunshot residue on his hands is enough for police to confirm him as the shooter. No one is harmed by Mya's silence.

Except that's not true either.

If she'd told the truth, River would have received punishment but also counseling. Finley and her mom would not have fled Alaska, and Finley could be herself instead of the guilt-ridden daughter of a heartless killer.

Everyone was harmed.

Finley and River most of all.

FIFTY-THREE

FINLEY, NOW

I burst into River's house without knocking. Lila is asleep on Bart's old recliner chair. She startles awake. "Finley?"

"Is River here or on the Gulf?"

"The Gulf?" Lila rises and trudges to the kitchen. "What are you talking about?"

"You know, crab fishing with his cousin."

"River's not there, butterfly. He got fired."

I cock my head. My breathing stills. River's been working almost every weekend since Valentine's Day. "When?" I ask.

"Did you two have a fight? Is that why he's sad today?"

"When did he get fired, Lila?"

She retrieves a bottle of vodka from the freezer and pours a splash into her drink. "He never showed up the first day, said he was too tired after the Valentine's dance. Danny fired him before he could start."

My stomach slides to the floor. He never showed up on the *first* day? River has looked me in the eye more than once and said he was busy working. Why is he pretending to have a job he doesn't have—oh God. My hand flies to my mouth. There is one reason I can think of and it makes everything clunk into place. Crab fishing is his *alibi*. "Jesus," I whisper. "Mya told me the truth. She and Eli didn't move the body. It was River. She's protecting *River*."

"What did you say?" Lila asks.

"He lied to me," I answer. "River's been lying to me for weeks."

Lila crosses the kitchen and pats my arm. "He lies to me, too, butterfly."

"Where is he?"

"Everyone's at the hut."

"What do you mean *everyone*?"

"The whole pack." She pouts her lips. "Please don't be mad at my son."

"I'm not mad," I tell her. I glide out the door and fire up the last snow machine. My mind takes in all that has happened over the past nine weeks as I process what Lila said about *everyone* being at the hut. All three of them are there. I'm not mad, I'm furious.

I squeeze the throttle on my snow machine and speed across the flat, scrubby Alaskan taiga. When I find them, they will tell me the whole truth about Valentine's Day— about what happened to Jason Walker—and then I will turn them over to the police.

Best friends aren't always the *best* friends.

My blood races as I imagine Mya, Eli, and River having another secret meeting without me. I don't trust them; maybe I never could. The trouble the four of us got into as children rushes back to me—sneaking out, cutting school, poaching salmon, and lying. The mischief ended after my dad died and Mom and I fled Alaska. Mom believes Dad's last act scared me straight, but that's not it. In LA, I met better people. It's that simple. I followed *the* rules instead of *Mya's* rules. Then I moved back.

"You ruined my life, Mya!" I scream into the wind.

And Jason Walker's life.

As I skim the flatlands, the spindly trees blur past and the pale northern sun reflects off the snow. There's the charred spruce Eli set fire to years ago. It's become a landmark on River's wilderness property. It means I'm close to the frozen pond and the fishing hut.

A wind gust tries to blow me off my seat. I slow the machine and scan the terrain. No matter what I find out about Jason, I'm in massive legal trouble. Nothing can change that now.

I gun the engine and the snow machine launches off a snowdrift and lands with a thump that tosses my body into the air. I miss the seat on my way down. Panicking, I squeeze the throttle tighter and the machine drags my legs through the snow. My shin strikes a rock and pain sizzles up my leg. Then the sled's double runners slide onto the smooth frozen pond, propelling it faster. Ahead is a brown shape, the fishing hut.

My hands break loose and I tumble free. The snow machine veers off as I slide face down across the ice like a hockey puck.

When my body eases to a halt, I flip over, gasping for air. Three figures stand outside the hut, their heads covered in hooded jackets—Mya, River, and Eli. Coldness engulfs me. One of the boys is carrying a hardwood bat used to bludgeon fish to death. He twirls it, and his spiked boots grip the ice as he walks toward me. The girl has wide, round eyes.

"Finley!" she shouts.

I curl into a ball and cover my head. Blood drips from my leg. "Stay back," I rasp.

"You're the one chasing us." Then they surround me.

My best friends.

FIFTY-FOUR

FINLEY, NOW

The fish bat slams the ice next to me. I flip over with my hands protecting my face, but River isn't attacking me. He's pissed at Mya and Eli.

"Look at her, she's hurt. This shit has gone too far." Spittle flies from River's mouth. His pupils constrict. He points the bat at Mya. "I can't do this again."

Do what again? Pain has rattled my thoughts. I point toward my bleeding leg. "I need help."

River's jaw muscles flutter. "Shit, okay. It's warm inside the hut. Let's go." Ignoring Mya and Eli, he carries me into the Madden About Fishing shelter and sets me on a bench. The others follow. River rifles through the hut's supplies until he finds a piece of twine, and then he ties it around my leg as a tourniquet. "I'll drive you to a hospital."

"No." Hot tears stream down my cheeks. "I'm not going anywhere until you tell me the truth. Your mom said you never showed up for your crabbing job, not one single day."

"Here it comes," mutters Eli.

I tug on River's shirt. "You lied to my face! How could you do that?"

He plops hard on the bench. "Please don't, Finley. Please let it go."

"You moved Jason's body, didn't you?" I shake him. "Tell me the truth!"

"Don't touch him." Mya pushes herself between us.

"God, stop protecting him, Mya." My voice rasps like sandpaper. "You lied to me too. You all lied to me."

"Not now, Fin. Okay?"

"Then when?! After my murder conviction? Or how about after I get released at age fifty and can't have kids or get a good job? You three knew Jason was dead this *entire* time." I yank on my hair, choking on my words. My tight muscles cramp. "You make me sick. All of you. You met behind my back. You"—I point at River—"you kissed me. You said you loved me."

I cry for a solid minute and then offer a long, slow clap. "This is for your performances when I told you I saw Jason at the restaurant and you pretended to believe me."

This hut is the very place where we celebrated Jason's miraculous recovery. I got drunk, felt good, and believed it was over. But it was just the beginning. My phone vibrates and I ignore it. My mom's been texting and calling since I stormed out of the house.

River's face pinches, but he's not crying or arguing. He's as flat as an empty balloon. "It's time to tell her," he says to Mya.

She gnaws her lip and Eli shifts from foot to foot. Their

cheeks are flushed, their eyes wide. Mya rubs her face. "Are we still talking about Jason?"

"Yes," River hisses, a warning lurking in his eyes.

My eyes bounce from one to the other. "What's going on?"

Eli frowns at River. "If Finley deserves the truth like you said, she deserves all of it."

"No!" River curls his long, artistic hands into fists.

"Then I'll tell her," says Eli.

"No, you fucking won't." River hauls back and punches Eli in the mouth.

Eli flies into the side of the hut and slides to the ice. He rubs his jaw. "Dude! What the fuck?"

"Why are you fighting?" I cry.

Mya drops to Eli's side. "You are an ungrateful bastard, River Madden. All our lies have been for you!"

River clamps his hands over his ears. "Shut up, shut up, shut up. Get out of my head."

Mya blows out a breath. "I'm not going to shut up. If you're sick of lying, prove it. Tell Finley everything."

I watch them, tearful.

River's golden eyes flatten to hard discs. His expression turns smooth, but it's not peaceful. He trembles with effort. He swings his head toward me and he spits out the words. "Yes, it was me. I hid Jason's body."

Mya shakes her head. "That's not what I'm talking about."

"Just let me fucking talk," says River. He turns his hollow eyes back to me. "I skipped out on crabbing to help deal with the . . . situation. I grabbed my truck and went back to the model home. You were right, Fin, it was wrong to leave the guy there. I tried to help him. I swear."

He twists his fingers together. "It was me, not them, who followed Jason's footprints into the woods. I found him collapsed in the snow and carried him back to the Chateau. He was totally delirious, but he was alive. Mya and Eli helped me load him into my truck. I—I planned to drive him to a hospital. We were on our way when he . . . well, I thought he fell asleep. I touched him and . . . he wasn't breathing. I pulled over and tried CPR, but I don't know how to do it right, or it was too late. He didn't wake up."

Tears roll down River's cheeks. "I panicked, Fin. He bled a little in my truck. My knuckles were bruised from when I punched him. It looked bad and there was no point in taking a dead man to a hospital. I drove him out to Girdwood and left him in a ditch."

"Oh my God," I say.

"He was going to die in the woods if I hadn't picked him up anyway," says River, his justification well-versed. "I called Mya and Eli and told them what I did. We agreed not to tell you. We knew it'd upset you."

I nod because yeah, I'm upset. "Why did you pretend to believe me when I said I saw him alive?"

"I wasn't pretending. When you said you saw him at the restaurant, I figured that maybe he'd passed out and not died, that maybe he'd hitchhiked back to Anchorage. I was glad." His head slumps forward into his hands. "None of us wanted you to feel guilty for his death, Fin. I'm sorry I didn't tell you the truth."

My brain chugs in slow circles. My phone vibrates again. My mom, looking for me.

River wipes his eyes. His hands tremble as he continues. "I'll tell the police what happened. I'll take the blame."

Mya throws up her hands. "You can't decide that on your own, River. We're involved too."

"I'm not doing what you say anymore, Mya."

Tension bubbles between them like a long-simmering sauce that is now burnt and ruined. "You know what?" says Mya. "Fuck the covenant and fuck our friendship. Tell Finley about her dad."

"*Stop.*" River blasts to his feet.

My head pounds. I feel like a train is barreling toward me. I rise from the bench, my weight on my good leg. "What about my dad?"

Mya grabs my hands and squeezes them. "Finley, your dad didn't shoot Bart. River did. River killed his father. I saw it and kept it a secret. I thought it was best for River."

"Best for River?" I step back, shaking my head. I could not have heard that right. I turn to River. "*You* shot your dad?"

He's silent.

"Did you know about this?" I ask Eli.

He frowns. "Sorry, Finny."

My eyes bob to each of them—my *best* friends. The pain in my leg diminishes as my blood pumps harder. My vision sharpens and my world collapses, revealing the three spiders behind the web of lies that have trapped me for years—Mya, Eli, and River. And me, the little fly. I recall a parable we studied in literature class:

*With buzzing wings she hung aloft, then near
   and nearer drew,
Thinking only of her brilliant eyes, and green and
   purple hue—
Thinking only of her crested head—poor foolish
   thing! At last,
Up jumped the cunning Spider, and fiercely held
   her fast.*

I entered their parlor of deceit, lured by flattery and false promises. I believed they loved me and wanted to protect me and care for me. But it was a ruse to silence me. I am done being quiet.

I accuse River first, my words grating. "You offered to take the blame for Jason as if you were doing *me* a favor. You told me not to feel bad about my murderous father and then tried to get into my pants. But all along it was *you*. You were the one hurting me."

River crumples. "I didn't sleep with you."

"Yeah, you're a fucking hero. Go collect your purple heart."

I whirl on Eli next. "You came into my house and *threatened* me. You warned me to be loyal to you, but you were *never* loyal to me."

He tries to say something.

I shut him up by hissing at Mya: "You swore me to secrecy while lying to my face. You said Jason left on his *own two feet*, but you helped carry him to River's truck. I thought you were protecting me but you were always protecting him. Is *anything* true?"

"It was for your own good," Eli interjects.

My head swivels. "You are *such* an asshole."

"Please don't be mad at Eli," says Mya. "Everything was my idea."

I give a hard, humorless laugh. "*That* I believe." I take another step back. My past implodes and explodes at the same time. Dad didn't shoot Bart. Dad didn't kill anyone. The information reshapes my memories as I bleed with fresh grief for my father. I gaze at them, the people who betrayed me. "You aren't my friends," I whisper. "None of you are my friends."

River's lips twist in agony. He steps toward me as if he wants to touch me or hug me.

I stumble backward, my foot punches through the unmarked ice hole, and I plunge into the freezing water.

FIFTY-FIVE

MYA, NOW

Mya rushes toward the splash. "Damn it, River. You didn't mark the hole!"

Finley pops up, flailing. Her screams freeze in her throat. Her painted fingernails claw at the ice.

Mya reaches for her just as Finley's head and long slender arms slide beneath the water again. "Help me!" she cries.

Eli plunges his hand into the pond and feels for Finley. His face twists. Thin chunks of ice float around him. "Finny!" he shouts.

Mya thrusts her arm next to his, swirling as if she's stirring soup. Finley is wearing a wool sweater and mukluks, heavy items that will drag her to the bottom. Her leg injury will make swimming difficult, and the water is not static beneath the ice. It flows in currents that can whisk a person away. "Finley!" She pushes her arm deeper into the water.

"Get the hook!" she yells.

River jumps to his feet and grabs the six-foot-long fish

hook and brings it to Mya. She plunges it into the aqua hole. "How deep is the pond?"

He squeezes his eyes shut. "Twenty, thirty feet."

Mya pushes the hook as deep as her arm will allow and feels for Finley's body. Her hand is so numb she can't feel the handle. Something cracks open inside her. This is her fault, all of it. She betrayed her best friend to protect her other best friend. She should have stayed out of it.

The hook bumps into something. "I think I got her!" Mya tugs on the pole, drawing Finley up through the deep. She spots waving blond hair, like tendrils of kelp. "It's her."

Eli grips the back end of the hook and helps pull. Finley's eyes are closed, and her jaw hangs open. The pole has hooked into her sweater. "She's unconscious." Mya's heart thumps against her rib cage. "Pull harder."

She and Eli heave, and then the pressure gives way as Finley's sweater rips and the hook comes loose. "No, no." Fin sinks back toward the bottom.

A woman bursts into the hut, startling all of them—Finley's mom. "Lila said Finley's with you." Her eyes land on the fishhook, the ice hole, Finley's abandoned jacket, and then on Mya. She lets out a scream.

The devastation on her face—the same devastation Mya witnessed the night of the backwoods shooting—opens her heart wider.

Mya rips off her jacket, sweater, and shoes. Eli's eyebrows lift to the sky. "Mya, don't!"

She dives headfirst into the freezing water. She can't save Finley Dunn from their lies, but maybe she can save Finley's life.

FIFTY-SIX

MYA, NOW

The pond swallows Mya with a neat splash. A deep, burning chill penetrates her limbs, and her heart gallops in rapid, erratic beats. It hurts as if she dropped into a lake of fire. Then a light appears. The Maddens keep a powerful flashlight in the hut, and someone has turned it on for her. The beam pierces layers of water that grow darker the deeper she swims.

She kicks toward the bottom with her eyes open. A large trout flicks past, studying her as it swims. She spies Finley, floating motionless, her arms and legs spread wide. Mya tries to kick harder, but her legs won't cooperate. Her head throbs from the cold and her scalp tingles—the only parts of her that aren't numb yet.

She hooks her hands into Finley's armpits and kicks toward the flashlight beam. Her lungs pulse with hot rebellion. The light grows brighter, almost blinding. She gives Finley a good, hard shove toward the ice hole.

A hand grips Finley by the hair and tries to pull her out, but Mya's weight creates a drag on Finley's body. She lets go of her friend and watches Finley rise. The flashlight beam wobbles as more hands tug Finley out of the water.

Mya's body spasms and her exhausted muscles fail her. She's dizzy and weak. The ice hole shrinks, and she realizes she's drifting away from it. The sudden departure of Finley's body produced a wake that sent Mya adrift, like an astronaut floating away from her ship.

Large hands grasp for her, and by their shape she knows they belong to Eli. The intimacy of that startles her. As his hands scoop the empty water, fondness fills her, and then peace. Her body stills. She's weightless and drifting. Her eyelids close.

Fight, Mya! The voice inside her head sounds an awful lot like her mother's. The peaceful feeling vanishes. Mya's eyelids spring open and she throws her flagging energy into kicking her legs. Her skull strikes the ice overhead. Her body skids below the surface, caught in a current. Face up, she drifts past the hut, watching the outlines of hemlock and pine trees slide past. Trapped on the wrong side of the ice.

I'm going to die, she thinks. A figure appears on the surface and drops to all fours, crawling after her and pounding on the ice, trying to free her. It's River. His mouth opens and closes as if he's talking to her. She has a ridiculous urge to explain that she can't hear him.

Then a second figure appears.

Empty of oxygen, Mya's body bucks and twists. *This is it,* she thinks. She slams her fists against the frozen crust and screams until her lungs are empty. Pond water flows into her mouth. Her body bucks again as liquid fills her stomach.

A heavy object slams onto the ice. A person circles their arm, twisting the object, and she recognizes their stance— it's Eli with his auger. No one can work an auger faster than Eli.

He's going to save me.

Mya's fear recedes. Her chest relaxes as affection warms her body.

I love him.

A smile graces her lips. Her eyes remain open, but her vision blackens. Mya drifts down . . .

down . . .

down . . .

toward the bottom of the pond.

FIFTY-SEVEN

FINLEY, NOW

I can't see, hear, or move, but I understand when I feel cold air on my skin that I've been rescued. Something soft wraps around me, then a finger enters my mouth and my stomach contracts. Water hurls out. Sweet, fresh air invades my lungs, and violent shivers engulf my body. A thought creeps sluggishly into my brain: *Death is cold.*

Mom is holding me and crying. "Finley!" She vigorously rubs my arms. "We have to get her warm," she says to someone.

An unfamiliar male voice answers. "Take off her wet clothes. There are extra warming blankets in the rig. We can't leave this patient."

My outer clothes come off, and I open my eyes. The cloud-filtered sun feels horrendously bright. An ambulance and cop car are parked on the shore. Mom must have carried me out of the hut toward help, but the first responders are occupied. Two EMTs and two police officers huddle on the ice over a prone figure.

Eli is nearby, watching them and chewing his knuckles. Tears soak his eyelashes. "Baby, don't go. Baby, I love you." He rocks back and forth. His auger lays by his side.

I crane my neck. "Mya?" I croak.

"Yes," Mom says as she peels off my soaked leggings.

A cop runs over with a warming blanket and helps Mom wrap me in it. "We need to get her back into the hut until the second ambulance arrives, I see there's a fire burning." Smoke pumps out of the hut's little chimney. The cop carries me toward it, holding me like a little girl, Mom at his side.

"Wait," I say. Mya's shape comes into focus. We pause on the ice. Two EMTs lean over her body, one applies rapid chest compressions and the other supplies oxygen through a mask. A puddle of vomit has frozen next to Mya's head. Her kohl-lined eyes are closed, her skin is blueberry blue. Her limbs hang limp. My mind screeches awake and reality crashes through. "Oh my God . . ."

"I know. Shhh," says Mom.

The EMTs prepare Mya for transport. Sweat drips down the forehead of the medic giving her chest compressions. His face is red with effort. "On three, let's move her." They lift Mya onto a gurney, and the medic sits with her while compressing her chest. "Help us across the ice," the other calls to the cops.

Eli trots by their side, holding Mya's hand. His eyes bulge as he pleads with her to wake up. I remember ten-year-old

Eli when we encountered a bull moose in the woods, not ten yards from us. It was the only time I've seen him scared. Until now.

Mya's black-dyed hair has dried in the wind, and it vanishes from sight as the ambulance doors close on her. Eli watches her go. "Your friend is in cardiac arrest," the cop says as we start walking again.

Trembles overtake me. "Will she be okay?"

He grimaces as we reach the hut. "A second ambulance is en route for you."

He sets me down, helps me inside, and seats me on the bench, still wrapped in the warming blanket, then runs back outside. I glance around the fishing hut. "Where's River?"

"I don't know. He was just here," says Mom.

My brain is still catching up, but I remember his confession. "Oh, Mom! I have something to tell you! River shot Bart four years ago. It wasn't Dad. Mya saw it happen." Fresh tears fill my eyes.

Mom's muscles tighten around me. "River shot his dad?" Her heart thuds against mine.

"My friends knew. They lied to me." I huddle closer, seeking her heat, her scent.

Mom's body goes stiff and her words are clipped. "We'll deal with that later. Where's the damn ambulance?"

While we wait, my eyes scan the hut, searching for another blanket or a scarf, anything that might help warm me up. A blank space on the wall catches my eye and my insides dissolve. The hunting rifle is gone. "Mom!" I sit taller, pointing. "There was a gun right there and now it's gone. Where is River?"

Mom sticks her head out of the hut and calls for an officer. The deputy enters the ice hut and I explain that River and the hunting rifle are both missing.

The deputy speaks into his radio. "We may have an armed teen on the property." Then to me, he says: "Where could he have gone?"

I skim the wilderness with my mind, flying over it like a bird. "Clark and Lois," I blurt out. "River likes to watch birds, it's how he calms down." I point west. "There's an eagles' nest at the top of a huge cottonwood tree. You can't miss it. It's where River goes to think."

"Got it," says the deputy. He and the officers from the first cruiser cross the frozen pond and disappear into the woods.

A fresh set of EMTs appear and they collect me from Mom and place me on their gurney. They check my blood pressure and temperature, strap me down, and roll me out of the fishing hut.

A rifle shot pierces the air.

I flinch as two eagles soar from their distant nest and vanish into the clouds.

FIFTY-EIGHT

FINLEY, NOW

The hospital releases me three days after I almost drowned in River's pond. The doctors command me to rest and take my medication for the foreseeable future. The cold water caused cerebral hypoxia. The doctors can't predict the long-term damage to my brain, but the quick actions of Mya, my mother, and the paramedics kept enough of my blood and oxygen flowing to prevent permanent disability. My tibia is broken and cast, but it's the least concerning injury.

Plunging into that water was my every fear rolled into one—freezing, drowning, suffocating—plus a fear I didn't realize I had: dying alone. I have zero survivor's guilt about my rescue. I got the second chance Jason didn't. I won't squander it stressing about my image or worrying what people think about me anymore. I will *do better*.

"I wish I could talk to Mya," I say from my bed.

Tears collect in Mom's eyes. "Ah, honey, you know that's not possible. I'm sorry."

I fall back onto my pillow. "I'm tired."

"Can I take these?" She points toward the newspaper clippings I've collected.

"No."

Mom grunts and scoops up my Jell-O bowl, then leaves my room. I pick up the clippings. Each time I read them is like the first time, but they don't upset me like they did at first. They're factual and clinical. They wrap everything into neat, consumable bites, like a spring roll. I turn on my lamp and read the headlines and snippets:

ONE PERSON INJURED, ONE DEAD, IN DROWNING ACCIDENT

Eighteen-year-old Finley Dunn and 17-year-old Mya Green required urgent medical care on Saturday from injuries incurred after Dunn fell through an ice-fishing hole on a private pond. Authorities described the dangerous 24-inch hole as not properly marked or supervised. Dunn slipped into the hole during an argument with friends. When she did not immediately reappear, Green dived into the icy water to save her. Green suffered a cardiac arrest underwater. She did not survive.

Each time I read it, I struggle to believe that Mya is gone. The part of me that loved her is very, very sad, but for now I've cried myself out. I move on to the next clip:

ANCHORAGE TEEN ARRESTED AFTER MURDER CONFESSION

Deputy Johnson with the Alaska Police Department had this to say: "Soon after arriving at the drowning scene, a witness warned us that a distraught member of their party had trekked into the woods and may have had access to a gun.

"Two officers, including myself, followed his tracks and found a male teenager sitting against a tree with a hunting rifle. When we asked him to drop the weapon, it accidentally discharged. The teen immediately released the rifle, and we took him safely into custody.

"The gun is registered to his late father, and he was in legal possession of it. While in custody, the 17-year-old confessed to the fatal shooting of his father, Bart Madden, four years ago. He is receiving treatment at the Adolescent Residential Treatment Program at Providence Medical Center and awaiting official charges in the death of his father."

Since the article posted, Mom told me that River also confessed to driving Jason Walker's corpse down the Aly-eska Highway and abandoning it in a ditch. He has been charged with obstruction of justice and misconduct involving a corpse, both misdemeanors. I can't believe that moving a corpse is a misdemeanor. It feels like it should be bigger, like a felony. River also named his accomplices, Mya Green and Eli Kalluk, in his statement. Eli was charged with obstruction of justice.

Due to the reopened murder case, River will have to face the consequences of shooting his father. Once my father's name is cleared, Mom will file an appeal to get his life insurance check. It's enough money to put me through a public university and open a retirement account for Mom.

I blow out a breath and glance at the latest article, which is about Jason Walker.

CELEBRATION OF LIFE FOR UNHOUSED ANCHORAGE MAN DRAWS HUGE CROWD

Hundreds gathered at the Anchorage Public Library yesterday to celebrate Jason Daniel Walker, age 28. Walker went missing on February 15 after a violent altercation with a group of teenagers.

I skip the part about us and our Valentine's party because the media doesn't have all the information. Not yet. I have an appointment with Detective Perez this afternoon. Jason's article ends with a statement from Brady Walker:

"My brother was ready to change his life, and it changed, all right. He died. His last high contributed to his death, but so did the reckless actions of Finley Dunn and her friends. Jason's situation was not their fault, but those teens knew what happened and didn't come forward. One girl paid for this mistake with her life. I don't want them to go to jail, I want them to spend the rest of their lives telling the truth. They owe Jason that. They owe me that."

With permission from Jason's family, the *Alaska Daily* published his poem:

A Heart Too Broke

Clouds glide
drift through my mind
a soul too sad
flying.
Sunlight falls
burns through my skin
a heart too broke
crying.
Dreams fade
sift through my soul
drifting, burning, dying.

FIFTY-NINE

FINLEY, NOW

Mom and I spot Cookie Green walking out of the police station when we arrive. Her hair is uncombed, her clothes are rumpled, and her eyes are red-rimmed from crying. She lost her younger daughter and she looks destroyed. She sees us and halts.

A sad, rasping noise emits from Mom's throat. She rushes to comfort her friend.

"No," says Cookie. "Stop."

I catch up to Mom. Is Cookie mad at us? Or at me? If I hadn't fallen through the ice, Mya would be alive. "I'm sorry . . . ," I start, but don't know how to finish. It's not my fault River didn't mark the ice hole or that Mya wasn't pulled out of the water in time to survive. Other things are my fault, but not those things.

Mom tries again. "Cookie, we—"

"I said stop." Cookie bends over, inhales a long breath, and then straightens. "You're going to hear this eventually, so you might as well hear it from me. I'm the one who told Mya to stay quiet. I knew your husband was innocent."

The silence that follows is deafening. My ears ring with Cookie's confession.

"It was the wrong thing to do," she says.

Mom's breath comes faster.

Cookie's head tilts in a way that reminds me of Mya. "River had been through enough and Dusty wasn't going to make it. I told Mya to keep the secret and let the police figure it out. I didn't mean to hurt you." Cookie wipes her eyes. "It's okay if you hate me."

"Hate you?" Mom rasps. "You're a monster! You let me— you let us believe—" Mom lunges at Cookie.

I grab her and Mom thrashes in my arms. It takes all my strength to hold her back while holding crutches. "Stop, Mom. She's not worth it."

The women stare at each other—each grieving, each destroyed by lies they either told or believed. There are no winners here.

"I lost *everything* that day," Mom says, gasping. Her body quakes.

Cookie's eyes flit toward me. "You didn't lose *everything*." She retreats to her car and drives away.

Mom drops into a squat, shaking hard. "I don't understand," she says, gasping. "I thought she was my friend."

I hug her closer. "I know, Mom, I know."

The police station door opens and Detective Perez leans outside. "You'll catch your death, ladies. Come inside."

We do as she says, and Mom composes herself in a small

interrogation room where Perez hands her a box of tissues. "Did Cookie Green speak to you on her way out?"

Mom nods.

"Well, I'm happy to report that we're making progress on clearing your husband's name, Ms. Dunn. River confessed to the killing, and Cookie just agreed to testify to the truth, but I must warn you: River was not of sound mind when he gave his statement. I'll interview him again once his doctor clears him to speak on the record. I don't expect a retraction, but you never know. Once lawyers and family members get involved, memories can shift. Still, with Mrs. Green's testimony, we have a good chance at convicting him."

Sadness for River creeps into my heart, but I shove it down. He lied to me for four years. Cookie and Mya lied too. The sadness cools into anger.

Perez grimaces. "There was always something fishy about that case. The motive was weak and River didn't have any scratches or other bruises to corroborate that he fell out of a tree. His medical history included a few suspicious ER visits. I believed River was involved in the fight somehow, but I never guessed he shot his father. Had we investigated the motive further, we might have come up with a different outcome. Without an honest witness, though, I couldn't support my theory and our lead investigator dropped that angle. I regret we got this one wrong, Ms. Dunn. I apologize."

Mom sniffles into her tissue. "What will happen to Cookie? She coached her daughter to stay silent."

"We'll charge her for that."

Mom grunts, and now it's my turn to confess. "Detective Perez," I blurt out. "I pushed Jason Walker down the stairs. I killed him." I close my eyes and brace.

Mom's sudden weeping fills the room and I have to peek to see if Perez heard me. She's sipping from her paper coffee cup. "Did you hear me?" I ask.

"I did," she says. "It's not news to me. Brady already informed me about your confession."

"Why haven't you arrested me, then?"

"Because of the autopsy report." Perez opens a file and pages through it. "It says here that Jason's injuries contributed to his *manner of death* but not his *cause of death*. He died due to a combination of natural and unnatural factors—illness, injuries, and his fentanyl ingestion. Besides that, murder requires malicious intent. Did you intend to end his life?"

"No."

Perez nods. "This is the coroner's summation: 'Jason Walker could have survived any one of his afflictions, but the combination of them was not survivable.' Meaning, the fall alone didn't kill him, Finley. His untreated illness and drug use contributed to his death. It's not cut-and-dried."

"But I pushed him on purpose." Now that I'm finally telling the truth, I'm telling it *hard.* I want to be punished, and Perez reads it on my face.

She glances at her papers. "River's statement indicates that Jason attacked the two of you first. Is that correct?"

I think back to how Jason charged out of the bathroom and tackled River. "Yes, that's correct."

"Jason shoved you into a wall and pulled out your hair by the roots, is that right?"

Mom grimaces and covers her mouth.

"That's right," I say.

Perez tilts her head. "Of course you pushed him on purpose, Finley. It's called fighting back."

Tears blur my vision. "But I was angry. I wanted to hurt him."

"To hurt him or stop him?"

I blink at her, trying to nail down my feelings. "I wanted to stop him. It . . . it happened so fast. I had a lot of feelings."

She nods again. "As much as you'd like me to arrest you, Finley, I'm not going to do it. I spoke with the DA after Brady reported your conversation and after we got the autopsy report. We reviewed all of it and he's not interested in levying assault and battery charges against you, and neither is Brady. Each of you was trespassing and the situation was extreme. It isn't a slam dunk case, but it's over. Do you understand?"

"But—"

"We understand," says Mom, pinching my thigh under the table.

"Good." Perez closes the file. "You lied and obstructed justice, Finley, and you made your plea deal for those charges. You aren't getting off scot-free, okay? You're paying for what you did, but you're not a killer." She smirks. "I would know. I'm an expert on killers."

Her words are like a benediction on my soul. I'm not a killer and neither is my father. "Thank you," I whisper.

"You're welcome. Now get out of my police station and don't ever come back."

"Yes, ma'am." Mom drags me out of my chair and out of the building. She pulls me into a tight hug. After a few minutes, she draws back and frowns. "Do you think I should submit a letter of resignation to Cookie or was calling her a monster enough?"

A small laugh bursts out of me. "I think it was enough."

"You know what, Fin?" Mom says as we climb into her car. "There's nothing wrong with this state. Our friends are what's wrong with Alaska."

"True, but if I get an acceptance letter to a college in California, I'm on the first plane out of here."

Mom grins. "A hundred percent."

I smile, feeling justified. A world that hasn't made sense in four years finally does.

SIXTY

The media dubs us "the most heartless teens in America." The internet blows up with memes, threats, and discussions about the high school seniors who assaulted the homeless poet and then hid his body. River, Eli, and I shut down our social media accounts. The world judges us under the stark illumination of hindsight. I wish it were that simple.

Over the days that follow, drone cameras capture images of Mya's resort-sized home, which the media replays whenever we're mentioned. Picketers continue to circle the entrance to Northwood Estates, and Brady Walker raises money for a new shelter called Jason's Home.

Cookie Green files for bankruptcy and her husband files for divorce. The money that was so important to her is gone.

Brittany deletes her social media photos and replaces them with one. It's a picture of her and Mya, playing in a creek when they were kids. Mya is making a goofy face and Brittany has her arm resting on her younger sister's head.

The caption reads: I wish I'd told you every day I love you. RIP bunny

Eli sends me a single text: I loved her Finny. Im sorry we hurt you. I miss her so much.

I delete his number.

A few weeks later, I visit River at Providence Hospital. It's April and breakup has started in Alaska. Melting snow creates muddy rivulets throughout the neighborhoods and sidewalks. It's fifty-five degrees, T-shirt weather.

I wait for River in a great room that's half-clinical, half-residential. Sofas, tables, TVs, games, and nurses populate the space. Residents visit with family or with each other. It's quiet, like a library.

River emerges from a hallway, wearing loose sweats, a T-shirt, slippers, and glasses instead of contacts. He looks smaller in here. "Hey," he says.

We stare at each other, a chasm of lies and kisses spanning between us.

He splays his hand across his forehead. "It's so fucking awful what I did. I'm sorry."

I'm speechless—which awful thing is he talking about? There are too many to discuss without me losing my temper, but I'm not here for that. I'm here for closure and tell him as much. "I don't want an apology, River. There's nothing"—my voice cracks—"nothing you can say to fix it. Nothing you can do to change it, but I'm glad you didn't hurt yourself with that rifle. How do you feel?"

"Medicated," he returns. "I'm talking to a counselor. It's helping."

"I'm glad," I say.

We sit for a long time, not speaking. Then River wipes his face and offers a medicated smile. "How are you?"

"Better. I'm serving my community service hours at Safe Spaces."

"Nice."

We make small talk and then say goodbye. It's anticlimactic. I understand I'll never see River again and it feels . . . okay. Some people shouldn't be friends *forever*. A burden lifts from my shoulders. The man inside River will pay the price for what the boy has done. The full adult price. That is enough.

Outside the hospital, I take a deep breath of Alaskan spring air. I received my acceptance letter yesterday and leave for Cal State Long Beach in the fall. Olivia and Imani are attending UC Irvine, but we'll be close enough to hang out like we used to. I confessed everything to them, and they were upset, but they didn't ditch me. Instead, they made me promise not to lie to them or anyone else, not ever again. I am grateful to have friends like these.

I'll miss Anchorage and living with my mom, but I need to figure out who I am so I can stand on my own two feet. Not everyone gets a second chance. I'm ready to make the most of mine.

• • •

The following day is Mya's celebration of life. Cookie scheduled it for after Jason Walker's celebration out of respect for what he went through. As Mom and I approach the venue, the first thing we encounter is a huge photo of Mya from when she was six years old. It's perched on an easel by the front door. My hand rises to my throat.

Mom steadies me. "Can you do this?"

I nod. "Give me a second." She leaves, and I stand in front of the picture alone.

Mya is wearing her favorite purple jacket and muddy boots over jeans. She's grinning, and one tooth is missing. Her eyes are as bright as sunshine on water. Tears swim in my eyes and my heart swells. I love *this* girl. We were best friends, chosen sisters. I trace the scar on my palm, remembering the vow we made when we were kids.

"What happened?" I ask the photo. The girl in the picture is silent, frozen in time.

I view Mya's lies in hindsight. She was thirteen when the murder happened and freaked out that River was pissing blood. She became more freaked out after River shot his father. Her overbearing mother convinced her to protect River by keeping silent, and so I can understand why Mya didn't correct the police when they assumed my dad shot Bart, and I can understand why she doubled down and protected River after he hid a dead body. What I don't understand is why she chose him over me both times.

River is fragile, I understand that now. Perhaps he needed her protection more than I did. I will never know for sure.

I close my eyes and transport backward, to days that were drenched in adventure and dripping with laughter, days when we believed in magic—when our stuffed animals could speak, kisses were gross, and growing up felt optional—days when our fathers were alive and our families formed a community. We can't go home again, not the way it was, not ever. My jumbled feelings unravel with a soft breath.

But I can move forward.

The days are getting longer, the snow is melting, and good memories of camping, swimming, and fishing with my father fill the dark spaces of my past. My childhood is behind me, but so are its secrets.

I open my eyes and face the little girl who died to save my life. *Mya.* Our protector. In the end, she told me the truth and set me free. She saved my life. In the end, she was brave.

Honesty isn't for cowards. That is the truth.

ACKNOWLEDGMENTS

Thank you for reading *The Trespassers*. I dedicated this novel to the homes I've left behind because there have been many—from Northern and Southern California to New Mexico, Colorado, Alaska, and Minnesota. Each time, I've left behind pieces of myself. They say you cannot go home again, and I think that's because you no longer fit into the role you once occupied. When Finley returns to Alaska, she no longer fits in with her friends. It's distressing, but in the end, it's okay. Some places should not be home *forever.* Some people should not be friends *forever.* It's okay to outgrow them. Sometimes it's better.

I treasure the friends who remain in my life. They might live far away, but they are close to my heart. They might be new, but they feel like forever. However we fit together, know that I love you.

The Trespassers would not have been possible without the assistance of my incredible support team. My agent, Elizabeth Bewley, immediately loved the idea of teens in Alaska! My #1 bestselling editor, Wendy Loggia, was excited to take the icy plunge with me on this new thriller. The entire team at Delacorte Press weighed in on the title, cover design, marketing plans, and publicity. My friends and writing peers—Shells Legoullon, Merriam Sarcia Saunders, and LB Schulman—read early drafts and challenged me to do better. Each member of my team, especially Wendy Loggia, contributed feedback that helped me shape the initial manuscript into something deeper, icier, and more impactful. I am grateful they leaped into my imaginary world and made it real.

Much love to my writing pals in SCBWI and across the globe; my dear friends, past and present; my adventurous book club gals; my church friends; my three children—Nick, Crystal, and David; the pets that watch me write; and my best friend forever, the one I will never outgrow, my husband.

Dear readers, without your eyes and ears, this novel is letters stamped onto an off-white page. You are the magic that brings the words to life. Thank you for reading. If you enjoyed the story, please share it with a friend.

ABOUT THE AUTHOR

Jennifer Lynn Alvarez is the award-winning author of eleven novels, and her young adult thrillers have been translated across the globe. She's an English Literature alum of UC Berkeley, a longtime SCBWI volunteer, a writing coach, and a speaker. When Jennifer's not plotting stories, she's hiking, daydreaming, or both. She lives outside Nashville with her husband and a cat with a misspelled name.

jenniferlynnalvarez.com